About the Author

Max Sebastian has written more than 20 novels, and regularly tops the bestseller lists for steamy couples erotic fiction. He began fooling around with naughty words on the Literotica.com website nearly two decades ago, and broke into the wider world of publishing in 2011.

Since then, Max has become well-known for sensual, steamy adventures in which couples explore thrilling alternatives to monogamous relationships, on their way to a very raunchy happy ever after — including menage stories, wife-sharing, hotwives, cuckolding and partner-swapping in various forms.

Max lives in London, England, and loves to hear from readers. Visit his website at www.maxsebastian.net.

facebook.com/writermax

twitter.com/maxsebastian

goodreads.com/maxsebastian

amazon.com/author/maxsebastian

Some of Max's Other Books
WEB: MAXSEBASTIAN.NET

WHAT'S MINE IS YOURS

MAX SEBASTIAN

MAXSEBASTIAN.NET

Second Edition (September 2020)

Cover image © nd3000 | BigStockPhoto.com

This is a work of fiction. All characters, organizations and events portrayed in this book are either products of the author's imagination or are used fictitiously.

Two Ships Passing in the Night

*W*e were like two ships passing in the night, offering friendly greetings as we went by, but scarcely stopping for long enough to even think about the loss of our sexual connection.

How did the passion between us fade? Our relationship had been so physical in the beginning. Yet a few years into our marriage, we seemed more like friends than lovers.

I guess the novelty of sex between us wore off, and as it did so, short cuts were taken. Neither of us made the effort we once had to make it special—and so we stopped feeling that it was special.

We entered that period in our late twenties where work was suddenly such a priority—we had to make something of our lives. Katie proved successful in her chosen career, while I floundered in mine, yet for different reasons we were devoting all our energies to our professional lives.

We were tired. Familiarity had settled our thrill of making love, turned it more into occasional relief than a flaming consumption of our passions. We could take sex or leave it, it was no big deal either way, if it happened it happened. Increasingly, though, it didn't happen.

Meanwhile, our all-important, self-defining professional lives were keeping us apart from each other. My work dried up to the point where often the only shifts I could get were night shifts. So while I went out to work, Katie was coming home and vice versa.

The fact that we hardly noticed much difference when we separated only went and proved how parallel our lives had become.

Our split was amicable, if any relationship breakdown can truly be said to be so. There was no shouting, there was no screaming, there was no throwing of the wedding gifts to smash against the wall in succinct analogy of our shattered dreams.

Katie simply stopped on her way out to work one morning and said, "I want more than this."

And the way she said it, I knew it was all over after five years of trying.

I couldn't deny that our relationship had settled into a platonic rut that made it little more than a shared living arrangement. And increasingly, that arrangement was a time-share where we did not see each other more than a matter of minutes each day.

My standard two days off per week didn't even coincide with the weekend very often, so more and more of those days were spent apart from Katie, and particularly since I had to continue my schedule of sleeping during the day and waking during the night. As Katie rose through the ranks of her profession, she came home more and more tired each week, so that our occasional evenings together could only ever be sitting in front of the TV, rather than catching up on our flagging intimacy. At the end, she just came home and went to bed, she needed the sleep. So we put less and less effort into making time to see each other each day.

Katie had urged me time and again to get another job, a day job. Oh, I didn't ignore her. I went for jobs—and got some. A football magazine here, a gossip rag there, a quarterly journal about pensions. They all folded while I was working there—or were simply pruning their work force in the light of dwindling sales—and I found myself back to taking night shifts on the Daily News, getting the paper ready for the morning delivery.

I was a sub-editor, and we were a dying breed. My job was to get news copy into shape for publication, adding headlines and picture captions and any other little details to spruce up a page. But the world was moving online, and there was less and less money available for correct spellings and impeccable grammar.

The night shift was a safe place for me to hang out while I looked for a proper job, but jobs for sub-editors were increasingly scarce, and while Katie encouraged me to find alternative work, it seemed my skill set and experience did not entice employers to take a chance on me doing something else.

"We just need a little more front-line experience, I'm afraid."

Or

"Look, thank you for coming, but we have a dozen Cambridge graduates with Nobel Prizes for literature in the running for this job."

Or simply,

"If you're not already doing this job for our biggest rival, we can't really consider you."

I didn't blame her for what happened to us. I didn't blame her for needing so much shut-eye—she was out saving lives every day, after all. One slip of the scalpel because of fatigue would end it all for some poor soul.

As far as I was concerned, she was frustrated with me

because I didn't have a day job. So I was working fairly hard to get a day job. I just couldn't face being unemployed in order to do that.

After five years of marriage, I guess I assumed our marriage was fairly bomb-proof, and that once I got myself back into the normal schedule, everything would be all right.

Could I have done more to find a better job? Possibly. But when you're married, you feel you have time to put things right if they appear to be headed in the wrong direction.

I was simply stunned when she told me she was done with this.

"Is it over?" was all I said in reply to her. Not even arguing that she should give me another chance.

All the while, my insides felt like they were burning up, corroded by acid. How could she just end our marriage?

By that point in our relationship, though, we were at the telepathy stage of communication. I was supposed to know what Katie was thinking at any particular point in time, and she didn't need to tell me what was up, what was wrong.

So she'd simply nodded at my question, said: "I think so. I'm sorry, Sean."

And I'd just shrugged, and said: "It happens."

It happens. Jesus. What an idiot. But when you're married, you have that strange sense of pride, that if your partner treats you outrageously unfairly, at some point karma will show her the error of her ways.

I felt so angry that Katie didn't want to give me any more time—not even an ultimatum—to get myself a day job so we could see more of each other, that she would just go and terminate things between us like that. So angry that I didn't want to be seen to stoop to begging.

Please take me back, Katie, I'll change, I'll do anything. I was afraid she'd think I was pathetic.

Well, she probably thought I was pathetic enough, since she was a talented cardiovascular surgeon, and I was just some numpty who corrected the spellings on the newspaper before it hit the news stands in the morning. Would begging her to take me back really persuade her to stay married with me?

So I couldn't show her how I really felt.

Seeing her walk off like that, without even looking back at me with any kind of regret, that she wasn't more upset about this—it horrified me. And I guess, looking back, she was probably feeling the same way about me since I was trying so hard to hold it together and act cool.

Inside, I was just a mess. But my brain was already going into denial mode just to protect myself from the trauma.

"You want me to move out?" I called after her, this Big Life Moment seeming such an anticlimax, turning into a fairly mediocre meeting-on-the-fly about what we should do to wrap things up.

"No rush."

And there really wasn't any rush. Well, we were like two ships, you see. Katie and I knew very well how to live in the same house and never see each other. It wasn't going to be awkward between us now we were separated, because when I came home from work, she would be gone for an early breakfast somewhere, and when I woke up after my day-time sleep shift, I'd vacate that little house in Fulham before she got home from work.

Ours really was the perfect diurnal time-share—and it hardly motivated me to get out there and find another apartment, particularly in London's nightmare property market.

I had vague thoughts that after a while she would realize that she missed me, and that separation wasn't the answer. Or, I hoped that perhaps intensifying my search for a day-time job would allow me to come to her with the surprise that I could now be a normal husband—and she'd take me straight back.

I suppose I was also wondering if I would eventually provoke Katie into saying something—leaving me a note or sending me an email. Passive aggression on my part, I guess. I hoped she'd get tired of knowing I was still around, and decide we needed to talk about this, even if it meant a formal divorce.

I was testing the limits of how long I could stay at "our" home before I reconciled with the fact that we were not getting back together. She wasn't pushing me for a divorce, so I wasn't pushing to get out of our house.

We were locked in a passive aggressive incomplete separation.

———

One good thing about being a night worker in the jobs market was that I could attend job interviews during the day and not have to take time off. It might mean a couple hours' less sleep during one of my daytime sleep shifts, but it allowed me to take whatever interviews were going my way.

I'd sleep as much as I could ahead of the appointed time, and when I returned from the interview I was often able to grab a few more hours' shut-eye to make up for the loss.

One evening, though, I'd had yet another interview end up with a "we'll be in touch" and a smile that wasn't matched by the eyes, and it just got to me. I went home to crash, aided by a nice tumbler or two of 18-year-old Talisker whisky.

When I woke, I was late for my shift at the News, and still feeling the Talisker spinning my head a little. I felt all I could do was call in sick.

Once I'd put the required call in to my line manager, our chief sub-editor, I lay back in the bed and felt the need for more sleep.

Only then I heard the rattle of a key in the lock downstairs—someone letting themselves in through the front door. Katie. Would she be angry to come upstairs and find me still in bed? In our informal arrangement, if I had a night off and was likely to be spending time at home, I'd decamp to the spare bedroom, a tiny little box across the hallway from the master, so that I'd avoid disturbing her sleep and keep to the unspoken terms of our separation.

Lying there spread over the large bed in the master bedroom, I wondered if I could spin the same line to Katie as I'd just spun with our chief sub-editor. Perhaps she'd have sympathy about my feigned illness. Perhaps seeing me still there in bed, she might be tempted to join me, even just for a friendly just-for-old-times'-sake cuddle. A spurned husband could hope.

Only when that front door opened, it wasn't just Katie's voice I heard. She was with someone else, a man.

It came as a total shock. I hadn't even thought that she might start dating again. God, I'd made so many stupid assumptions. That I might get a proper day job and we could immediately be a normal married couple again.

I hadn't even considered the possibility that Katie might want to see some other guy.

Shit—was she sleeping with him? I guess she had every right to be doing whatever she wanted with him, we were separated.

I had to quickly and stealthily exit the bed, grabbing my clothes and smoothing down the bedsheets in the process before dashing across to the spare bedroom.

I sat on that tiny little bed in the dark and listened to the murmur of voices as they went through to the kitchen downstairs. I felt like an idiot. Cowering in that room, the hot flush of shame and embarrassment overwhelming me at the sound of Katie merrily entertaining her new friend, I just wanted to scuttle out of the house. Only, there was no way I could escape now without making some kind of scene.

It was already late, and Katie did not seem to be showing her date to the door, saying goodbye. I just sat on the tiny little spare bed, holding my knees, shaking as it hit me: Katie and I hadn't sex for months. At least six months. Maybe even a year.

Had that been what she'd meant when she told me she needed "more than this"?

Jesus, it hadn't even seemed like that long to me since we'd had sex. It hadn't seemed like an issue. I guess my sexual urges had just faded in the time that the passion had dwindled in our relationship—but perhaps Katie hadn't responded in the same way. I should have seen it. It didn't help that we hadn't talked about it, but I should have realized.

In the dark, I tried to keep calm by telling myself it was inevitable that Katie would want to see other people now, but that even if our sex life had dried up, she must be in the early stages of seeing this guy and she'd be sending him on his way soon. I figured I could simply go and talk to her once she'd said goodbye to him, and tell her I'd seen the error of my ways.

Crap. I really never even considered the possibility of Katie dating someone else. I guess I had assumed she had been so absorbed in her work that she didn't need any kind of a social life.

I was burning, shaking with jealousy. Praying that she hadn't started sleeping with this guy, that there might be some way she'd give me another chance.

But I heard her from the kitchen, sounding so happy, her laughter ringing through the house and its thin walls. I wanted her to be that happy, but not because of him. It thrilled me to hear her being so joyful, but it made me realize how long it had been since I'd heard that.

It sounded to me, though, that she'd brought him home for sex.

It terrified me that I was now too late to do anything about it.

I was trapped in that little spare room. If I went down there and confronted her, I'd embarrass her in front of her date. It would only make her hate me, only thwart any attempt I might have to win her over.

Could I leave enough evidence to make her realize I was home, though? Perhaps she would be persuaded not to carry her date through to its full conclusion.

What could I do, though? I crept out and put my jacket prominently on the banister at the top of the stairs. I took off my tie and dropped it on the floor by the bathroom.

I turned the bathroom light on.

The only other thing I could do to hint that I was home without alerting her date to my presence was to close the spare bedroom door while I was inside and turn on the light. Hope she picked up on the signals.

Only, she didn't. So as I lay there on that tiny little bed, I heard them clomping up the stairs, chatting and laughing, and apparently from the sounds of it, stopping briefly to kiss and peel off various items of clothing on the way up to the master bedroom.

"I think you just can't handle your drink as well as me, and you're scared of what I'll find..."

"Scared? Try me."

In the still of the night, I heard everything. I heard Katie flirting with him, I heard her kissing him. It filled my stomach with acid.

"Does that feel like I'm scared?"

"Mmm... no, not scared..."

I should have just walked out of the house, just left right there and then. But I still felt the need to avoid embarrassing Katie in front of her date.

"Okay, but I do have a procedure in the morning."

"You know what's one of the best ways to burn off alcohol?"

"I can imagine."

"You don't need to, though. Imagine, I mean."

Then that dark little curiosity kicked in, and I wanted to see what was going on. As if the pain of hearing them together wasn't enough to punish myself for being so stupid about our failing marriage, I wanted to go the whole hog and watch what she was doing with this new man, to find out who he was and how I stacked up.

I pulled myself up off the bed and edged open the door.

"You know it was a national disgrace that you ever got married."

"You're so sweet."

"There should be a law against women as hot as you getting hitched."

As if it wasn't all bad enough, I suddenly felt an added pang of unease as I faintly recognized the man's voice.

Peering out through the crack in the door, I could see they'd left the bedroom door wide open. Inside the master bedroom, Katie's full-length mirror stood in the corner to offer me a complete view of everything that was going on. I was stunned. Not only by the fact that she lay there in a white shirt and panties, another man lying with her in nothing but his underwear, kissing his way down her chest.

A jolt of shock stabbed me right in the heart. I recognized the man: it was one of my good friends, one of my few remaining friends. Grant.

"If there was a law against vaguely attractive women getting married, all children would be hideous."

"Good business for our clinic. And who ever told you that you were 'vaguely' attractive?"

The man who had set Katie and myself up in the first place, a member of our wedding party, was now here in my home, lying in my place, flattering my wife in preparation for sleeping with her. Christ, how long had it been since I'd actively told her she was beautiful? After a while being married, it had felt to me that I didn't need to say things like that—or that she'd feel I was somehow obligated as husband to say such things. But I could see now that she'd probably needed me to say those things.

Grant was taking full advantage of my failings as a husband.

I just stood and watched him, sharp, acidic anger mincing up my insides.

I was too damn tired to do anything, though, and it was too late. Our marriage was over.

Katie was giggling, pushing him up from her, kissing his mouth. God, she looked so beautiful, her sandy blonde hair all mussed up, flowing down over her shoulders like a wild waterfall. How had I ever come to take that for granted?

"Hey, easy, tiger!"

"Come on, I've been thinking about this all day. Quit stalling."

I couldn't stop watching her. I was like a rubbernecker gazing at a horrific car crash, I couldn't look away. I couldn't believe she was doing this, couldn't believe what pain it was causing me, and yet I could not tear my eyes away from them.

I was punishing myself, but I was also just plain curious.

Katie shoved Grant over onto his back, kissing his mouth forcefully. The hand that wasn't supporting her body was roaming all over his gym-toned body, sweeping down to the sizable bulge in his underwear. Feeling out his package.

"Help yourself."

"Thank you, I will."

God, how long had she been seeing him? I'd had a drink with Grant not long after our whimpering separation. He'd attempted to cheer me up, all evening telling me she'd calm down and that we'd get back together.

And now he was lying there on my marital bed, and my wife was kissing him deeply while reaching into his briefs to pull out his wincingly large cock.

Breathing suddenly seemed to be difficult, the air too thin for me as I watched my Katie stroking another man's cock, her closed fist slowly pumping up and down that obscene pole.

She broke away from their kiss, smiling, so excited. Something I hadn't seen for so very long. She brushed her hair out of her face, and then bent down over him, her mouth opening to allow her tongue to touch the tip of his cock.

She licked around his tip, and then she was stretching her lips around him, taking him into her mouth, as much as she could fit of that huge thing, at any rate.

"Fuck, you're a filthy whore..."

He was so brash, so uncouth. But she was purring like a contented kitten as she rubbed that thing all over her face.

"Suck it, Jesus. Suck it..."

I felt so angry at Grant for lying back against my pillows to enjoy her mouth around his thick cock. I think, as I watched, that my former friend took on the focus of my wrath. By comparison I wasn't so angry at Katie. I'd let her down: somehow it was understandable that she'd need someone else.

She looked so happy, so elated to have this new cock in her hands, in her mouth.

I watched her fellating him, and still found myself thinking perhaps this would be it: it was their first date, she'd go down on him and then send him off on his merry way. That it would be all right, that it wasn't really sex if it was just a blow job.

Only, who was to say this was their first date? First dates didn't usually involve intimate dinners at the woman's home followed by kissing and oral sex in the bedroom.

I watched her rise from his shaft, kiss him again and then finish pulling his underwear completely off him.

Then she was kneeling up to peel her own underwear down her thighs, and after dropping them behind her, straddling his hips as he lay there on his back.

"I am going to ride you until I can't walk tomorrow."

"Your rounds are going to be fun in the morning."

"I'll get a first-year to take me round in a wheelchair."

My heart was threatening to pummel its way out of my chest cavity, the butterflies in my stomach were turning into meat-eaters. Katie was naked other than an open white shirt, sitting on another man, letting him guide his huge bulbous cock up to her open and available pussy.

No, no, no.

My Katie was giving another man her bedroom eyes as she eased slowly down on him, taking his bare cock inside her. Christ, they weren't even using a condom—and they were both doctors.

"Oh my sweet Jesus that feels so good..."

"Take it, bitch. Take it, you filthy goddamn married bitch."

I gasped, and had the two of them not been breathing heavily themselves, they might have heard me. Slowly at first, she began to ride him, and I could see even without the benefit of the full-length mirror his huge cock disappearing between her firm buttocks—and I could see each time she rose up on it again that it was glistening with her wetness.

We were still technically married. She was having an affair.

"You talk to your mother with that mouth?"

"She thinks I'm an angel. That turn you on?"

"No, that would be this unbelievably huge cock inside me."

I felt stunned watching them. Somehow, my brain acted to prevent permanent damage by numbing me to the pain. It still hurt, but it allowed me to even appreciate just how beautiful Katie was in the full throes of passion. Perhaps, if I told myself she was only doing this for the sex, because her sex life with me had dried up, I could even tell myself this meant nothing, and see this as just Katie satisfying herself with some kind of living sex toy.

I couldn't deny I was hard watching her. And the things she was saying to him only made that worse.

"It's so big... you're splitting me open..."

"Fuck... how do you do that to me?"

"Just like that.... just like that... just like that..."

I'd never seen other people actually having sex before. This was like pornography, only starring a woman I loved.

Only, the fact that this was the woman I loved now started encroaching on that veil of numbness that had been protecting me from pain for a short while.

Grant wrestled her over, and now she was laying back down against our pillows, arms wide, breasts bared so her stiff nipples revealed just how turned on she was, her legs parted so that her new lover could drive back inside her.

She closed her eyes and moaned like I hadn't heard in years as that enormous thing entered her, stretched her, filled her.

"Oh God... oh God... oh God..."

Jesus. Grant was a surgeon, like Katie. He was wealthy, he had a Porsche. And he had a huge cock. You just had to hate a guy like that.

And now he was fucking my wife and plainly making her feel incredible.

"Sweet Jesus... sweet Jesus... sweet Jesus..."

It was worst of all when he kissed her, locking his lips over hers as they writhed against each other in our bed, or brushed his lips down her neck, her hand affectionately holding his head as he did so. The fact that this might be more than just sex felt like knives carving up my life-sustaining organs.

Katie looked exquisite, her face flushed and pink, the perspiration beginning to show in her hair. Grant had everything a man could ever want in life, he could have had any woman in the world, probably, and he had my gorgeous wife.

And watching them hit their peak, I was so confused I came without even touching myself, without even removing my pants.

*A*fterwards, I lay in the dark, overcome with emotion. I felt hollow, half of me ripped out and thrown away. My life, as I knew it, was over. My future with Katie was gone.

I cried, quietly, into the pillows on that single bed in the spare room, my body seizing up with painful sobs.

Grief, I suppose, that was delayed from the original break-up, which I had somehow told myself at the time wasn't real, which I had assumed was some kind of cry for help on Katie's part to get me to try harder to find a day job.

I was in mourning, only I had to lie there in that depressing little room and listen to every move and whimper as Grant made love to my wife over and over again. I could smell their sex as well as hear it. I was sitting through the funeral for our marriage, and I had a full-on erection right there in church.

And Grant had unbelievable stamina. Was it just because she was new to him? Because he'd coveted her while she'd been mine, perhaps. Or because he got off on the fact he had stolen her from me.

"Oh God... I'm coming again..."

I bitterly observed how much louder Katie was with him than she'd ever been with me. I tried creating fantasies in which she was faking it, but it didn't help much.

I even wondered if she knew I was there, if she'd read my little signals, and this was her attempt to either get me to move out for good, or punish me for neglecting her in our marriage.

By the morning, when they were finally gone and I was peering into that awful room, seeing her panties and her shoes and her skirt and everything else strewn around the floor, the bedsheets all messed up like Katie never ever used to leave them, the mustiness of past sex still in the air, I actually received a text message from her.

Katie: oh my god, I'm so sorry. Saw your things this morning and realize you must have been in last night. I'm so sorry – I didn't mean for you to find out like that

That made my blood run cold.

I guess it was some kind of an awkward conversation opener. But I was too devastated just then to reply.

I took one last look at the bedroom, feeling the sad, regretful atmosphere of an era passing. Then I left, with no intention of ever setting foot in that house again.

2

Fish out of water

*T*here's something foreign about the daytime when you're a night worker. I sat in a cafe pushing a full English breakfast around my plate at just past noon, and felt just plain wrong for being awake at this hour.

No wonder Katie had felt distant from me. Even my days off were really nights off, and I still generally spent the daylight sleeping so as not to wreck my sleep patterns.

She had always been able to see me at transitional times, but those times always had one or other of us tired after a long work shift. When I returned home tired from work at about 7am, Katie would be waking up and getting ready for work. When I was waking up and getting ready for work at about 8pm or 9pm, she would be slowing down ready for bed.

I might be able to have dinner with her, although that would be merely her breakfast, not time for a slap-up meal. My breakfast time was too late in the evening for her to eat her dinner with me.

On my nights off, she had been able to see me all evening, though she missed most of my awake time because she went to bed about 10pm or 11pm.

Increasingly, though, as she had risen through the ranks from trainee surgeon on up to resident and so on, she was late home from work, which ate into our transitional time together.

No wonder she'd felt that our marriage had ceased to be.

Here I was now, after the most miserable morning of my life, not really eating the food on my plate, locked in self-imposed exile outside what had been my own house. I felt like an outlaw.

Jesus, there wasn't even anyone I could really dial up to vent my sorrows to, either. It seemed to me that all my friends had been Katie's friends, and really they had been Katie's friends before they were mine.

If I went and jumped in the river right now, if I had a funeral at all, I'd have nobody in attendance, I was sure of it.

My insides had been ripped out, nobody in the world cared about me any more, and I was homeless.

Sitting there in the cafe, I realized I didn't really have much of anything to call my own any more. My suitcase suddenly looked very small. I might have the technical claim to half the house after all the divorce proceedings were finally over, but it was her house really. She'd bought it before we got together. I was going to have to find somewhere else to live.

That afternoon, I dragged my puny-looking suitcase up to King's Cross where a classified ad in the Evening Standard had suggested I might get a ludicrously cheap hotel room, and sure enough £23 was sufficient to get me a semi-clean cubbyhole that was just about big enough for me to store my suitcase in, if I didn't mind keeping it on the single bed that dominated the space.

I traipsed into work at 10:30pm, early for the usual 11pm start for our shift, feeling strangely cut off from the world around me. I hoped the night might bring some interesting news stories to absorb my attention, but feared that nothing could do that right now.

"Heart broken by a cardiac surgeon. There's some irony in that somewhere."

My co-worker Henry Robinson didn't offer me pity, and I was hugely thankful for that. I wasn't quite sure how to respond to pity. As far as he was concerned, my marriage had ended ages ago, I'd just managed to ignore it.

"Could have been worse," he said, glancing across from his computer screen, which was zoomed in on a picture caption for a shot of Prime Minister David Cameron having an egg thrown at him on a visit to Manchester.

"Could have been worse?"

"Well, she could have been sleeping with a member of your family, for instance. Or she could have plotted to have you killed so you'd finally move out of that damn house. Or she could have waited until you were asleep, stolen your kidneys, then fled the country to sell them on the black market..."

"I suppose so," I said. "Suddenly I feel quite fortunate."

Henry, I realized to my great surprise, was suddenly the only real friend I had left in the world. All the others, essentially, would go to Katie in the divorce settlement.

Grant had been my go-to drinking buddy—and look where he ended up.

My old friends from college—well, I hadn't been in touch for a long time. Henry was all I had left. And I'd always treated him merely as a work colleague—the guy I always happened to sit beside when our shifts began because we went to journalism school together.

He did make the night shift bearable. We had inane conversation for hours on end while our fingers went about our paid employment on virtual autopilot.

We did have a little more in common than just our journalism training—Henry, like me, had been attempting for years to get out of the night shift game so he could devote himself to his wife and their future. But like me, he would get something on another paper or a magazine, and then he'd suffer the regular staff cutbacks, or when a title folded, or when he decided the work was so badly paid and mind-numbingly tedious he was better off coming back to the night shift.

We'd look through the job ads together, we'd apply for things together, and we'd trade stories on how we got on with the interviews if we were actually awarded any.

And generally, we made each other feel less guilty about being washed-up hacks in their early thirties who hadn't made it to the big leagues.

"My word she had the biggest hair I've ever seen. I couldn't stop looking at it. I was trying to work out just what the hell was holding it up, what the hell could hold it up. All I could come up with was some kind of adamantium structure..."

"And by then she'd probably decided you'd looked at her hair for long enough?"

"Ten points to that man, Sean Ruskin. She gave me that withering look that told me not even to expect a phone call."

But thus far I'd never really gotten to know Henry

socially—outside the office we'd always had our separate social worlds, and never the twain shall meet. Even the mentions of our personal lives within our conversations had been sporadic at best—Henry's marriage a couple of years back had been about the only time we'd really talked about anything significant in that direction. And I hadn't even been invited—although since the ceremony itself had been on some far-flung exotic island, only a few family and friends had been invited.

Bottom line was, I knew little about what Henry got up to outside of work, and vice versa. What a great thing I had going with the only friend I had left in the world.

"Was he really naked?"

"Naked?"

"The big ugly man you watched—"

"As the day."

"So you could see his—"

"I suppose so."

"And?"

I looked at Henry's raised eyebrow, and the twinkle in his pale eyes, and couldn't avoid breaking out into a wry grin, whatever the state of devastation my personal life had become.

I said: "You ever see that Kevin Bacon movie, Tremors?"

Henry sucked the air in through his teeth at that. "Jesus. No wonder she boned him. You should have no shame, my friend, no shame at all."

"Thank you. I'm not sure that makes me feel better."

Henry nodded. "You know she's been buffing him for a while. Probably since she ended things with you."

"It's possible."

"Dinner at her place? And then they left in the

morning for work together. You going back there after we're done with this shift?"

I suddenly felt deeply distressed about the cruddy little hotel room I had waiting for me in King's Cross.

"I can't."

He shrugged, "There's a room for you in our place, if you need a little space, a little time."

I looked at him, this guy I'd shared three years of my life with, yet hadn't ever bought a drink for, and I was struck by just how decent he was. I did enjoy spending time with him, I did enjoy our conversations about politics or celebrity gossip or the finer points of underrated movies while we shuffled words around the pages of the Daily News each night. While we simultaneously sifted through the journalism industry jobs boards for vacancies that never seemed quite what we were after, or never had call for a couple of bums with three years of night shifts on the more recent end of their resumés.

"Seriously?" I said. "You'd really be okay if I stayed a little while? I'm sure it would only be a day or two."

Henry had smiled that great beaming Labrador Retriever smile and it was decided: "You stay as long as you need, old man."

I can't adequately say what an extraordinary relief it was to be offered a place to say by a friendly face.

In the morning, after our shift was over, Henry took me home and showed me around his small but perfectly respectable apartment in Chiswick, a fairly affluent part of West London just down the District Line from our office at Victoria.

He lived in an apartment building just off Turnham Green, the small park at the heart of Chiswick that seemed as much like a village green as anywhere could be in a London borough, complete with a little church in the middle. It all had a wonderfully welcoming atmosphere for a man who had suddenly become homeless.

It felt strange to be in Henry's company outside of the office, but I think the strangeness stemmed from the realization that I knew this guy so well, having worked with him so closely for three years, and yet I'd never seen his apartment before. Hadn't even seen a picture of his wife.

"Your wife's going to be all right about this?" I asked him as he showed me into the spare bedroom, which seemed to me not much smaller than the master bedroom.

"Oh, sure, she's very easy going," he said, not really giving me the solid confirmation I needed that Mrs Robinson wasn't going to come home from work that evening and scream at her husband for bringing someone home unannounced.

I felt Henry was really going above and beyond the call of duty. Jesus, he even gave me a spare set of keys for the place.

"While you're here, until you're ready to take the next step, this is your home as well, old man," he said, and I just felt like weeping.

I didn't have time to spend much of the morning with him, however. I had to head back out to the Tube Station, and journey back to King's Cross to fetch my meager belongings from that cruddy hotel. Supper was a quick bite in McDonald's, where they were naturally serving breakfast, but by the time I returned to Henry's apartment and let myself quietly in, my new flatmate had gone to bed.

I didn't mind. Amid all the hurt and confusion

surrounding the break-up of my marriage, it felt good to have a proper bed to call my own. It made me feel a little less homeless. After a long, long day, I was happy to settle into a new but supremely inviting bed and collapse instantly into a deep, deep sleep.

3

Drowning sorrows

*T*he first time I met Henry's wife, she was perched on the edge of the couch in the little cramped living room as I emerged from 'my' bedroom that next morning.

"Hey," she said, smiling in amusement at the gormless expression I presented her fresh from my sleep.

"Uh hey... Michelle, right?"

At least I knew her name. It felt more than awkward that I'd worked so closely with her husband for three years and had never met her before. More so than the fact that she'd caught me in this disheveled, under-dressed state, wearing nothing but a bathrobe prior to my shower.

"Certainly is," she said, surprisingly brightly, her accent taking me a little by surprise. So, Irish, then? Or American. Just needed a few more words...

"You must be Sean, right? Henry's told me so much about you."

American, then. She leaned forward to offer me a dainty handshake.

She was certainly attractive, I was impressed—Henry

had done well for himself. Oh, a third party might have told you she was nothing special—girl-next-door looks, an innocent charm, cute enough—and perhaps they'd be right, Valentino would probably never have put her on a catwalk.

But sitting there in a simple gray blouse, dark skirt and pantyhose combo that showed a fair amount of cleavage and thigh, Michelle Robinson was wincingly cute, from her long flowing brown hair and bright aquamarine eyes to her full lips and trim, yet curvaceous figure.

She was younger than Henry and myself, perhaps five or six years so, and while her lipstick and makeup was subtle in tone and application, the mascara and dark liner around her eyes gave her the Cleopatra look girls of our generation generally did not affect.

I caught a hint of her sweet perfume as I lingered a second too long over our handshake, and for some reason it surprised me that I would react to her in that way. I guess it really had been a while since I'd thought about all things sexual.

"Uh... right, nice to meet you," I said, suddenly a little embarrassed that the wife of my only friend in the world had stirred the base impulses of my masculinity in that way.

She didn't even hesitate a moment over my clumsy pause, in my mind that showed her grace and easy confidence.

"I heard about what happened..." she said, her reminder filling my stomach with the molten lava of grief once again.

I shrugged, trying to seem bold. "Happens."

She wrinkled her nose sympathetically, "Hurts, though, right?"

I nodded, offering a grateful smile as I kept my eyes

politely on hers, doing my utmost not to linger on the exquisite swell of her cleavage or that smooth, taut expanse of nylon-clad thigh. What was I, some kind of sex-craved teenager? What had happened to me?

"Michelle's on her way out to night school," I was startled by Henry's voice coming up behind me. "But she'll join us later."

"Join us?" I was confused.

"Night off, remember, Squire?" Henry grinned like a court jester.

Of course—it was one of our two nights off for the week. That was some relief. Henry and I had tended to coincide with our nights off since the early days, since we had both come to recognize that if one or other of us was off separately, the remaining partner faced a long shift without the usual inane conversation to ease through.

"Oh, right," I said, giving a momentary dazed expression that attempted to hint to my kind hosts that I was merely still half-asleep, rather than a touch on the dim side.

"We have an appointment with the Pride of London, my friend," Henry stated firmly, making me wonder what he was getting at before he added, "and Michelle's keen to join us for one or two when she gets out from business school."

Michelle was smiling at the prospect of helping Henry cheer me up, and there was a note of pity in her pale face.

"It's very kind of you, but—"

"Then it's agreed," said Henry, who always had that vigor in his voice that could not be denied, and could not be derailed. Henry had decided to help me drown my sorrows, and so that was what was going to happen.

I guess I was faintly relieved that my first night off after moving out would not be spent completely alone.

"Great," I said, nodding, smiling at them both, trying

not to look too intently at Henry's attractive wife for fear of offending them.

Henry didn't seem fazed about anything, though, and I doubt even had I been obviously staring at Michelle's pert breasts that he would have taken offense. He hadn't even bothered to dress in a bathrobe in front of his new house-guest—he was standing there as though he'd just claimed Mount Everest for England, wearing nothing but faded plaid boxer shorts, his pale bare chest sporting a light dusting of his red hair.

I let him head for the shower first, since he was virtu-ally undressed for it already, and because I got the feeling that spending time with Michelle might help keep my mind off the painful issues in my life.

"So business school, huh?" I asked her, slumping down on the armchair to which I hitherto had only been making vague overtures toward.

She smiled, joking easily, "Somebody in this marriage has to have a little ambition."

"Right," I said with a smile that was at least a little self-deprecating, since she was commenting on my job as well as her husband's.

"Henry has us doing very well," she said, backtracking on her semi-cutting remark, "but I think he sees his trust fund as a little more potent than it probably is."

I nodded. I'd never really seen Henry as a trust fund kid, he was so very down-to-earth. But I suppose with his plummy voice and the way he carried himself, the hints of the upper class were apparent.

"And anyway," Michelle grinned, an expression that really lit up her face, "I can't just sit around and be Henry's wife."

"No," I said, nodding appreciatively, though the devil inside me was imagining how it must be to have a wife like her sitting around waiting for you. To me it was a wonder that Henry managed to pull himself away from her long enough to get a night shift in. I suppose anyone looking at Katie would have said the same about me. Idiot.

"So what kind of business do you see yourself going into?" I asked, trying to conceal the weirdly adolescent feelings I had for this beauty sitting just a few feet away.

"Sports physiotherapy, something like that," she said. "I majored in sports injury and recovery."

"Right," I said, knowing nothing whatsoever about her field that might help me in a conversation. With an empty head, I reached for a phrase one always tended to use whenever a new acquaintance revealed their profession or intended profession. "Well, they'll always be demand for it, of course."

It was sufficient to maintain the conversation. Michelle said: "I think so. The government might be selling off school playing fields all over the country, but people will always need exercise and sports."

It was curious to hear the American accent commenting on our lowly British government in such familiarity as she did, but then Michelle was English-by-marriage now. To me it just pronounced her simmering intelligence, which only made me envy Henry more.

"Michelle teaches yoga and aqua-aerobics by day and studies by night," Henry said proudly as he stepped forth from the bathroom again. "It's why she's so bloody gorgeous, but she's overdoing it if you ask me."

"I'm not overdoing it," she smiled modestly, bemused at her husband.

"It's very impressive," I said. "Where do you take your classes?"

"Imperial. It's not too bad, actually."

Then I was in the shower, keeping the temperature of

the water way down to try to keep my mind off the idea of Michelle Robinson in a yoga outfit, or in a swimsuit, at one of her day-time classes. I could do without having an erection on my way back to my bedroom.

God, Katie really did have a point about how our sex life had fizzled.

---

*W*e were in a little pub just off the top-end of the Fulham Road, which wasn't far from Michelle's business school in the South Kensington area. Henry had plenty of really nice drinking holes near him in Chiswick, but he didn't seem to like the idea of his wife traveling on her own at night—so we were taking out consolatory drinks close to Imperial College.

"You seem to be doing pretty well, old man," Henry said as we found a booth in the dark recesses of the Duchess of Corby. "If you don't mind my saying."

I didn't feel it. I felt cold and weak. Henry wouldn't want a huge sob story, though. I said, "I think I'm probably still in shock."

As Henry and I drank our beers, I did find his company somewhat calming, at least.

"I had my heart broken by a girl in school once, you know," he said candidly. "Couldn't get out of bed for two months, you know."

"Really? I am sorry."

Henry shrugged. "I was young, green, unworldly. Sure. I wasn't the confident man-about-town you see before you these days," he smiled. The man had one of the most infectious smiles there was. "Oh, Penny Milner. I had all these syrupy feelings for her—really sappy stuff. Thought we'd grow old together, the whole caboodle."

"It's so sad when it happens like that."

Henry sniffed. "Then one day, I saw her doing handstands with Tommy Doherty. I knew I'd lost her forever."

"Handstands? How old were you guys?"

"Six, seven? I guess she was probably eight."

That night, Henry's infectious optimism gradually built me back up into some semblance of manhood, albeit the kind of semblance that couldn't entirely walk straight while headed to the bar for a refill. Midway through the evening Henry and I decided to establish ourselves at the bar itself, where we not only cut out the transport link between drinks, but also found a few young ladies milling around nearby.

Henry would, from time to time, instruct the bartender to top up one or other of these women, who appeared to be younger even than Michelle—college students, perhaps —and occasionally this seemed to draw them over into conversation, which was pleasant enough. It took a drink or two of my own before I cottoned on to what he was doing.

"Are you trying to get me laid, Henry Robinson?"

He clinked glasses with mine, spilling a sip or two of his White Russian into my Mojito to make my drink a little cloudy.

"You know what they say about falling off a bike?"

"That it's no way to win the Tour de France?"

"Not unless you're Lance Armstrong on drugs. No - when you fall off, you've got to get straight back on and just keep going."

"I thought that was falling off a horse."

"Bike, horse, cardiovascular surgeon. It makes no difference these days."

What can I say, he cheered me up no end, whether there were holes in his logic or not. I was almost in a good mood by the time Michelle joined us after her night class—just about inebriated enough to temporarily forget about Katie.

I was also inebriated enough to find myself flirting with the wife of my only friend in the world. The odd thing was, it wasn't all one-way.

Michelle seemed to be quite flirtatious herself. To begin with, I assumed she was just being friendly, making me feel comfortable since I would be living with them, trying to keep my mind off things.

The frequent light touches she gave me on the arm, the hand, maybe a brief shoulder massage when she was asking us what we'd like for the next round—it was a little more than friendly.

I thought maybe she was just a tactile person, perhaps it was connected to her job as a yoga instructor, her ambitions in the sports and leisure field. But she was really smiley around me, looking at me with those big blue eyes just a fraction too long.

I didn't think she meant anything serious by it, she didn't seem the type to cheat on Henry—but then none of what she did that evening was kept hidden from Henry. He saw everything she did, and seemed completely unperturbed by it.

We stayed out until the small hours—Henry and I locked on the nightshift schedule, while Michelle was young enough to make it through the night, even though she had work to go to in the morning while us nightshifters had our regular daytime sleep.

She had all of three hours' shut-eye before she had to get up again to get ready for work.

On the way home, Michelle was walking between us, arm-in-arm, and I decided that she and Henry must be so solidly secure in their relationship that no amount of flirting with Michelle was going to threaten anything. It made me feel safe, and a little warm inside.

Later, I lay in my bed unable to sleep, much like the night before, only this night was full of thoughts about Michelle, not Katie. Memories of the soft brushes of her hands, those sweet curves, the heart-stopping smile. Hearing her moving about in the next room, the walls being not exactly thick, I looked over toward the door of my room to see that I'd left it open a good crack.

From my darkened little bolt hole, I could gaze out and watch the exquisite Michelle Robinson wander through to the bathroom, and then after a shower back again, wearing nothing but a little purple bra and panties.

And I guess I felt in that moment that it might be nice being around my friend's wife while I got my own life back on track.

4

No way back

I woke later than normal, finding that my usual alarm had not hauled me out of sleep since my phone had run out of juice. Its battery had probably died a long time ago, but such was the distraction Henry had provided since sheltering me from the storm, I hadn't noticed.

My stomach seemed to fold in on itself as I eventually located my charger and powered up my iPhone, only to find a missed call from Katie. She hadn't left a message, but even so, it was the first sign that she'd really wanted to contact me for a while, it felt strange. Heart-breaking, all over again. I guess I felt guilty, too, about not replying to her last text.

God, Katie. I was a little surprised at how effective our night out had been at distracting me from thoughts of her.

I did miss her. I missed the cozy familiarity of her being around. Her comforting smell, the easy smiles that hadn't been so easy recently. How long had she been miserable? Had I missed the signs?

But my concern for her welfare quickly segued into

pondering whether she'd been courting Grant for a while, and perhaps had just taken the need to move to the sexual phase with him as the time to end our marriage. It made me feel slightly betrayed, though it had been my fault she'd felt neglected, my fault I hadn't appreciated her.

I didn't call her back, I didn't know what to say to her. It might even have just been a butt-dial, and I'd phone her to find that she hadn't meant to call me.

At work, I told Henry about the missed call. He said simply, "She knows you've moved out. Probably just wants to make sure so she can turn that bedroom of yours into a sex dungeon."

"She knows?"

"When you slept there, did you used to tidy up the bedroom after you left, like she did?"

I paused, said, "I made the bed, cleared up any stuff I left lying around."

"But did you do it to her standard?"

"I suppose not."

"So then. She knew as soon as she came back to an unused bed that you moved out. Probably just wants to know when you're going to pick up the rest of your stuff from the house."

That was probably what her call would have been about. When did I plan to finally remove all traces of my presence from her life, so she could finally move on and forget all about me?

"I should just clear out my crap, huh?" I said to him. "Let her get on with her life."

"We'll take the car on the way to work tomorrow," Henry said, quickly coming to my support in the kind of tone of voice which made it impossible to politely turn down.

"*Y*ou think she was an item with Grant before she told me she wanted out of our marriage?" I asked Henry later, as we sat in Henry's battered brown Austin Montego, a car so ancient it might well have been left behind in the British Isles when the Romans went home.

Despite the logic of it all, it was still bugging me that Katie had already moved on.

I couldn't deny that our marriage had fallen flat, or that I didn't completely understand Katie's reasons for needing another man. Under the surface, I was even intrigued by her being with another man now—curious about how she'd be with someone who wasn't her husband. I was even happy for her, that she might be finding fulfillment with someone else.

Then of course there was that funny feeling I got thinking about her with someone else, turned on by her sexual revolution, in a way that I could not quite comprehend.

It did hurt that she might have been already looking for the attention of another man before calling it quits with me. I didn't have any proof one way or the other.

I was just confused, conflicted.

"I don't know, old man. Some women might be of the opinion that you shouldn't jump ship until you have some-where else to jump."

Henry was breathing out smoke as though he was trying some ill-thought-out method of camouflaging our presence parked just a few hundred yards down the street from my front door—or Katie's front door, as I had to think of it now.

"You talk to her since seeing her with him?" Henry asked.

I shook my head.

"Got to talk to her."

Henry passed over the joint, and I found myself accepting it without a second thought, despite the fact that I probably had a better track record keeping off drugs than the Pope. I'd smoked a cigarette for all of a month at university, as a vague attempt to get a girl interested. But I didn't turn down his offer now.

I'd spent my youth sternly opposed to illicit substances, certain that I'd one day grow up to be a crusading journalist. Well, what was the point objecting now? I breathed in long and slow, feeling the hot fumes filling my lungs. You couldn't argue with the powers of relaxation that it inspired.

"Maybe you just have to give it time," he said. "Let her sew her wild oats. Maybe when she remembers how awful most men are, she'll find she misses you, misses the stability of your marriage."

"I don't think I have a problem with her being with another guy," I said slowly, feeling no need to rush in my response, or in anything I was doing. Feeling that the slower I communicated, the slower I moved, the slower I did anything, the wiser it made me appear.

"It's not so much the fact that she was sleeping with him," I said eventually.

"It's not?"

"God, it seems so weird. Katie. My wife. Fucking another man. It's just... I never thought it would happen. And now it has..."

"But it's not the sleeping with him that gets to you?"

"I don't know... it's the fact that she doesn't need me

any more. I'm completely out of her life, I'm nothing to her. I didn't even affect her in five years of being with her."

"Nonsense, old chap. You've affected her plenty. She just has other needs—she needs to fuck."

The F-word sounded odd in Henry's plummy accent, it even made me chuckle.

"You know, seeing her like that, with Grant, I actually felt myself wanting to sleep with her again. First time I feel like I've wanted to for a long while."

I thought I'd get Henry cracking a joke at that, some kind of witty remark at my expense. But he simply nodded, said: "Perfectly natural. Rivalry gets the blood up, doesn't it? You see a guy making moves on your girl, your body responds by turning you on to her desire like never before."

It made sense. This strange mixture of jealousy and excitement was some leftover relict of prehistoric times when cavemen routinely clubbed each other over the heads to steal their women.

Feeling I had some kind of explanation actually felt reassuring.

"Plus, it's just plain hot knowing the woman you love just got herself off on the biggest dick you've ever seen," Henry added with a smile.

It was nearly seven o'clock in the evening. We'd arrived here a little later than planned after my sleep overran, and I'd spent the last fifteen minutes slumped in the creaky black leather passenger seat wondering if we'd have time to get into the house, retrieve my things and get out unseen before Katie came home from work.

The trouble was, I didn't have any real clue what time she got home from work these days. I really didn't want to be there when she came back, and be forced into some kind of conversation.

I wasn't sure I even wanted to see her, I wasn't sure whether I'd cope.

My insides were quietly burning. The fear that she'd return home, perhaps dragging Grant in with her for the purposes of banging his brains out, stabbed at my heart. I was probably most terrified of seeing that she was obviously happier without me.

"I guess if I'd just moved out straight away, as soon as she told me it was all over, it would have been easier," I said.

Henry puffed on the joint. "You can't say that for sure."

"Maybe. If I hadn't seen her with Grant..."

Henry laughed, though not in an unkind way. "It's no good searching the hypotheticals, my friend. There's no do-overs here."

"I suppose not."

"I mean, what if she'd originally come to you, said she had concerns about your lack of sex. Maybe even said she'd been hit on by someone at work, and it made her feel... wanted... in a way her husband hadn't for a long while. What then?"

"I would have tried something. Quit my job, maybe. Made my job search more obvious to her. Made more of an effort to... you know... sleep with her."

"Effort. It shouldn't be effort."

"No, but marriage is something you have to work on. I just didn't realize what aspects I should have been working on."

Henry nodded. "Maybe she thinks you did. You know how women can be—they communicate with you using signals they assume you can decipher."

I sighed. "Maybe I would have just said to her go ahead and have fun with your colleague, Grant or whoever.

But we could still be married, still be best friends, still know that we'd spend our lives together and when life settled down..."

The weed probably helped stir that funny feeling inside me at the thought that if she had outright come to me and said she wanted an affair with another man, I probably would have preferring allowing her to just do it than lose her completely.

It must have been the weed that made my cock start stiffening in my pants at the thought of actually letting Katie sleep with someone else just to save our marriage.

But then, my strange thoughts were interrupted by the arrival of Katie herself.

We saw her walking down the street in a shorter skirt than I'd ever seen, arm-in-arm with Grant, no less. Looking completely blasé about everything. In fact, I'm sure it wasn't my paranoia that gave me the impression she was happy. Slightly flushed with the excitement of a new relationship, perhaps, sex with a new man.

That hurt. The jealousy was like a knife being jabbed into my chest and twisted around.

God, look how comfortable she seemed in his presence, how right. They were both doctors, both surgeons—on a level, peers. He could understand her in ways that I could not, he could satisfy her in ways that I could not. And that faint glow about her was testament to her newfound satisfaction. I felt sad that it took someone else to give that to her.

Gutted, in fact.

But wasn't there a flicker of something else, almost like dark and perverted excitement, that my comfortable and stable existence was being shaken up so brutally, that life was about to change?

Perhaps, even, the caveman inside me felt some flicker

of arousal at the idea that sex was in the air—even if it hadn't happened very recently between these two lovebirds walking up the street, it was doubtless going to happen very soon.

The confusion inside me came from the idea that Katie looked somehow more attractive to me, more sexy, because she was now accompanying another man to our house with illicit intent. While I could not deny the searing pain from my jealousy, and the hurt from Katie pulling the wool over my eyes for god-knew-how-long, for some reason I'd never felt as drawn to Katie sexually as I was now—even compared to the early stages of our relationship.

I figured it was part of the whole shock thing. My brain finding complex ways to cope with the pain of betrayal.

"She doesn't love him," I said. I was confident about that, although it was perhaps the biggest fear I had. Grant was so brash, so loud, so slick, so aware of his good fortune. I couldn't imagine that Katie could love someone like that.

It was just a physical thing.

Part of me wanted to run down the street and tell her she was forgiven, that I understood why she was fooling around with Grant, that there was no reason to stop if she did it the right way. Yet what was the right way? I wouldn't want to know about it, but I wouldn't want her to deceive me.

Another part of me was angry. I had lost her, I felt there hadn't been enough opportunity for me to save our relationship.

"She's going to spend the night with him," I said, my tone flat, neutral. A statement in which I was merely testing my own feelings rather than making any real complaint about what was happening.

It almost felt as though I didn't really care any more.

Grant could have her. But that slight feeling of nausea was still there deep down.

"Come on," Henry said, knowing full well that now Katie was home, there was no way we'd be going in that house. "We can try again after work when she leaves."

By the time our shift was over, and we were heading back to the car Henry had parked in the Victoria Station lot overnight, I was in no mood to fetch my things from Katie's house.

I'm not sure I even wanted any of my belongings—anything I retrieved would be indelibly marked by our marriage, whether it was bought by her, bought with her, even simply used while we were together, it had memories ingrained.

I had to move on with my life.

5

Night on the town

*a*t least in the beginning, the pace of living with Henry and Michelle was frenetic. Five nights a week, Henry and I were working, two nights a week we all went out for heavy sessions in the bars and restaurants of Soho, Shoreditch, Clapham, Brixton, Camden or Islington —wherever Henry dragged us next.

I couldn't complain—we had the day time to sleep, and it took my mind off things with Katie, which was what I badly needed just then.

At one point, Henry came down with a touch of summer flu that had him permanently parked on the couch in front of the TV for a few days, swaddled in blankets and moaning about his various aches and the constant streaming of his Rudolf-red nose.

As I emerged from my day's sleep, I had assumed that evening I would crash in front of the TV with him, and when Michelle got back from business school, we'd all have a quiet one in honor of Henry's condition.

"So what're you up to tonight, Squire?" Henry asked me as I slumped down on the armchair with my evening's breakfast. He seemed like he was in need of some distraction from his plight.

"Actually, nothing much," I said. I felt as though I was letting the side down, having no plans, but I hadn't anticipated that Henry would be sick, leaving me to my own devices. The past couple of weeks, each time it was a night off, we'd wordlessly prepared ourselves, grabbed a bite to eat perhaps, and headed out to meet up with Michelle and start a night of drinking and chatting—and as I noticed and increasingly looked forward to, flirting. There was no Sean-making-independent-social-engagement-plans.

Henry was just being polite, though, hinting that I shouldn't be diverted from doing whatever I wanted on my night off, just because he was out of action.

"I guess I could have a fairly quiet night," I said, trying to lightly insist that I didn't feel put out not going out because he was sick.

"You fancy watching a movie?"

"Sure," I said, thinking he was going to order one through On Demand, or switch over to a movie channel.

"Great—Michelle's been dying to get to that new Godzilla remake."

I knew full well the one he was referring to was just coming out at the movie theater, it wasn't available on demand, on DVD, or anywhere else for the small screen just yet.

Henry wanted me to go out for the evening with his wife without him? It gave me some pause. I mean, I was certain it would be nice spending time in Michelle's company, but this would be the first time spending an extended period of time by ourselves. What if things turned awkward? Conversation might run out with Henry gone.

Our flirting had always seemed safe with Henry around—what would it be like without him there?

It wasn't as though I was going to start hitting on her while we were out at the movies, I supposed. I did have some self-control. I just didn't want things to seem suddenly awkward because Henry wasn't there—because that might suggest to us that the flirting when he was around was also inappropriate.

Yet I looked at his innocent—some might say 'naive'— face and now worried that if I refused, he might take it as a suggestion that I disliked Michelle somehow, or that I didn't want to do him the favor of escorting her to something she wanted to go to.

"It's supposed to be quite good," I said neutrally. "Better than the last remake, anyway. Wouldn't have thought that was her kind of movie."

I had no real idea what her kind of movie was, we hadn't really discussed that particular topic as yet.

"Oh, she's a total geek when it comes to movies," Henry said. "She'd be so thrilled if you went with her since I'm so bloody feeble at the moment."

I heaved an internal sigh. The thing was, a huge part of me was singing a silent Hallelujah just then at the thought of spending some time alone with Michelle. The thought of being in her presence, of having those occasional brushes of her hand, of spending the evening chatting and gazing upon her beauty, that set off fireworks inside me after so long without real female attention.

"I think it would be fun," I said, concealing any reservations I had. "What time's it showing?"

"Nine. She's coming back here to change first, there's no rush."

We watched one of the Alien movies while waiting for Michelle to return home—the third one, the underrated

David Fincher-directed one, which I'd always quite enjoyed.

"And how're things without me?" Henry kept the conversation ticking along, naturally, while I silently tried to brainstorm some discussion topics to draw from if Michelle and I ground to a conversational halt later that evening.

"Oh, it's not too bad. They persuaded Magnus to come back for a shift or two, since his baby's sleeping the night these days."

"Well, that's something. That Barker guy they got in when Sheila got the plague worked like a diabetic crack whore."

I spent the half hour wait trying to keep calm, trying to tell if Henry had any reservations whatsoever about Michelle and I going to the movies together—he showed no signs of it.

My attempts at being zen were shattered as soon as I heard Michelle let herself in the front door, and she emerged from the little hallway, all perky and pretty and gently flushed from her stroll home from the Tube station and from the fact that as an exercise aficionado, she shunned the elevator.

"Hey, you're watching without me? I love this one!"

Henry laughed. "It's in your iTunes library," he said. "You can watch it whenever you want."

"It's not the same without company," she rolled her eyes at hubby, but offered me a beaming smile, saying: "So we're going to Godzilla?"

I felt my heart lift at being able to answer in the affirmative. God, how could I ever deny such a woman? Even if I'd previously said 'no' to Henry that evening, I knew just by looking at Michelle that one little plea from her and I'd have committed to being her escort anyway.

"Fantastic!" she said. "It's got great reviews. You all set to go? I just need a quick change."

We had plenty of time, but Michelle's quick change was anything but fast. She'd come home wearing sweats —she'd gone to her MBA class straight after work, so it was fair enough she felt she needed a shower. But it took a while, and then it took even longer for her to dress, and then she was applying make-up for a fair amount of time.

When she eventually emerged her make-up was applied to impress, her hair brushed and flowing beautifully down her back, and she looked incredible in a black and silver summer dress that simply took the breath away.

She looked as though she was dressed for a night at the Oscars, not a casual visit to the movie theater with her husband's friend.

And her plunging neckline plunged so far that it took very little imagination to picture her shapely breasts. Was she even wearing a bra? If she was, it was cleverly engineered.

I put every ounce of effort into avoiding a gasp as she stepped between Henry and I, and approached her husband for a brief kiss on the lips, filling the room with her sweet fragrance as she did so.

"You look amazing," he said to her, but while I waited for him to add some suggestion that she was overdressed for a movie, or some kind of command to put on something more appropriate for an evening with his friend, he didn't.

Was he really going to allow her out of his sight wearing something like this?

"You will try to get some sleep, won't you?" she said to him. "I don't care if you throw your body clock off, you need sleep."

"Yes, dear," Henry said, and as Michelle turned to me, he gave me a playful eye-roll about his wife's mothering.

"Ready to go?" she asked me.

I had one of those moments where I just did not know where to put my eyes. The way she was looming over me as I sat in that armchair, her short, short dress and those lithe legs in elegant black nylons —

"Uh... yeah," I fumbled, eventually setting my eyes on hers. "Am I supposed to be in a suit for this movie?"

She grinned at my jokey flattery of her wow-factor, but it wasn't entirely a joke. It did look a trifle ridiculous walking out with her dressed in jeans and a casual blue shirt.

I walked slowly with her out of the apartment, leaving Henry plenty of time to come to the decision that he did not want his wife spending the evening with another man looking like that. But he never got up from the couch, never called out after us, never said anything after the last:

"Have fun, you guys!"

*W*hile we were out, I did notice that other women were wearing summer dresses, and a lot of those dresses were quite short. I guess the summer had arrived, and it was a warm evening. Katie had tended to wear trousers, as did the friends of hers we socialized with on the increasingly few occasions I could manage it with my nocturnal schedule.

But as we hopped off the bus at Hammersmith to venture into the little Cineworld movie theater on the corner opposite the town hall, and queued up for our tickets, I did notice quite a few male eyes—and some female— checking Michelle out.

I actually felt a little buzz from having them checking her out, thinking she was with me. Almost pride, I guess you might say.

As we were standing in line to get tickets, I noticed—how could I not—that her nipples were faintly visible through the dress, or at least their impressions against the thin material. So she wasn't wearing a bra, despite her intense attention to her appearance before we came out.

I think other guys must have noticed too. It wasn't particularly cold in that movie theater—was she quietly excited by attracting a little attention while we were out on the town?

My eyes remained a fraction of a second too long on those little raised points over her chest, and as I drew them back to her eyes, it was fairly clear she'd noticed where I'd been looking. At the realization, I swear I saw the corners of her mouth edge upwards. Had Henry been aware she was not wearing a bra for this evening's night out?

"You guys go out to the movies much?" I asked her, a lame conversational gateway that was the first thing I could think of to distract from being busted.

"We used to before we got married, but it's only once in a blue moon these days," she said, not dwelling on the fact that she'd caught me red-handed.

Then she said: "Henry said you'd been hoping to see this one for a while."

"It's supposed to be good."

"You weren't put off by the last Godzilla movie?"

I managed to avoid reacting to this little inconsistency, since Henry had told me Michelle had been the one itching to see this movie.

Had Henry engineered this evening for some reason? A husband seeking an evening's peace while he was feeling unwell. My ears burned a little, but I let it go.

"You know, I didn't mind the last Godzilla movie that much. Everyone says how bad it was, but I thought it was okay."

"You like bad movies too?" she was amused at our sudden connection. "Or, movies that are supposed to be bad."

I laughed. "That's the thing, isn't it? Every movie is bad for someone. Bladerunner was panned when it came out —"

"That took a director's cut to reverse, though, so I'm not sure it counts..."

Well, we were in a movie theater. If you can't talk about movies there, where can you? The rest of the wait for tickets, and then for the latest remake of Godzilla to start, we debated great movies that had had terrible reviews when they came out, and it was an easy conversation to have. Nicely time-filling for a guy worried about getting too close to his best friend's wife.

When the trailers started, and all talk in the auditorium ceased, I felt thankful that we would have 123 minutes in each other's company without having to worry about how we were getting on away from the chaperone eyes of Michelle's husband and my only friend in the world.

I assumed that once the credits were rolling, we'd slip out of the theater and be back on the bus to Chiswick by the time the house lights came back up.

But Michelle was not headed for the bus, she turned right out of the theater, away from home.

"Tell me you don't want something more than soda after that!" Michelle grinned as I flashed a confused expression at her as she walked backwards away from me up towards the more lively end of Hammersmith.

"I guess..." I said, not wanting to be seen as an old fuddy-duddy by this younger woman.

"Come on—we can start at the Dartmouth Castle."

"Start?"

Well, what damage could a few beers do?

The thing was, it wasn't just a few beers. We got talking, and my fears of running out of conversation during the evening quickly evaporated—even before the booze really sank in, it felt so natural talking to her, opening up about my past, grilling her about hers, we could have filled dozens of evenings.

I think I was relieved after the first drink that we were able to get on with each other without Henry being present.

Only, what was now concerning me was that I might be in danger of developing a little crush on my friend's wife. I felt I could really have done without something like that.

Don't get me wrong—it was wonderful to spend time with her. Every moment I was with her felt like I was in some enchanted world. I was breathing her perfume, I was sitting a few feet from her, gazing into her eyes across the table, and I was the only person in her focus that whole evening.

But in my situation, things could get seriously awkward if I started doing more than simply admiring her from afar.

That evening I could find distraction in the simple fact that actually, she was really quite an interesting person having grown up in rural Iowa before moving to Chicago after her parents' marriage broke up, and of course her relocation across an ocean.

"And you decided London was the place to make a career out of sports and fitness?"

"I only came for a year in college because I minored in history and I wanted to see castles, but hey, I liked it."

"So you stayed."

"Also, I met Henry while I was in my college year here. That kind of decided it for me."

"And the immigration authorities just let you stay when your student visa ran out?"

She smiled. "Oh no. I had to go back to graduate from college. That was another year—"

"And you were still with Henry?"

She shrugged, "It was only a year, we managed things long-distance. Henry spent far too much on air fares, so we saw each other every other month or so. There was light at the end of the tunnel."

"You guys must have really fallen for each other."

"He's a real sweetheart," Michelle grinned, and it seemed as though she lit up the entire place. I felt glad for Henry that he'd met someone like Michelle, that he'd found The One, but I can't say my chest didn't burn a little with pure envy.

"Then when you graduated, you were able to live over here?"

She held up her hand, flashing him the ring. "Henry asked me to marry him, so..."

I think talking to her, seeing how strong her bond was with Henry, actually settled me down, calmed my fears, made me see her in a slightly different light. Having any kind of crush on such a woman would clearly be ridiculous.

Having her grill me about my backstory actually helped me return my perception of her to safe platonic territory. I didn't particularly want to talk about the death of my father, but it was a fundamental part of who I was I suppose.

"You were thirteen? I can't imagine how awful that must have been."

"It was pretty hard to deal with. But if you think about it, there are a lot of people out there in the world suffering more."

"Still. Nobody should have to go through that."

It felt a little funny to be talking so openly about my past. I guess Katie and I never had shared much, beyond the initial getting-to-know-you while we'd dated. Details had come out here and there, of course, along the way, not least on visits to her family or when socializing with friends. But after we settled down, the sharing of the anecdotes and prying into the past had fizzled long before even our passion had cooled off.

I suppose I'd always thought I had a fairly unremarkable background, but Michelle prized a fair amount out of me. It was quite a surprise to find myself running through a Cliff Notes on my own personal romantic history. The alcohol helped.

"She was called what?"

"Magda Cum Laude. Well, that wasn't her real name. Magda Swietek, actually. Polish. But she had a certain reputation for... well, vocalizing, shall we say, when she was... enjoying herself."

"That is terrible. And she knew you guys called her this?"

"We may have kept that particular information from her."

"Boys can be so cruel."

"Oh, and girls don't inflict psychological damage on each other at all?"

"Yeah, I guess so. Girls can do it so much more effectively than boys."

As I discussed the more significant girlfriends I'd had before Katie, I did find myself keeping back one particular detail. A lot of the girlfriends I'd had, especially at school and in college, had started out dating my friends.

No wonder I hadn't kept in touch with any of my friends from college.

It was kind of embarrassing how many times it had happened, too. Why had I always pursued girls my friends had dated? I wasn't the most socially forward of guys back at school—those girls were the only ones I'd really hung out with, I guess. So perhaps it had only been natural for me to form attachments to them, or at least desire them.

Magda Swietek: I remembered her, of course, but it had been Eddie Dorlan who had dated her first. And when they'd split up, and I started seeing her myself, I remember how frosty things became with Eddie. At the time, I'd just turned all self-righteous—if he disliked me for dating a girl he no longer wanted, then he couldn't be a very good friend, then, could he?

Only, with hindsight and a little more maturity, it was easy to see that my friends hadn't wanted to hang out with their exes, and didn't want to think about me being with their exes, either.

I'd really messed things up in my social life.

But, what could I do about that now?

Still, Michelle being the wife of my only remaining friend, I saw no reason to tell her of my running proclivity in the world of romance. Katie had been an exception to that rule.

Katie was like the diametric opposite now, of course: she was now dating a friend of mine, Grant. He'd always been a friend of hers, too, but still. I suppose it was karma to some extent.

Anyway. The point was, talking everything through with Michelle helped me to stop trying to impress her, and helped me to relax. It didn't mean I ignored the array of cleavage on show thanks to that dress, or the way her azure blue eyes made me shiver all over whenever they connected with my comparatively dull brown eyes, but I was able to cool it, treat her more like a platonic friend.

The only thing that disrupted my state of calm was the fact that she could not sit still, at least rarely longer than a single round.

"Come on—I know a great place around the corner," she'd say, but we'd end up piling into a cab and driving halfway across town before the next place.

We ended up traipsing between bars in Soho, a fair shout from home. I guess she was younger than Henry and I, just a few years out of college, more likely to want to do everything everywhere, rather than slump in one place to just drink the night away. She was also a lot fitter than either Henry or I, and that was a mainstay of our night out —her constantly having to drag me along, with yours truly huffing and puffing to keep up, and Michelle hopping along all bright and sprightly as though she'd been drinking caffeine all night instead of alcohol.

Oh, I'd seen it before on our nights out with Henry, plenty of times, but with Henry laid up back home, Michelle seemed to feel the shackles were truly off, and her bounding along London's streets was twice as bouncy.

"How does Henry ever keep up with you?" I asked at one point, bowing over and gasping for oxygen before my lungs exploded.

"Oh, he does okay," she grinned. "You wanna see if Harry's is crowded? It's just 'round the corner. They have good cocktails in there."

I straightened up, hands on my hips, which is actually

better for sucking in air than bending over, as I remembered from my old rugby days. "How about we find somewhere that does a good mug of warm cocoa," I suggested, "and we sit you down and pump a few gallons down your throat? That might calm you down a little."

She giggled and flashed me a mischievous look that accepted that her marathon-style bar crawling might be a little unfair to the uninitiated.

"I do have a lot of energy to burn when Henry's... not in the mood," she said.

In the neon lights of the Soho streets, I could see those little bullet nipples of hers once again, straining against her dress, and it brought back the whole burning, pulsating, blood-pumping desire to me that I'd just about managed to repress. God, she was a horny minx, and it was plain as day that she wasn't getting enough of her usual dose of physical attention from her husband. It made her seem so devastatingly alluring to me.

"Well, I think I burned off most of my energy three or four places ago," I complained.

We started walking over to Harry's, a bar on Poland Street I seemed to recall had a couple of absinthe-based cocktails that could send a rocket to the moon and back.

She grinned. "You need to join one of my fitness classes, Mister."

"I think I tend to be sleeping when you have your aqua aerobics classes," I said, silently thinking that I'd probably look a fool doing one of her classes along with seasoned regulars.

"No, I run a few training classes on Chiswick Common after people get out from work," she said. "They'd be perfect."

"Well, I suppose I could try..."

"And none of the guys that do it are particularly advanced."

"Okay, I'll give a go some time."

"Next one's Monday. I'll hold you to it!"

I nodded, sighed, feeling the bonds tying me to this dazzling creature getting stronger and stronger by the moment. I'd need some good recovery from this night of debauchery before attempting anything like real exercise, though, I thought.

However, a round of the aforementioned absinthe-based mind-blowers later, and Michelle had some real exercise in mind.

"You want to take me dancing?"

"You're kidding?"

"Of course not—it'll be great fun."

---

*N*aturally, I had no ability to refuse her, so we ended up in a little basement club on Frith Street, shaking to a thumping beat among a mob of sweaty twenty somethings. I felt old, but there was distraction in the form of Michelle in that dress dancing close to me—and as things proceeded, increasingly closer.

It was one of the most intensely erotic experiences of my life up to that point. The fact that such a beautiful young woman was dancing with me, surrounding me with her scent, her athletic frame moving so gracefully to the music, made me feel alive like never before.

I had her pretty smile constantly breaking out as we danced, and those sparkling eyes of hers shot lightning bolts through me with every glance. Her occasional touching of me became less and less occasional all night, and I wasn't going to stop her, though I was careful not to reciprocate with any subtle contact of my own.

The thought that she was working off her pent-up sexual energy with me made the blood rush between my legs. I had to be careful to keep my hardness from pressing against her as we danced, giving the game away. I think once or twice she may have detected it. I just hoped she would be too tipsy to remember come the morning.

One time, she purposefully bumped into it, and there was no way I could conceal it from her. She giggled and looked all wide-eyed at me, her jaw dropping in a silent gasp.

But damn it, this was my friend's wife.

I mumbled something about needing the restroom, and excused myself, a little terrified that word would get back to my friend that I'd taken his wife out dancing and had pushed my erection against her body while we danced.

After I got back, Michelle behaved herself, and we even managed a little slow dancing without infringing on Henry's territory.

On our way home, however, I couldn't help but think about the way she had been pressing against me. She really was trouble.

*W*hen we got home I was thinking how Henry was both seriously lucky to have such a gorgeous wife, while also being unfortunate in that it was quite possible she could not fully contain her insatiable libido.

I mean, that thought only added to her allure in my eyes, but I could see that if Henry wasn't careful, one of these days Michelle might be tempted to stray.

Perhaps—and I told myself so—her forward behavior with me that night was a one-off, and alcohol-fueled, part of her effort to divert my attention from my own failed marriage.

It was the early hours of the morning as we parted ways in the narrow little corridor between our respective bedrooms, and Michelle kissed me demurely on the cheek, almost as though she was aware things might have been close to bending the boundaries of appropriateness for us a little that evening.

"Thank you for a wonderful night, Sean," she said, with another of her pretty smiles. "I had so much fun."

"Hey, any time," I said to be polite, though I'm not sure I could handle that kind of night too frequently. "I had a great night too."

And then she was gone, leaving the last look at her in that dress burned on my retinas, complete with the slight sheen of perspiration from our energetic end to the night, a slight flush on her cheeks and her exposed chest, and those stiff little buds of hers perched atop her mouthwatering peaks.

I silently wondered if it might be obvious what was going on if I took a cold shower just then.

Turning into my own bedroom, I found myself considering the evening, wondering whether anything we'd done together would actually be offensive to Henry. It depended how jealous he was as a person.

I couldn't really picture him jealous, just as I couldn't really picture him angry—that never happened.

Was Michelle simply a highly flirtatious person, was she like that with other guys as well, perhaps at her yoga classes or in the personal training sessions she held in the park a few blocks away?

Was Henry aware of how she was with other guys if he wasn't around?

All these concerns of mine reflected my own marriage collapse, of course. I think it wasn't entirely selfless thinking, either, since if Henry was caught in a similarly failed marriage, his resulting misery added to mine might make our working lives that much more intolerable. One of us, at least, had to keep up their spirits.

After our night out, I couldn't really see Michelle as the type to do something behind her husband's back, though. She adored Henry, that much was clear. It was just her obvious and powerful sex drive: was that enough to push her into infidelity?

I found myself amused that my fears about Michelle being unfaithful with other men was so obviously linked to my own jealousy, that Michelle might be unfaithful with men other than me. It made me laugh, recognizing how awfully self-centered I could be sometimes.

Climbing into bed, a noise from outside my room stopped me, silenced me.

A quiet, female moan. Undoubtedly Michelle.

I felt my heart skip a little. There was another moan, a little louder. I crept to my door, and opened it a crack. Now I heard the silky sounds of Michelle breathing heavily. A warm tingle sparked up in my loins. God, she was so sexy. And here was me thinking we'd come home and Michelle would simply slip into bed and call it a day, despite her being seriously horny after our dangerous dancing.

No, she was horny, and she was tending to it. I was certain.

Oh, I should have left her to it, should have allowed her some privacy, but I was so turned on, so curious more than anything. I opened my door a little wider, and her moaning became louder still. I wondered for a moment if she was in the living room or in the bathroom—but the sound seemed to be coming from her and Henry's room.

But Henry was supposed to be out of action, wasn't he? He wasn't even able to take his wife out for a quiet movie at a theater 10 minutes away on the bus.

I slipped out of my door, figuring that if anyone caught sight of me, I could easily turn it into simply visiting the bathroom to clean my teeth before bed.

The sound was certainly coming from Henry and Michelle's room—was Henry asleep while she was tending to herself?

God, the way she sounded, her sighs, her little moans, the way her breath caught in her throat in response to the sensations swirling around her body—it was the most erotic thing I could remember.

But then I heard Henry's voice softly, barely more than a whisper: "You're so wet..."

I heard the wet smacking sound of lips kissing bare flesh, and it was suddenly clear to me that Michelle was not tending to herself. She'd woken him up, or else he'd been awake when we'd returned home. He must have wondered why we'd gotten in so late, having meant to just go see a movie.

Maybe I'd imagined Henry's voice, his words an illusion drawn from the sounds Michelle was making in her sexual bliss.

But then he said quietly: "Must've been a good night."

I felt the envy and—though I had no right whatsoever —the jealousy injected into my stomach. I also felt a strange tinge of disappointment, that Michelle had gotten so worked up, so aroused by our dancing, but then she'd come straight home to wake up her husband to deal with it for her. I guess a part of me—that unforgivably selfish part —had wanted her to come home unfulfilled, her desire for me increasing. Even though I didn't want to be put in the situation where I could choose to actively commit adultery with my best friend's wife.

Michelle moaned loudly, and then I heard her say: "Oh, it was. You know how much I like dancing..."

What was he doing with her? God, did I really want to see? Could I really handle that? If simply listening to them made my stomach feel so tight, my heart threatening to jump out of my throat, how would I react to watching Henry making love to the woman who made me feel such longing?

"Naughty girl..."

"Oh... oh my God..."

"You like that, huh?"

"Right there... right there..."

A little gasp from the pretty brunette, and I felt certain he'd entered her.

Her moaning intensified, her pitch rising rapidly into a feverish soprano.

I suddenly felt a little foolish: Henry and Michelle's marriage wasn't in trouble. Not even close. They seemed as passionate to me as a couple in the very first stages of romance.

My stomach lurched into a state of mild nausea. I shouldn't have been listening anyway. I backed into my room again, forgetting any idea of even going to the bathroom before bed on this occasion.

Headphones in, music on, I shut the saucy sounds out of my world.

6

The arrangement

*T*he next evening as we headed off for work once more, I was struck by just how well Henry looked. I felt certain he hadn't been faking his illness to begin with, but surely he couldn't have recovered so much from the mess I'd seen on the couch as Michelle and I had ventured out to the cinema, to what I saw now?

He seemed like a new man.

It wasn't until we were out of the apartment, away from his wife, and strolling past Turnham Green up to the High Road on our regular walk to the nearest Tube station, that Henry mentioned what was at the forefront of both our minds.

"So you did have a good time last night?"

I looked at him, trying to gauge his true feelings. Did he want me to tell him I had a great time, that he had been right to suggest we go out anyway, even if he didn't manage to go with us? Or did he want to hear that it just hadn't been the same without him, that Michelle had been miserable without him and I had missed the wit and erudition of his standard conversation?

Was he prying to check that nothing untoward had happened the previous night?

But this was Henry. Henry the Labrador Retriever, Henry the guy who just did not have pretexts or subtexts or whatever-the-hell-texts I was supposed to worry about when someone sent me on a night out in the city alone with his wife.

"We had a great time," I said, opting for the honest yet guarded option for an answer. "Really. It was just a shame you couldn't make it."

He smiled, and as had often seemed the case with Henry, he made me see that really, honesty was the way forward. There was no point in trying to spin things, engineer the response I thought Henry most wanted.

"Michelle had so much fun," he said.

"We both did. She's... something else."

"Isn't she?" a grin. Pride, it was definitely pride. There was no hint of jealousy in Henry, no hint of suspicion. "You took her dancing!"

A jolt of fear shot through me—was he angry that she'd danced with me, at how it had gone?

"I think... well, it was more like she took me dancing."

"God, I can't stand dancing. And I'm useless. So thanks for doing that, old man."

Henry seemed genuinely grateful to me, for taking over his dancing responsibilities. I felt a huge obligation to tell him, to warn him about how strange it had been, at how flirtatious Michelle had been, and how dangerous it had seemed to me at the time.

I felt compelled to warn him of my past history of stealing girlfriends—but it was so difficult to know how to tell him. Naturally I didn't want to throw myself on a sword and force my moving out, but I also didn't want to cast dispersions on Michelle, to smear her character with the suggestion that if Henry wasn't careful, she'd cheat on him.

"She has a lot of energy," I said after a pause. Coward.

"She definitely has that. When we first met, I never felt the need to keep up with her. I assumed we'd only be going out for a few weeks, maybe a few months at most."

"She was only over here for a year, right?"

"Right. I guess the Henry back then saw that as quite a nice little limit on things."

"Nice?"

Another broad Henry grin. Mischievous, amused, and yet a touch remorseful for his old ways. "I was not the kind of chap you would ever have thought would become a married man—and a happily married man at that. I took my fill of womankind, and always wanted more."

"Until Michelle came along."

"She changed me, there's no question about it."

"Well, it just shows how good you guys are together."

He nodded. "It does..."

"But?" I could hear in his tone the 'but' coming.

Another nod. "But... well, increasingly I suspect I can't keep doing this."

I felt a kick to my stomach. What was he saying? He was having problems with his marriage? The thought that this perfect couple might have some hidden fracture horrified me. Strangely, just then I felt a deeper sadness for Henry and Michelle than I did about the very real collapse of my own marriage with Katie.

"You can't—"

Henry sighed. "I want to, I do," he said. "But she gets bored when we have evenings in together. Unless there's a seriously good movie on, we have to go out. And then... well, she still has a lot of energy left by the time we get home."

I felt my ears burn, my face flush at the thought of just how the two of them worked out that excess energy after I brought Michelle home to him.

"She has other friends, right? That she goes out with while we're at work?"

"Some. Most of her real friends are in the States, of course, but she has a few friends from her MBA class, and from her gym. But the guys from the gym don't drink and her friends from business school don't fool about on school nights."

"Leaving her the nights when we're off work?"

"Exactly."

As we strolled across Chiswick Common, where Michelle ran her extracurricular fitness classes, across to the Tube station, I was desperately trying to think of suggestions—but what could I suggest? Did they have dating services for women to find other women merely for friendship? They had a lot of things on the Internet these days.

"But it's no reason to... you know... split up...?"

I blurted it out after a long pause between us was beginning to get out of control. My biggest fear for them, I guess, and it was a genuine fear. I knew a small part of me —the part that had waited quietly for Eddie Dorlan to break up with Magda Swietek so that I could make my move—rejoiced in the thought that Henry and Michelle might somehow split up, go their separate ways. The rest of me had learned, and knew well that if Henry and Michelle went their separate ways, that would be the end of my seeing Michelle. Henry was my friend. And Michelle had no reason not to go back to the United States if she no longer had Henry.

"Split up?"

Henry looked at me aghast, and then started laughing. "Oh, no, I'm not saying that at all."

A wave of relief swept through my system.

"There'll be some kind of solution to it," I said, smiling, trying to make light of my drastic interpretation of where Henry was going with this.

"We just need to find a few ways for her to use up her energy."

"Exactly."

"So how about helping a fella out?" Henry said as we proceeded across the crosswalk toward the Tube, yelling a little to be heard over the engines of the rush-hour traffic stopping to let us pass.

"I'm sorry?" I wondered if I'd heard him correctly.

On the other side of the road, we could hear each other a little better. Henry said: "You guys had a great time together last night—what say we make a regular thing of it?"

"Regular?" I felt stupid. Henry wanted me to take Michelle on regular nights out without him?

"If you and I staggered our nights off a little," he explained as we rounded the corner into the Tube station, "I could have a night out with her, and you could have a night out with her, and we could all have a night out together, and that would give her three nights out a week, instead of two."

"You'd still be going out twice a week," I pointed out, though just as some kind of distraction to the clamor going on inside my brain at the prospect that Henry truly wanted me to take his beautiful young wife out on my own one night a week.

"It would make her happier," he said with a shrug, "and maybe she'd be more willing to have the occasional quiet night in with me."

I could see his logic. God, it wasn't as though he was asking me to sleep with her. It was just a friendly night out once a week, to keep her occupied, diverted. Shoulder some of Henry's burden from having an energetic spouse.

Through the turnstiles, and up the steps to the platform, I felt the conflict going on inside me—the celebrations that I might get to enjoy more evenings out flirting with the lovely Michelle, along with the fear that one day we'd get overly tipsy and do something inappropriate, something that threatened Henry's happiness with her.

"What do you say?" he asked as we got to the platform, the nearest train being two minutes away according to the display.

What else could I say?

"Well, I suppose... sure, why not?"

While Henry and I had always scouted the job vacancies during our evening shifts, for a few weeks I was also pouring over apartment rental listings, room share websites and the like looking for somewhere to take my next step in the grown up world.

We talked about that, and Henry's advice was not to accept something sub-standard.

"You know you can stay with us as long as you like," he said. "Not worth moving out unless you can find something genuinely better."

"You're a gentleman, sir."

I could only respond with quiet gratitude, my tone of voice clear in its appreciation but also hinting that I didn't want to put them out, I didn't want to keep disrupting their privacy. The truth was, I didn't really want to move out. Chiswick was a wonderful part of

London, in which I probably wouldn't be able to afford to live on my own.

Of course I enjoyed living with Henry, extending the repertoire we'd always had in our nightshifts together. Michelle was something else. She was like the treat you don't quite believe you deserve to enjoy as much as you do.

On the few occasions we saw her during the working week, I'd catch flashes of her in her yoga clothes, or her swimsuit, or even a glimpse of her underwear from time to time. She didn't seem worried about using the whole of the apartment when getting changed—wandering through the living room half-dressed because she'd left her make-up bag in the bathroom, perhaps, or her hair dryer in the living room.

Sometimes I'd get up during my daytime sleep period to use the bathroom to find her hanging out watching TV in nothing more than an old t-shirt and panties. Apparently trusting that I was asleep—and yet she must have known the chances were high that I might get up now and again to use the facilities.

I also got to see a fair amount of her during her fitness classes out in the park. She ran them on Chiswick Common after the nine-to-five so that local commuters could get out and do some regular exercise out in the open air. I joined as promised, and it did actually make me feel good.

I wasn't the only person in the class sneaking surreptitious glances at her in her tight fitness gear. But it motivated me to attend, and Michelle may well have caught me looking a few times and never let on that she minded. Her smiles even suggested she enjoyed it, if you interpreted them that way.

Settled into that apartment, with a new regular exercise regime and a couple of close friends who really seemed to enjoy spending time with me, my self-confidence definitely started to pick up again after the devastating blow wreaked by Katie's dismissal.

Over those first few weeks, I started wondering if I would ever move out of their place. I guess I expected to at some point.

Having the certainty that this was only temporary did mean I no longer feared the constant flirting with Michelle. I enjoyed it. She seemed to enjoy it too. Henry didn't say anything about it, but he couldn't have missed it. I guessed he just had total trust in his wife, he knew she wouldn't do anything risky.

After my eavesdropping of their encounter following our night out, I purchased ear plugs specifically to ensure that when Henry and I got home after work, or when we all came home after a night out, they had their own space upon which I did not encroach. Besides, I didn't think I could handle overhearing more of Henry satisfying Michelle.

Only, as time wore on, and I felt more and more settled in that spare room, I actually started to feel a little uncomfortable in my close relationship with Michelle. I was taking her out one night a week, and seeing her one night a week with Henry, and it seemed that I was spending as much time with her as he was.

It made me feel guilty: I had invaded their nest like a cuckoo, yet the two of them needed their own personal space, I believed.

In quiet moments where the guilt started to eat at me, I also felt the surviving pain from losing Katie—and that pain made me feel certain that I should be doing more to try to re-engage, reconnect with my wife than to enjoy myself in Michelle's presence. I might have accepted it was over mentally, but my heart was still finding it difficult to let go of the idea of Katie.

I kept resolving to call Katie. But then each time I'd pick up the phone, I'd back down. Thinking that she hadn't called me since that night, since that text she'd sent. She probably wanted to just move on.

I guess it unnerved me that I might call her and she'd say something like, "Oh, you just reminded me: I've got to get the divorce papers sorted out."

Meanwhile, I started making excuses why I couldn't go out with Henry and Katie, or why I couldn't manage to take Michelle out on our regular nights—purely to give them a chance to be together exclusively with each other. It meant spending even less time with Michelle, which ate at my insides, but I felt I had no choice.

And when I did go out with her, I toned it down.

I was still perfectly friendly, I was never distant, never outright shunning her. I just tempered my behavior—my smiles were polite and friendly rather than flirtatious or suggestive.

Then one night at work, when we were talking about something or other during which the subject of Michelle came up, Henry said to me: "You do still like her, don't you?"

His words felt sharp to me. Like he'd discovered the true extent of my burgeoning crush on his wife.

"Like her?"

"Michelle. It's just... well, it just seemed like you've been avoiding her a little recently—avoiding me when I'm with her."

He'd realized, then. I felt butterflies stirring inside my stomach for some reason, at the idea that I'd gone too far, perhaps, that I needed a certain amount of flirting with Michelle or else Henry would feel we weren't getting on.

"She's great, Henry, really. I've just been trying to give you guys a bit of space. You know—because I still haven't found a place."

"You're not still griping about that, old man?" he said. "Look, I wonder if it might not be a good idea to come to some kind of arrangement on that score."

"Arrangement?"

"Well, you know, so you can just stay. We have a spare room, we're not having kids any time soon. You need a place—we're well located."

"Oh. But you guys need your own place," I said, but liking the idea of a permanent arrangement.

"We do fine. We've talked about this—maybe you could just rent the room from us. But if you're not so keen on Michelle..."

I smiled, and then my mouth nearly got me in trouble. "If anything I like her too much," I said, my heart palpitating as I realized how dangerous my over-sharing of information could be. "Any man would be quite envious of you, Henry."

Henry gave me a broad grin. "She is pretty special, isn't she?" Then he gave a nod, adding: "Then it's settled."

S o I became a lodger. But after that little chat, I also knew I couldn't afford to completely end my conviviality with Michelle.

Sure, that fondness for her was not going to go away—and I was not going to free myself from the simmering burn of jealousy as I saw my friend disappearing off with her to bed at the end of our nights out together. Yet managing my feelings carefully, I found I could be playfully flirtatious with her, almost as though I was an older brother or gay best friend.

I was able to loosen up and enjoy her sporadic flashes of flesh, allowing them to fuel my fantasies behind the scenes, while on the surface teasing her about it with reminders that she had another man around the house now, a man who was not her husband.

I caught a slight smile here, or a raised eyebrow there on the occasions my glimpses of her skimpy clothing were a little too lingering, but I think she liked the attention, my noticing her exposure only ever seemed to spur her on to do it more.

When I was with her, even just lounging around, my pulse quickened noticeably and my breathing accelerated in step. It was actually slightly thrilling to be straddling that edge between the deep attraction on my crush and the control I needed to keep from embarrassing myself.

I just treated it all as a bit of fun.

And my relationship with Henry was so relaxed I could tease him a little about his wife's tendency toward being semi-naked in our apartment—dropping hints she was after me, and so on.

He either laughed it off completely, or made the kind of joke that sometimes made my heart quiver.

"We could have some kind of arrangement," he might say, grinning in his innocent manner. "I'm sure she'd like that."

7

An invitation

*S*hould I have felt guilty that my loosening up about the whole living with Michelle thing took my mind off the whole collapsed marriage thing with Katie?

Well, it hadn't been me who had decided to call time on our marriage. Having a good time with Henry and Michelle, though, particularly the flirtatious Michelle, it did make me feel a strange remorse that I wasn't obsessing over Katie, that I wasn't doing everything in my power to win her back.

I did feel that Katie wasn't the type of person to make such a huge decision and then change her mind. But still.

All those thoughts came rushing back to me as Henry and I came out of the Daily News building one morning after the end of our shift to find a familiar face standing on the curbside, presumably waiting for yours truly, dressed smartly ready for work.

"Hi, Sean."

"Alicia. What are you doing here?"

"You haven't been answering your phone, or responding to her emails."

It felt like a huge injustice to me that right then, that she was making it out as if I was the one in the wrong. But really it was my own sense of guilt that was making her words seem like criticism.

"I don't check that email address any more."

"She worries about you, Sean. She misses you."

I really didn't feel like slugging it out with Katie's sister Alicia in the early morning, after a whole night's work. And she was so much more intelligent than me. God, two sisters: a surgeon and an eminent human rights lawyer. What genes they had in their family. I must have been such a disappointment as a son-in-law.

"If she misses me that much, she could have come herself."

Alicia sighed. "She was worried that if she showed up, it would hurt you."

I nodded. I suppose it was nice that Katie was so thoughtful. In between banging Grant.

"Well, I'm fine, so you can go tell her," I said, keeping my chin up. Then, changing the subject, "How's Paul? You guys still aiming for September?"

Alicia looked pale, drawn. I think I was most surprised at how she seemed to be taking this, not that Katie wanted to get in touch with me. I'd always liked Alicia. Despite her lofty achievements, she'd always looked beyond my lack of career success, always accepted me in their family.

She ignored my reference to her wedding plans. She wasn't moving from the subject. She said, "You were her best friend, Sean. For five years, you were her best friend."

"That wasn't quite enough, though, was it?" I felt the anger bubbling up now, such an ugly emotion, something I usually avoided at all costs, probably to my own disadvantage in life.

"She's just been working too hard... she's at that stage where she's successful at her job, she thinks everything else in her life should be just as perfect."

"Well, I wasn't perfect. I don't think any man ever could be."

She sighed again. I didn't like arguing with her, and it wasn't because she was more intelligent than me, it was because when you argue with someone, you want the points to hit home—only this argument, the points were supposed to hit home with Katie, not her innocent sister.

"I guess Grant must be pretty perfect," I added, and regretfully, my words had barbs on them.

I saw in Alicia's dark eyes that I was right to assume Katie was still seeing him, and I felt my heart squeezed as a result.

"She loves you, Sean. She just doesn't know what she wants right now."

I shook my head. This depiction of Katie as confused, wandering about without knowing exactly what she was doing—it didn't fit with the person I knew her to be. She was a very bright, very driven, very talented young surgeon.

"Katie's a beautiful heart surgeon, what the hell does she need from someone like me? She can have whoever she wants."

"She does want you, Sean. You have to understand: you're her vacation from everything, from her high-pressure job. She needs that. She'll come round..."

"And in the mean time, I should just wait while she screws Grant for a while?"

As I said it, I felt that strange tingling in my loins again. Something about the idea of letting my wife enjoy the thrill of a new man for a while, before she came back to me—it was a thrill to me, though the acid burn of anger and jealousy could overwhelm those feelings if I let them.

At that point, Alicia seemed to notice Henry standing next to me, spectating like some kind of sports fan. I saw her give him a not-so-subtle glare that had it been words, would have said to him: "Do you mind?" I saw Henry respond silently to her non-verbal request for privacy with the kind of expression that replied to her: "Not at all, do carry on." Completely missing her subtle point.

I had to cough to avoid smiling or even laughing at Henry for showing Alicia so plainly that he was interested, perhaps even entertained, by all this gossip.

Alicia sighed, her eyes flicking back to mine as if she could tell instantly it wasn't worth snapping at someone like Henry.

She said: "Grant's just an old friend. She never had any interest in him other than his..."

"Oh, so that's okay, then? She only wants his huge prick. So I should just go ask her if she'll take me back?"

Alicia pursed her lips, perhaps regretting being pushed to come here by her sister. "What I mean is, she doesn't love him, never has," she said. "She doesn't need him, she doesn't even really like him."

That did make me laugh, though without any hint of humor or warmth.

"She just has certain needs, and with you guys leading separate lives recently..."

"Was she seeing him before she ended our marriage?" I asked Alicia, my voice suddenly sharp, this being an important point I wanted to know.

"No, not at all."

"Was she thinking about it? Was she talking to him about it, telling him to wait until she'd got rid of me?"

"No, Sean, she's not like that," Alicia insisted. "Katie and Grant... go way back. We all knew each other back in school. She's never had... romantic feelings for him. She just kind of... well, they got together occasionally if they both happened to be single."

"Friends with benefits? And it's only when they're both single."

"Not once after she met you." Alicia sighed again. It had to be awkward for her, she didn't want to be here talking about this stuff on the street. "Look, just talk to her, please? For me? She really has been a complete mess about this. She had to take two weeks off work..."

The way she was talking about Katie did not fit with the way Henry and I had seen her with Grant outside her house.

"I'll think about it," I said, and it felt to me as though I was caving. What did I have to talk to Katie about? She'd moved on, she was seeing someone else.

Alicia nodded, and actually seemed mildly pleased I'd said that. It was some kind of result she could take back to her sister.

"This is yours," she said, stepping aside to reveal a small suitcase sitting nonchalantly behind her, something I recognized as belonging to Katie. "She thought you'd want them. The rest of your things are still where they always were if you want to go fetch them some time."

"Thanks," I said.

"She wants to be there if you go to pick up the rest of your things," Alicia pleaded unnecessarily. "She wants to talk to you, Sean."

"I said I'd think about it, didn't I?"

She nodded. "I need your new address, Sean. For the wedding invitations. Katie doesn't know where you're living."

God, I hadn't even thought about the prospect of attending Alicia's wedding. I suppose I shouldn't have been surprised she still wanted me to go.

"I'm just staying with a friend at the moment," I said, and then gestured toward the Daily News building. "You can send anything for me here."

"Don't even think about not coming," she said stiffly, before wheeling on her feet and striding off down the street toward Victoria Station.

8

PDA

I think, looking back, I saw the situation with Henry and Michelle as a kind of antidote to what had happened with Katie. Although I knew I couldn't have Michelle, it was a nice distraction, and kept my thoughts away from the dark despair that was ever present in the background, ready to consume me if I let my guard down.

Katie was such a huge loss to me, I could hardly comprehend it. And yet Michelle made me believe that losing my wife did not leave me with a destiny of permanent loneliness.

As the summer rolled on, the warmer weather and familiarity seemed to collude to encourage Michelle to wear increasingly thinner and skimpier clothes in public, and if it was possible, to be even more revealing in our apartment.

She'd wear tiny strappy tops that showed significant sections of her bra beneath, or that left her midriff uncovered, emphasizing her flat stomach and the alluring swell of her breasts. If she was wearing anything at all to cover herself from the waist down, other than leaving it to the bottom portion of one of Henry's shirts, it would invariably be the shortest of skirts, or hotpants which left little to the imagination.

In our flat, I'd catch more frequent glimpses of her panties, and her flirtation became borderline outrageous at times. I even caught a brief flash of her in the shower on one occasion, when she failed to close the bathroom door properly—and what a sight, though she had her back to me at the time.

Though I kept myself in check publicly, privately Michelle filled my every waking fantasy and at night, my dreams. I felt pretty pathetic about it a lot of the time, but there was little I could really do.

Meanwhile, both Henry and Michelle attempted to pair me up with this girl or that during nights out. None of their attempts worked out, I guess my heart wasn't really in it just then. I didn't need another girl, I was happy enough to have a break, and perhaps merely dwell in my infatuation with a friend's better half.

My attendances at her late-afternoon fitness sessions in the park continued, and I forced myself to go even when I was feeling lazy. I think it was really taking affect on my body, too. I felt trimmer, leaner, healthier.

I could always see the other guys in her class checking her out in her skin-tight leggings and lycra tank tops, and enjoyed seeing their faces as they watched me escort her home at the end of the sessions. She did look stunning.

Some months into our living arrangement, I felt almost as though I was spending more time with Michelle than Henry was.

I guess seeing how strong Henry's bond was with his wife, my concerns about my influence on their marriage softened, which only made me feel a little more relaxed flirting with Michelle.

And I got the impression as they spent more and more time around me, Henry and Michelle seemed to feel more relaxed with each other around me.

Too relaxed, perhaps.

The first time it happened, I had been running errands after our usual work shift, returning home in time for my usual sleep shift to find my roommates enjoying a little intimate time together in the living room.

"Sorry!"

I breezed through to my room, a little startled by the brief flash I'd received of Henry's blindingly white butt clenched as he thrust into his pretty wife, lodged between her legs on their otherwise drab brown sofa.

I received a "Sorry!" in return from Henry as I passed through trying not to look, but it was a gasp uttered by Michelle that made me turn—just for a moment.

What I saw before disappearing into my room made me rock hard. It wasn't the fact that she was naked on our couch. In fact, I only really caught a glimpse of her bare breast, since Henry lent her his body for concealment. No, it was the expression on her sweet face as her eyes locked onto mine for that flicker of a second.

In her gaze, there wasn't any shock, horror or revulsion at me for stumbling in on them screwing on their couch. There wasn't anger for my intruding on their intimate moment. Those big blue eyes of hers were filled with unbridled lust, and in that one glance suggested to me that she wanted me to watch, she wanted me to desire her.

I probably imagined it, but in that glance, I felt her lust directed at me, rather than the man between her legs. She was, undoubtedly, more than pleased that I could be there to witness her like that.

I closed my door to the sound of giggling.

I emerged only when I heard the two of them leave the apartment to spend a little more of Henry's day off together. Like me, Henry would probably be in bed by noon. In the mean time, I planned to just watch a movie on TV until I was ready for sleep.

I could smell a slight musk in the air as I came out of my room, blended with the lingering traces of Michelle's sweet perfume. It intensified as I collapsed in front of the television.

Michelle.

It made me tremble a little, thinking that I was breathing traces of her arousal, and from the memory of her looking at me straight in the eyes while she lay there completely naked, my friend still inside her.

I closed my eyes for a moment, just breathing in that scent, imagining it was me, and not Henry between her thighs.

I think I could have controlled myself, maybe moved on with my evening, had I not noticed the scrap of black material poking out of the sofa cushions. As soon as I caught sight of it, curiosity got the better of me, and I duly fished out Michelle's panties from where she'd left them.

Jesus.

It seemed to take me a few heartbeats to realize what I was holding. Had she done this on purpose? Surely after you have sex, you look for your clothes before going anywhere. Maybe she'd gotten changed before going out. Or maybe it was all part of her underlying plan to flaunt herself in front of me.

I shook off this ridiculous but growing sense of paranoia, but couldn't resist pressing them to my nose, breathing in the scent of the beautiful brunette's arousal uncut.

Sure, my sense of being utterly pathetic was strong, but this infatuation I had seemed to be stronger. Certainly stronger than I'd ever had for any other girl—even Katie, if I could believe that.

A few days after first catching them out in the living room, I saw them again.

Were they doing this on purpose?

It was after a usual night out, during which the three of us had been to various bars, and actually gotten into a little karaoke for an hour or two in the West End.

After another evening of Henry and Michelle applying the pressure on me to begin dating again, I eventually grew tired and decided I was better off heading home for a little sleep. Henry and Michelle were keen on staying out longer, and I was happy enough to give them some time to themselves.

I was in bed and asleep when they came home, but as usual with my room, I left my door open a crack to help with the ventilation.

Having only managed to get into a shallow sleep, I was soon woken up as the two of them fumbled around on their return, banging cupboards in the kitchen and clinking glasses as they continued their revelry with a little sampling of Henry's personal vodka supply.

I rubbed my eyes a little and from my bed, could see through the gap in my doorway, from where I actually had quite a good view of their living room.

What I saw made me catch my breath.

Both Henry and Michelle were standing there topless - Henry wearing only his chinos, Michelle just her skirt, neither of them wearing shoes or socks—and as Henry leaned up against the living room doorway, kissing the pretty brunette, Michelle was wrestling with Henry's belt.

She was standing on tip-toes as she kissed him, side on to me, She had the most wonderfully graceful curves.

A jolt of red-hot shock shot through my chest. Were they really going to do it out there? Merely assume I was asleep? They didn't seem to be trying to keep quiet.

I felt the natural urge to step up and close my door, but then as I sat there in my bed, I stopped myself. Why should I? They were so determined to do that in the communal area of the apartment—why should I accommodate them by shutting myself away in a poorly ventilated box room?

I was swayed by my curiosity and the raging lust I felt for Michelle—was it wrong to attempt to live vicariously through Henry, to actually see him indulge in his cute brunette?

But I did feel the gentle burn of envy and—perhaps, jealousy, considering my entirely irrational sense that Michelle was somehow 'mine' because of the crush I had on her. Sitting there in the dark, I was in a state of shock, horrified at what was going on as well as brutally aroused. Yet I could not stop myself from watching, my whole body fizzing with energy at the prospect that I could actually see the exquisite Michelle making love.

They did look good together, Henry and Michelle, though she had to stand on her toes to reach his mouth.

I felt a twinge of jealousy blend with my lust as I watched her unfasten his belt, drag his chinos down his thighs to reveal his large, rigid cock. And then she was sinking to her knees in front of him, kissing his stomach and around his loins.

Michelle gazed up at him with adoring eyes, and for a moment leaned back to brush her long brown hair out of her face, and I saw how hard her nipples were on her pert breasts.

As he merely stood there, still holding a tumbler full of

vodka, she grasped his manhood in both hands, and then slowly licked her way up his shaft.

I found I was holding my breath as I watched her slip his tip inside her sweet mouth.

My Michelle was sucking another man's cock.

Watching her sink down on his length, part of me wondered if that might have been me standing out there, if I'd responded to her flirtation in a certain way. The rest of me felt certain she would never betray her husband, and I think I felt most comfortable with that latter thought.

Henry held Michelle's hair back as she bobbed on his hardness, and he was guiding her rhythm as she sucked him. Each glance up at his face, as she licked and kissed him in between deep sucking, was filled with that same warm affection that made me feel strangely jealous, instead of merely envious.

My subconscious, my heart, held a torch for her, and every time she smiled at Henry, that torch was dampened a little.

After a while, Henry slumped to the floor, and for a moment I wondered if he'd finished. Holding his swollen shaft for her as she sat in his lap, her skirt now gone, he showed me he wasn't spent.

I couldn't quite believe what they were doing right in front of my eyes. She was straddling him, sinking on his lap in the hallway, and though I couldn't quite see it from this angle, I knew he was inside her now.

It took my breath away. Henry, fucking my crush. They might be married, but my insides didn't care.

She rode him, bounced on him, moaning in that sweet soprano as he fucked her. They were saying things to each other, speaking softly, but from that distance I couldn't hear.

They were beautiful together - Henry was surprisingly

trim for someone I never saw exercise, and Michelle was all toned curves and brightness. He pushed her forward, onto all fours, and then I watched as he entered her from behind, thrusting into her like some kind of beast, so that I could actually see his hardness disappearing into her shapely rear.

I thought they were both about to come, and I knew I wanted to watch, my whole body burning with lust and jealousy.

As their pace accelerated furiously, Michelle's moaning became gasping, and I felt a curious gratitude that she was enjoying herself so much, that my beautiful Michelle was being satisfied - even though it wasn't by me.

Henry continued to talk quietly to her as he thrust into her, and Michelle visibly responded to his words, whatever they were. Then at the last moment, I suddenly froze as I saw her head turn—and she was looking directly at me.

Could she see me in the dark, watching them? Surely not. But she was staring at my bedroom door, as though wondering if I could be enjoying the display.

And strangely enough, I was. Michelle's smile was as broad as I'd ever seen it as the two of them grunted and groaned and shuddered and shook with the force of their combined orgasms. She was looking at me, mouthing the words "oh God" over and over, her breathing out of control. In that moment, it was Michelle's unbridled joy at fucking Henry that made me feel good - I couldn't quite understand it, but that was how it was.

I just really got off on her sexuality and the sheer delight she took in it, even if it meant I could not have her myself.

And then I was out of control, shocked to find myself shuddering in time with the couple outside my room.

Afterwards, I felt a touch of guilt at what I'd done, at

watching them. I told myself that they might even have seen me, might have known I could see from my door, and yet that hadn't stopped them.

Yet I felt a nervous flutter inside, knowing that my resolve not to fall for my friend's girl was quietly breaking down.

Michelle was driving me crazy.

The guilt didn't stop me from taking an interest in their sex life, though. Didn't stop me obsessing about Michelle, living vicariously though Henry.

And then I got caught.

9

A step too far

*I*t was just another morning after work.

As was often the case after a day off, I felt the need for a good breakfast after my first shift back, and suggested to Henry as we clocked off that we head for our favorite greasy spoon cafe for a full English breakfast.

Henry actually seemed to blush slightly, and declined my invitation.

"Michelle's... well, she's told me in no uncertain terms to get my posterior back home."

I nodded, not needing much explanation to know what Henry was meaning. I felt that familiar tingle starting up down below at the knowledge that sweet Michelle was horny, that my good friend was about to go back to our apartment and ravish her.

"Fair enough," I said, giving him no grief—wanting him to go home and indulge in her so that I might stoke that strange burning feeling inside me, as the envy and the jealousy blended with the pure, uncut arousal.

"Recently..." Henry said, and it was the first time I'd

ever really seen him stumble over his words. "She's been particularly... demanding."

I caught a slightly odd look from him, a look I don't think I'd had from Henry before, so I couldn't entirely interpret it.

I tried to play down the hint of tension between us, though I knew full well he was talking about Michelle's libido.

I tried to make light of it, joking, "Maybe she's been flirting with someone at her yoga class."

I don't know what I was thinking. It was the kind of teasing that one red-blooded male might use on another, with both of them knowing that the idea of one of their girlfriends actually flirting with another man would be like a nuclear blast for their relationship.

I suddenly felt terrified that I had drawn attention to Michelle's flirting with me over that summer.

But Henry simply shrugged, and didn't seem at all concerned, saying without a hint of being unserious, "Probably something like that."

"Best go home, do as she wants, huh?"

He nodded. I know it was after work and everything, but in that moment, Henry just seemed worn out to me.

I think I noticed it because it surprised me so much. A husband with such a gorgeous wife gagging for sex all the time should feel like the luckiest son of a bitch in the world, right?

"You know," he said, smiling as though he was joking too, now, "sometimes I wonder if perhaps I don't need help with all this."

He seemed serious, and I didn't quite know how to take it if he wasn't joking. I just nodded.

Before we parted, I mentioned the need to shop for a wedding gift for Katie's sister Alicia, basically hinting that

I'd be away from our apartment to allow him time to see to Michelle's needs.

Only, as I scanned the morning newspaper, eating my much-required full English breakfast alone in a half-full cafe, I couldn't help feeling tempted to violate my promise of vacating the apartment. Now that I knew what was happening, I couldn't dispel the thoughts from my mind, that Henry was about to slip under the covers with his cute little wife, that she might be sleepy and he'd wake her up with his mouth.

I imagined him sliding into her willing pussy, and how her face would melt into a picture of pure bliss.

I sat there in the cafe behind a group of construction workers chugging tea before their morning shift, and I felt the familiar tickle of jealousy at my Michelle being taken by someone else. And I embraced those feelings. Surely it was better to let go, and enjoy those sensations, rather than see them as negative, and let them boil up inside, to potentially sour my friendship with Henry?

I felt such a draw—I'd seen them before, but an addict couldn't ever get enough. How could I possibly keep myself from heading straight home after my feed?

Besides, I had started feeling that Henry and Michelle knew of my watching, that they perhaps enjoyed the risk of being discovered, or that they might even have a thing for exhibitionism.

Hadn't Henry told me in plain language that he was going to go straight home to see to Michelle?

Well, it was my home too now. I abandoned any ideas of shopping and headed straight for the Tube, and the half-hour journey back to Turnham Green. I was fizzing all over on the way home, even at the prospect that I might merely hear Michelle being taken again.

Silently, I fantasized that she was mine, that she was

only having sex with Henry to tease me before letting me take her for the ride of her life. In my fantasy, I didn't feel an ounce of negativity toward Henry for being with her before me—somehow, I had mentally converted him into some kind of human sex toy, who she would simply play with to warm up for me.

Quietly letting myself into the apartment in the hope of catching some obvious signs of the passion going on inside, I felt suddenly crushed to find the apartment as quiet as I was being.

Was Michelle still sleeping?

Their bedroom door was closed, so it was possible that Henry was simply respecting her last remnants of sleep.

I stifled my sense of disappointment—if anything, it held my sudden burst of mad lust in check, making me recognize that I had been stupid to imagine I could simply come home and enjoy some kind of free sex show starring the woman of my dreams.

I remained quiet, though, respecting Michelle's right to sleep if that was what she was doing. I slumped on the couch in a shady living room, not bothering to open the curtains. I didn't even turn on the TV. My mind was racing, I wouldn't be able to focus on it anyway.

After a few moments, the door to Henry's room opened quietly and Henry himself darted out.

From where I was sitting, I had a direct view into their room, and I could see the end of their bed, and a chair by the wall. From what I could see, the bed appeared to be made, and the curtains were certainly open judging by the amount of light that was there.

Was Michelle even home?

Silently, I laughed at myself for trying to mentally will my roommates into bed with each other. I knew I was going to have to seriously chill regarding the concept of

Henry and Michelle being together if I was going to remain comfortable living with them. Otherwise, I'd have to find another apartment.

I saw Henry pad back into the room bearing a mug of cocoa, which was one of his pre-sleep rituals, without turning to even acknowledge me. Had he even seen that I was back? I guessed that he had felt so certain that I was out shopping, that he wouldn't even look for me in a living room he assumed to be empty.

I was about to flip on the TV, however, when suddenly I heard a girlish giggle, proving Michelle's presence in there. What were they up to?

Henry hadn't closed their bedroom door when he'd gone back in, so naturally it drew my gaze. My heart rate was picking up noticeably, and I began hoping that since they didn't know I was home, something might actually happen.

There was another giggle from Michelle, and then I saw her walk slowly into my field of view. She was wearing a fairly simple yellow cotton tank top and a little denim skirt, very cute and girl-next-door. The way she was dressed, I wondered if she hadn't just had an all-nighter with her other friends.

I felt myself tingling all over to see her like that—but I was also afraid, afraid that she'd see me lurking in the darkness and be revolted.

She sat tentatively on the chair, looking over at Henry, apparently in conversation with him, though I couldn't hear what they were saying. I felt trapped where I was: if I moved now, it would draw attention to the fact that I had been watching. I would have to go directly past their open doorway to reach either the kitchen or my own room.

Looking over at Henry, Michelle pulled up her top to

reveal a dark red bra containing those sweet breasts of hers.

God, I couldn't look away.

It seemed plain that she assumed there was no one else in the apartment. When she slipped the button of her jeans skirt and wriggled out of it, she acted as though the door to their bedroom was closed, as though they had complete privacy.

She stood briefly to remove her skirt, and my hardness was nearly bursting out of my pants to witness her, so stunning in that little crimson bra and panties, and the way her hands gracefully skirted over her curves down to between her legs drew my gaze to the way her underwear clung to the shape of her mound.

She sat, and looked over at her husband, flashing him a lusty, smoldering pout as she now slipped a bra strap over her shoulder, slowly allowing it to fall and reveal a bare breast, and her stiff nipple.

Oh God, Henry was a lucky man.

Giving him his own private strip show—and yet so into it herself. She was so very hot.

She was touching herself as her bra finally came off, cupping her breasts, crushing her nipples between fingers and thumbs, looking so hungrily at Henry. I don't know how he resisted her. I was only seeing her side-on, and yet seeing her hand slip down into her panties, I felt the strongest urge to go straight in and beg for the honor of pleasing her.

"You like this?" I heard her saying to Henry, her voice still quiet, but the phrase unmistakable. I didn't hear Henry's reply.

I did start to hear her heavy breathing, her quiet moans, however. It sent shivers of arousal down my spine.

I was so hard to watch her fingers stirring between her

thighs, to see how she stretched her legs wide for her husband, and teased him by pulling her panties tight against her sex.

Off came her panties, and I received a few tiny glimpses of her perfect little pussy before she covered it in her hands. The tidy little strip of hair on her mound seemed so glamorous to me, so sexy when I was used to Katie's bushier style.

She was so alluring, leaning back in that chair, displaying herself for him, touching herself, satisfying herself, losing herself in the feelings. There was something so wicked in watching her—I think when I was getting my sex education from men's magazines and the early Internet, there was a sense that girls didn't touch themselves, particularly if they were in relationships.

Did Katie ever let me watch her like this? I don't think so. Even though we were married, we were best friends, we knew each other intimately, masturbation was kind of personal for us, it had a stigma that kept it secret, unshared. I suppose I had never let her see me doing it—but then, women don't really want to see that kind of thing, do they? They probably assume it is the same for guys. They might think we'll feel somehow inadequate to watch them take care of themselves.

It was so hot to see Michelle doing this for her husband, I felt so envious of him.

Henry now walked into view, still wearing his shirt and pants from work. I was surprised at the self-control he displayed—I would be a lust-crazed wreck if Michelle had performed like that for me. But then I suppose, Henry was married to her, it would be different for him. Would the passion fizzle even for a couple so obviously into sex as these guys?

He stepped beside her, touched her knee, then brushed

her hair out of her face with his hands as she smiled up at him and continued touching herself.

Cradling her head, he kissed her mouth tenderly, and I felt that familiar tickle of jealousy to see the affection he shared with my crush.

Then he was kissing her neck, her breasts, his hands wondering over her smooth skin, enjoying her as I so desperately wished I could. She responded to his touch, her moans becoming more intense, her head tilting back to cope with the feelings two pairs of hands could draw from her body.

Oh, Katie. How I had neglected her. It was obvious to me now.

As Henry knelt between Michelle's legs, clearly about to taste her, as I craved so very much, something seemed to disturb him.

I hadn't heard anything—I certainly hadn't made any kind of a sound myself. Perhaps there had been some noise from the street that I hadn't noticed since I was so focused on the sound of Michelle slowly building herself up to a sweet climax.

He turned his head, and I felt an electric shock pass through my heart as his eyes locked on mine.

He looked at me for what seemed like an age before he reached over and swung the bedroom door shut to take back their privacy.

I felt terror in those moments, and it was mainly because of the neutral expression on his face before he had shut me out. I just could not interpret it: was he angry at me? Upset? Horrified at my intrusion? Had I read the two of them completely wrong in attributing some kind of exhibitionist flair to their activities?

I was suddenly desperately afraid that I'd just lost the one friend I had left in the world. And, I guess, that I would never get to see my crush again—there was no way he'd let me even lay eyes on Michelle after that point.

I heard her orgasm, but it no longer aroused me, I felt so awkward.

I could hardly burst in there and apologize. What could I do? My insides felt as though they'd been torn out. I would have to wait. I would have to grovel on my knees and beg for Henry's forgiveness. Even then, I might salvage a friendship, but I'd probably have to move out.

I really did leave the apartment to go gift shopping for Alicia's wedding after that. Traipsing around Oxford Street with no clue what to get, my state of mind did not help with the retail inspiration.

I suppose the various weddings I'd been to in the last few years had been those of Katie's friends, and Katie had handled the whole gift thing.

But I was both trying to assess and re-assess what Henry's state of mind might have been judging from his expression in that moment our eyes had locked, and trying to work out what the Hell I would say to him the next time I saw him, taking into account the various possibilities for how he might have felt about my transgression.

After tours around most of the large department stores, from John Lewis and House of Fraser to Selfridges and even a quick dash down to Knightsbridge in the hope that Harrod's might spark some kind of brainwave, I ended up returning home empty-handed.

My strategy for dealing with Henry would take the form of either simplifying the facts—came home quietly as I'd thought Michelle might be asleep, then you opened your door prior to Michelle's strip show and saw me—or the claim that I'd had my mind on other things—namely, Katie—and I'd been so distracted I hadn't actually seen anything while I'd been there sitting in the living room.

They were both lousy options. I could hardly tell my only friend in the world that I had a crush on his wife, and I'd come home instead of shopping in the perverted hope of witnessing or hearing him making love to Michelle.

As I re-entered the apartment, my heart in my throat, I was a little surprised to find that the whole place was empty.

Michelle had gone to work, of course. But Henry wasn't there, either. His bedroom door was open, and inside the daytime was full. I ducked my head around the corner to find it empty, the curtains open.

What did I do? Did I call him? Or text him to find out what was up?

Jesus. It was like we'd been out on a first date or something, and now I didn't know when was the right time to make that follow-up call to avoid appearing foolish.

Oh, perhaps he had some errand to run. It was easy to be tempted to use the daytime to get things done when you were a night worker. A day worker who is supposed to go to sleep at night is helped by the fact that most shops close in the evening.

By 1pm, Henry still hadn't shown up for his sleep shift, and I had chickened out of calling him. I decided to try to sleep on it, and if he wasn't back later, I'd see him at work.

Only the thing was, after a fitful sleep, I woke up and there was no sign that Henry had been back to the apartment all day. His bed hadn't been slept in, I was fairly sure of that. And when I got to work that night, I found that without telling me, he'd switched his days off around, and wouldn't be in that night.

So, I had a fairly atrocious night shift to get through,

without the usual opiate of conversation to help alleviate the tedium. Two or three times that night our resident Darth Vader, otherwise known as chief subeditor Sue Collins, crept up behind me and discovered my sly attempts to surf the web during the quiet moments.

I felt like a shit, let's face it, and it was my own fault.

I had completely misread Henry and Michelle. I had stumbled on them enjoying their private time together a couple times, and they hadn't made a stink about it, so I had wrongly assumed that they must have somehow liked the fact that I'd seen them. Purposefully sneaking home in order to catch them, when I plainly knew they'd be thinking I was out running errands, was pretty bad.

It wasn't quite stealing a friend's girl, but it was fairly atrocious behavior.

By the end of the night, I was resolved to admit everything to Henry—my crush on his wife, my illicit pleasures at hearing them together, even perhaps my personal history of coveting other men's girlfriends. I'd volunteer to move out of the apartment, and hope that over time, I might rebuild his trust in me and save our friendship.

Maybe I needed to bite the bullet and get some kind of therapy.

I could meet Katie for coffee, too, and apologize for being such a boring schmuck, while I was in this mood for rebuilding my life from scratch.

I left work on the dot at 6am, and with a nice empty Tube carriage all the way home, got home in record time, my heart pounding all the way.

And when I returned to the apartment, there was still no sign of Henry or Michelle.

The place didn't look as though anyone had come here since I'd left for my night shift. I felt a heavy stone drop in my stomach: this really was serious. Had I upset them so much that they'd vacated the apartment?

Well, I was in a gloomy mood. I skulked around the apartment, watched The Mummy from Michelle's iTunes account in the hope that the delectable Rachel Weisz might take my mind off my troubles, and then grabbed breakfast at Sam's Brasserie when it opened at nine, pouring over the headlines of the Guardian in the attempt to distract my thoughts.

A man who betrays all his friends feels seriously lonely, as it turns out.

Back at the apartment with the intention of slowing down before my sleep shift, and of course there was still no sign of my roommates. I started wondering if something had happened to Henry and Michelle that was totally disconnected from my perversions—perhaps a close relative had fallen ill, or something like that.

You'd have thought they might have left me a note of explanation, dropped me a text or an email. But if it was something serious, why should they think to inform their blundering roommate?

It was my night off coming up, so I wouldn't see Henry then. Perhaps I'd just have to have patience. They might be working things out between themselves, they'd gone somewhere to cool off or manage the upset I had caused, before returning with fresh energy to force me out of their home.

Well, I might not have been sleepy just then, but I knew the importance of maintaining my diurnal schedule.

Just as I was finally settling down in bed, however, I heard the front door being unlocked, which made me jump. Then there was the sound of the front door opening and closing as someone came in.

I quickly hopped out of bed and pulled on my jeans, thinking that if Henry had finally returned, I needed to catch him before he went into his bedroom and shut himself inside.

Fastening my belt, my mind was spinning trying to recall the carefully worded scripts I'd worked out for what to say to Henry when I finally did see him.

Jeans on, there was a quiet knock on my door.

Well, this was it. Do or die.

10

A secret revealed

*O*nly, as I opened my door, it wasn't Henry standing out there waiting to confront me over what I'd done. It was Michelle.

My heart did a little pirouette. Then, after a moment's joy for seeing her again, I felt deep despair blackening my insides. Where was Henry? Was he so angry with me he had to send his wife with the orders for me to leave?

"Hey," she said, trying to seem like her usual cheerful self, but not being entirely convincing about it.

"Hey," I said, my tone of voice attempting to convey innocent confusion about what was going on. "Is Henry with you?"

"No, it's just me," she said.

God, she looked good. She was all made up, her long dark hair down for once, flowing down over her shoulders in beautiful waves, her eyes were even more startling than usual with elegant mascara, and a touch too much eyeliner. She was wearing a burgundy dress made of some kind of lacy, flowery fabric that gave her a hint of the gothic.

A simple little gold pendant on her chest guided my

eyes down to her full cleavage before I realized I really ought to be keeping my eyes on hers.

Had she smartened up to give herself the confidence to do what was needed, to tell me to get out of their lives for good?

"Is everything okay?" I asked her, my tone still suggesting I was unaware that anything had changed between us.

I noticed the nervous quiver in her eyes, the way she licked her lips, and it only made me more anxious, stirring the butterflies in my stomach.

"Yeah, everything's fine," she said, flashing a half-smile.

I don't think I'd ever felt so awkward. I just couldn't quite face the confirmation that I knew everything had gone bad between us all, and it was my fault. And yet it was plainly clear that something very, very unusual was going on from the fact that I was even talking to Michelle in this way across my bedroom threshold.

And I was trying so hard not to react to her beauty, yet she looked stunning, and every breath I took was saturated with her syrupy perfume.

Taking my hesitation from not knowing what to say as some kind of prompt, she said: "Henry sent me over here."

"He did? Is he okay?"

"He's fine."

"He's seemed kind of... I don't know... preoccupied recently."

I don't know what I was doing. Attempting some subtle ploy to shift blame for what had happened onto the fact that Henry might not be thinking straight just at the moment, for some reason.

"I don't know if you remember him talking to you... about me," she said.

I was a little baffled as to where this was all going. I

said: "Henry often talks about you, you're the light of his life."

She nodded, not responding to the flattery, and the note of sadness in her eyes made me feel suddenly that I had misinterpreted everything going on around me—that actually, it wasn't me in trouble here, but Michelle and Henry.

Was their marriage in trouble? Why on Earth would it be?

"Has he ever said anything about me... about the fact that I'm quite... high-energy?"

I saw her tremble a little.

"I think he may have mentioned it occasionally," I said. "But in a good way. He's always loved that you're so full of energy."

Why did it feel as though I was trying to persuade her to give him another chance? Had she decided, like Katie had with me, that she wasn't compatible with Henry because her sex drive was so much more? Or was I reading too much into it, jumping to conclusions based on what had happened in my own marriage?

She was somewhat younger than her husband, and it was said to be natural for a man's libido to slow down after his twenties, while a woman's only stepped up and up.

Were they splitting up? In which case what was Michelle doing here?

"Look, do you want to sit down?" I asked her, thinking how long this conversation was getting to be hovering in my doorway. "Why don't I get us both a coffee..."

She nodded, "That would be good."

Coffee at this time, of course, would obliterate my chances of getting to sleep. But I didn't care about sleep right now. I was terrified that Henry and Michelle were about to call time on their marriage for pathetic reasons, not unlike how my marriage had ended.

And I suppose, that dark little part of me deep inside, the part that stole friends' girlfriends ever since school, was hoping that Michelle had come to me to ask me to elope with her, to Hell with my best friend. But I couldn't listen to that part of me.

I left her to get comfortable in the living room while I made coffee, and when I eventually came in bearing Nescafe's finest, she was sitting on the edge of the armchair, leaving me to slump on the couch trying not to dwell on the way her short dress revealed an expanse of shapely nylon-clad thighs.

"Did Henry ever say anything about not being able to keep up with me?"

I sighed. The coffee was not going to lighten the mood. "Perhaps," I said, thinking that perhaps honesty was the safest route here. "He might have said he needed a little help to cope with you."

I put on a comedy old fogey voice to try to play down the seriousness of all this, adding: "I guess we're getting older, Henry and I, we can't keep up with you young-uns any more."

Michelle cracked a smile, which made me feel at least a smidgeon better, and seemed to take some of the tension in the air down half a notch.

"I'm sorry, I guess he put you in an awkward situation," she said.

"I don't know I'd say he did that."

"He did get you to take me out all those times, didn't he? Using you like some kind of escort."

I smiled, thinking it the best way to lighten up the atmosphere here. "I wouldn't have said that was particularly awkward—or any kind of burden. I enjoyed it."

She shuffled back in the armchair, and seemed to relax a little.

"Are you two okay?" My question was, perhaps, my first offensive move, my first attempt to get at just what the heck was going on here.

"We're good," she said, and then flashed the warmest smile, making me feel quite considerable relief. "We're better than good, I think. Only... Henry's been... confused. Recently."

"Confused?"

She nodded. "The thing is," she said, "about a year ago, we got to the stage in our relationship where we were finally comfortable talking about our pasts... you know... our past relationships."

"Right," I nodded, sipping my coffee.

"I guess I had a bit of a secret to share," she said, tiptoeing around the big reveal.

"A secret?"

She looked me straight in the eye, as though both needing to know I was okay with what she was about to tell me, and also defiantly declaring that if I wasn't okay with it, she didn't care, to Hell with me.

"I told him I'm polyamorous," she said. "I guess it was a bit of a surprise to him."

"Polly-what-what-what?" I asked, attempting to lighten the atmosphere in here, before recognizing that if this was some kind of condition or disease, I should probably be a lot more sympathetic in tone.

We'd talked about each others' pasts during our 'dates'—but while I'd kept the secret of my thing for my friends' girlfriends, she'd clearly been keeping a secret of her own.

"Polyamorous," she said. "I don't really believe in

closing myself off to one single person when it comes to love."

I narrowly avoided spraying coffee all over the carpet, but it was a little humiliating having to retrieve my jaw from where it had dropped to the floor.

"I see," I said, trying to act calm, crossing my legs and placing my hands on one knee as though I were some kind of New York shrink used to dealing with this kind of situation all the time.

Her eyes flickered over my face, I think trying to gauge what my real feelings were about her revelation.

"You're into dating more than one guy at once," I said, nodding gently, doing my best to sound as though this was no big deal to me. Doing my best not to imagine Michelle stuck in the middle of some kind of Caligula-style Roman orgy.

She smiled - it was a welcome return for that particular expression, which always had lit up her face like nothing else.

"I was," she said. "I also believe a person can fall for more than one person, and if it's all out in the open, on the level, honest and truthful with everyone concerned, there shouldn't be a problem with loving more than one person."

I nodded and frowned, like I'd digested this particular fact, now it wasn't an issue.

"So," I prompted her, "Henry couldn't deal with it when you told him?"

She shook her head, "Oh no. Actually, the complete opposite. I was surprised."

"He was okay with it?"

She gave me a wicked look, which seemed to light fires in my stomach. "More than okay with it. It kind of... interested him."

I nodded. For Henry to accept this fact about Michelle

perhaps explained why he'd always been so tolerant about her flirting with me, ever since we'd met. I wasn't sure what that meant, though.

"This poly..." I started.

"Polyamory."

"Polyamory. Is it, like, a Mormon thing?" I tried to appear non-judgmental. I wasn't judging, either. I didn't really know enough about the Mormon faith or any other kind of faith to make anything like a judgement. Michelle was American, after all, it wasn't out of the question that she might be a Mormon.

"No, nothing like that," she said, taking her last mouthful of coffee. "I'm not really religious at all."

"But now you're married," I said, my tiny sips making my coffee last a little longer, "Presumably all that poly... amory... belongs in the past?"

"That's what I thought," Michelle nodded. "Only... when I tell you it interested him... well, it didn't stop interesting him, if you know what I mean."

I had to make it seem like I knew what she meant, of course, to avoid appearing to be a complete idiot. But I really didn't have a clue what she was saying.

If Katie had come to me in the middle of our marriage and confessed to once being polyamorous, dating however many men at once before she was married, I'm not sure how I would have reacted. Right now, after separating from her, the absence had definitely made my heart grow fonder, which probably fed into the strange arousal I felt whenever I pictured her dating another man, even sleeping with another man. She was a beautiful, insatiable woman who was out of my league, and now that other men could have her, it was plain to me what I'd lost.

Henry still had Michelle, though. What did she mean that he was 'interested' in her polyamory?

Giving her the impression that I knew what she was talking about, however, offered her the unfortunate signal that she didn't need to provide any more explanation for just what the Hell was going on around here.

"So where's Henry now? Where've you guys been, anyway the last couple days?" I asked, floundering a bit.

"We decided to stay at a hotel," she said, putting her coffee mug down on the little table beside the armchair. "We wanted to get away from everything and just talk."

"Talk?"

She nodded. "About all this. About my polyamory."

"And Henry's... still there?"

Another nod. "He's staying a couple more days, he says."

"Oh. But you aren't?"

She swallowed, and looked me straight in the eye again before saying: "No. He sent me over here to seduce you."

11

Full disclosure

*T*his time, I did manage to splatter coffee all over the place. It wasn't pretty. I think the only positive that came out of the situation was that I didn't get any of it on Michelle.

It made her laugh, though. I guess that was a big positive. It might sound sappy, but I don't think there was anything I did in my normal day-to-day life that was anywhere near as satisfying as making this particular girl really crack up.

"He did what?" I asked, my ears burning in the knowledge that people had been talking about me behind my back.

I grabbed some paper towels and carpet cleaner from the kitchen, and Michelle helped me to mop up the carpet, my coffee spray reaching an impressive range.

I couldn't help but notice her proximity to me again as we cleaned things up together. This time my head spinning with the apparent fact that Henry had sent this gorgeous creature over here with the express purpose of fulfilling my every desire.

I also considered the fact that very probably, the whole idea was simply too good to be true.

"I think to start with," Michelle said as we pressed the paper towels down to absorb the spilled liquid, "he really didn't understand where I was coming from."

"He didn't?" I could empathize with my absent friend.

"He seemed to get this impression that because I don't necessarily believe a person should be restricted to one soulmate, that I wasn't happy with just Henry."

"Oh, right."

"He thought somehow that I must need other guys as well, or I'd never be happy in the long term."

"Was he right?"

"Well... no." As we wiped down the counter, our arms brushed against each other. It made me catch my breath - something electric seemed to pass between us as her velvet skin touched mine, even just for the briefest of moments. "The thing is, just because I believe it's theoretically possible for me to fall in love with more than one person at once—and I guess I have in the past—doesn't mean I need to be in love with more than one person."

"But if someone else came along and swept you off your feet, you'd be open to that?"

"I don't really know," she said. "It isn't as easy as just deciding I'm poly, and then sleeping around with whoever's available."

"No."

"I met Henry knowing he was monogamous, and accepting that was the case. And while I've been with him, I've never needed to even look at another man."

I recalled all her flirting over the past weeks and months—but then all that came after she'd revealed herself as poly to her husband.

She pulled herself back up into the armchair while I

finished up applying the carpet cleaner, and I caught a brief glimpse up her dress, seeing that she was wearing thigh-high stockings, rather than standard hose. Jesus, she really had dressed for seduction.

"He's a good guy," I said, trying not to let her know I'd seen up her dress. "Of course you didn't."

Though the temptation was severe, I felt my years of ruining friendships finally begin to pay off, knowing that I had to resist this offer of Michelle that Henry had laid out before me. I didn't entirely know why he'd sent Michelle over here to me on a plate, but something about it all felt just too dangerous.

If this wasn't some kind of friendship test, which I would fail by jumping eagerly into bed with this divine woman, then perhaps it was Henry testing himself, and his reaction to his wife implementing her hidden polyamory. We might all test it out, and find that Henry really didn't care for it—with our friendship ending in the process.

Presumably Michelle had talked this over and over at length with her husband—well, that was what the past few days had been all about, wasn't it? They'd been holed up inside a hotel somewhere, discussing it and figuring out what they did about it. But after all of that, they'd come to the conclusion that Michelle ought to come over here and fling herself at me, and I wasn't sure that was the easiest answer—though every ounce of my being wanted it to be.

"Look," I said, "I'm kind of awake now…"

"Sorry," Michelle looked as though she'd only just remembered that this was my usual time for sleeping.

I shook my head, "No, it's fine. Look, why don't we go grab a bite to eat somewhere?"

It hadn't been so long since I'd had a big breakfast at Sam's, and it was still fairly early for lunch, but I felt the need of a table between us, and some time to talk all this through.

"Sure," she said, a trifle taken aback at what a simple but effective suggestion it was to just get out of here, to go for a nice quick change of scene. "That would be nice."

"You have time?"

She shrugged, "I'm not working today."

---

*T*he midday air was seriously warm, which seemed to relax us both as we strolled over toward the High Road and the cluster of restaurants that lay just before Chiswick Police Station.

As we walked, Michelle even felt confident enough to hook her arm in mine, as she would have done ordinarily on one of our weekly dates, which I now started to believe might have been a way for Henry to test how he felt about Michelle pursuing her polyamorous nature with me.

I took the fact that she wasn't actively trying to avoid me as testament to her realizing she was safe with me. That I wasn't going to jump her bones simply because her husband had had the startling idea of sharing her with me.

"It's been a whole year since you first told him," I said as we walked, feeling like some kind of relationship counselor trying to tease out the explanations about her condition.

"When I first told him about it... I don't know, I thought from how we'd been talking about Henry's past relationships, that I'd just be able to get it out there, and we'd move on, leaving it in the past."

"But he didn't let it lie?"

"No. I suppose there was some truth in the idea that since I was polyamorous in the past, it wasn't something I could just switch off when I married Henry. But just because I might feel ethically okay with having an affair, wouldn't mean it wouldn't hurt my husband if I went out and did it."

"Only, he didn't take it that way?"

"He kept thinking it was my nature, that I needed to feel open to other relationships. I'm not sure if he was right or wrong."

"So what happened?"

"To start with, he just asked me a lot of questions about it all. About what had happened to me in the past. About how I felt about it now we were married."

"And how did you feel about it?"

She shrugged. "I don't know, I was happy with Henry. I didn't need any more than that. Maybe I was even happy with monogamy."

We found a table in Zizzi's, an Italian chain restaurant that was nicely empty considering the early hour, but at least it was open and serving lunch. We had a table in a fairly shady corner, and there wasn't anyone anywhere near to pick up on our conversation other than the waitress, who was efficient picking up our order.

I ordered a bottle of chilled white wine, and some olives to snack on, then Michelle opted for a prosciutto salad while I went for a bowl of carbonara.

The wine raised Michelle's eyebrows until she reminded herself mentally of my inverted time—this was kind of nighttime for me.

In the end, she joined me for a crisp glass of Frascati, perhaps recognizing the benefits of a touch of alcohol for our discussion.

"So Henry approved of your polyamory when you told him, right?"

She shook her head. "Actually he wasn't exactly

obvious one way or the other. He wanted to find out more about it, and because it was me, and he loved me, he seemed determined to see it in a positive light."

"And after you'd explained everything to him?"

"Well, he needed a bit of time to think about it all, to let it all sink in," she said, taking a sip of wine. "I mean, I made him understand that I wasn't itching to get out there and meet other men. I was committed to our marriage—and all the vows that went with it."

"It must have been something he needed to get his head around," I said, trying to imagine how I'd react if this had happened to me, if perhaps it had been Katie who had come to me and said she was polyamorous.

I suppose anything would have been better than Katie coming to me and telling me she wanted out of our marriage because she wasn't feeling fulfilled in the bedroom. But after all the strange, confusing thoughts I'd had ever since she had called time on us, I couldn't help thinking it would have been quite exciting to discover I had a polyamorous wife, and actually say to her that I was happy for her to be polyamorous.

"I guess so—even though it didn't have to be. He could have forgotten about it, and our relationship would have been just the same as it ever was."

"But he didn't forget about it, did he?"

"No."

She looked around the restaurant, double-checking that we were out of earshot.

"One night, a little while after I told him, Henry came out with us when I went out with some of my friends from business school. I didn't really think anything particularly unusual happened, but when we got home... well, Henry was kind of all over me."

"He always is, isn't he?" I joked.

She smiled. "But back then... I guess you could say things between us had... well, settled down a little. I wasn't surprised. Then this particular night, he was just crazy. It was like when we first got together."

"He liked watching you flirting with your friends from business school," I said, adding one and one to make two. It all made sense as to why he'd seemed happy for Michelle to flirt with me, and later encouraged me to take her out on private dates, just the two of us.

"That's what he said," she nodded. "I mean, I told him there was nothing going on with me and any of my classmates, never had been. He just said I was naturally flirty with them—and he thought they obviously wanted me."

"And what did you think, that he found that... exciting?"

"I was confused," she said. "I guess when I was back in the States, back in college, my only experience with the whole polyamory thing was of guys who... well, tolerated it, but didn't really want to know about the other guys in my life."

"They weren't polyamorous as well, then, your boyfriends back home?"

"No. And I fell for a couple of guys who would not deal with it at all. Thought it was all a crock of shit, I don't know, but they weren't letting me date any other guys but them."

"But wait, you never told Henry about any of this when you first started dating him?"

Michelle flashed a warning glance, and our conversation paused while we waited for the waitress to lay out our food on the table, ask if we needed anything else, then drift away again.

"I'd been over here long enough to know things are slightly different," she said as I tucked into my carbonara.

"I mean, in London you don't even date more than one person at a time when you're just... you know, dating. The instant you start seeing someone, you're exclusive."

"And here was me thinking that was normal every-where," I laughed.

She shrugged, "It probably is. I guess in my circles back home, you weren't really exclusive with a guy to start with, until you both decided you were going to try it—and then you were really a couple. But in London, I liked Henry so much, I wasn't going to fool around with his expectations. I just went along with the whole monogamy thing."

"But after that night you guys went out with your class-mates, what, he started thinking about you becoming poly again?"

She nodded, and waited to finish a mouthful of her salad. "I guess to begin with, I was just adamant I wasn't going to... that I didn't need any other guy. Henry teased me a little about it here and there, and it wasn't all that serious. But when he brought up the subject in bed..."

"Things got exciting?"

She blushed. "It really got him going," she said. "The thing was, all the time I was in a poly arrangement in college—and it was the same for this other girl I knew there, who was also poly—the guys didn't want to know about the other guys, each relationship I had was kind of isolated from the others. You didn't talk about other guys with any of your boyfriends. It was different with Henry."

"He was interested in seeing you with other guys?"

I was hardly touching my pasta, I was so interested in what Michelle was saying. It was like a detective at the end of a murder mystery detailing how the crime had linked up all the little clues you'd read about all through the story. Michelle was explaining Henry's secret mindset, and it made sense of a load of his behavior up to this point.

"Well to start with we only talked about it. He wanted to know more about my past boyfriends, in serious detail, too. I wanted to understand where he was coming from, why he wasn't jealous about all this. Well, he was jealous, he said, but for some reason he enjoyed those feelings, and at the same time was turned on by the idea of me being this sexual free spirit.

"And he wanted me to fantasize about being with other guys while we were in bed. I mean, it really got him going. It was insane."

"But you were okay with it?"

She smiled, "Who was I to complain? I told my husband I was poly, and it turned him on like nothing before. I never felt so... well, adored. It just seemed to make him love me more, and want to give me the gift of other men to have fun with."

"So long as you told him all about it."

"Something like that. For me, I had to get used to that, to making up stories while we made love, creating these fantasies that I'd been out seducing other guys while Henry was at work through the night."

It was slightly off, talking about all this with Michelle, of course, because I was not her husband. It seemed too intimate for a conversation between roommates or even good friends.

It felt like betraying Henry, except that Henry had sent Michelle over to ask me out. As far as he was concerned, right now we might even be sleeping together, I wasn't sure.

"Then, after a while, he brought up the idea of maybe... well, maybe doing it for real," she said, and took a somewhat immense gulp of wine.

"That must have been a real step," I said, not quite knowing what to say to all this.

She said: "It was a little unnerving—and I was supposed to be the poly one. I just kept thinking that Henry had never done this before, before we got married. He'd never seen how some guys say they can accept a poly girlfriend, only a little way along the line, they decide actually they can't and they want to break it off with you."

"You thought he wouldn't be able to handle it?"

"He wasn't sure either, but he wanted to try. He said he didn't want to be the one putting restrictions on me just because he was my husband."

She took another mouthful of salad, and I just looked at her, thinking how fortunate I'd be if I really did get the chance to know her a little more intimately. I could just fall into those blue eyes and drown in her beauty.

But even with so many signals going in my favor, I felt a deep need to avoid hurting Henry. It made me feel slightly uncomfortable that I was some kind of test for them—that I might be offered the forbidden fruit, only to have it torn away from my grasp because Henry might suddenly decide he couldn't do polyamory after all.

I asked, "So you started thinking about me? I mean when it came to making it all real. Was that before or after I came to live with you guys?"

Another sip of wine, and I was topping up her glass. "We thought maybe I should date a stranger," she said. "We went to bars and I sat on my own, waiting for guys to come hit on me—and Henry watched. It was kind of exciting, especially for Henry as it turned out."

I tried to imagine how I might feel watching Michelle being picked up by other guys. Or Katie. I could even feel a pang of jealousy, particularly when I thought of Katie, and imagine that in controlled conditions, where it was all part of some sex game and not some real form of cheating, it might prove quite exciting. You just wouldn't know what would happen, or who she would end up going for.

"You enjoyed it?" I asked her. I don't think there'd be any point if it was just for Henry's benefit.

"I did," she nodded. "It made me feel single again—you know, very occasionally, I think you miss not being available when a hot guy looks your way, or even shows some interest. This was like saying I could have that again if I wanted. The freedom. Only, some of the guys noticed I was married, and that was too much for them—some of the guys asked if my husband knew what I was up to, and when I said he liked me doing this, they couldn't handle that..."

"It would be a little difficult for some guys to understand," I said.

"Yeah. I mean even in the States, most single guys want you to themselves if they're going to have you. Henry said maybe I should try taking off the ring, but I said from the get-go I wasn't going into this making guys think I was single."

"You'd probably have to tell them at some point, right?" I suggested.

"Exactly. So we tried something different, we tried some online dating—again, laying it all out that I was happily married, and that my husband was letting me explore a little extramarital fun."

"And how did that go down?"

Michelle smiled, but not with her eyes. "Oh, you know. Plenty of interest, as it turned out, but the guys all... well, they kind of creeped me out. I mean some of the pictures they seemed to think I wanted to see..."

She stuck her fingers down her throat, and it made us both laugh.

"And then you came along," she said, and her smile turned genuine.

I took another sip of wine, and said: "So was I invited to live with you guys after Henry decided I might be someone you could date, or did he figure I might be good for you after I moved in to your apartment?"

Michelle smiled, "I think Henry always liked you, and maybe in the back of his mind when he offered you a place to stay, he wondered if we might get along."

I nodded. What did I care if Henry had ulterior motives for letting me stay at his place? I mean, what incredible ulterior motives!

"He obviously liked you, and we did have a spare room," Michelle said, checking herself as though feeling she needed to reassure me I would have been invited to stay even if I hadn't been a candidate for dating her.

"Well, it was much appreciated," I said, my tone making it clear I didn't care one way or the other why they'd let me stay. "You were both very welcoming at a point when I really, really needed it."

The waitress came back to clear away our plates and ask us if we wanted anything more—dessert, coffee, whatever. I didn't know what I wanted, but we sent her away without adding to our bill.

"I think you were someone that Henry felt he could trust," Michelle said once we were on our own once again. "That if we went down this road and you seemed uncomfortable at any point, we would be able to stop, and you'd be fine about everything."

"Right," I nodded.

Then she gave me a wicked smile, "And when I first met you, I definitely liked what I saw."

I felt the butterflies in my stomach start fluttering again at that, and the fact that there were faint impressions of her nipples pushing quite clearly against the thin material of her dress.

"I have to say, though," she added, "I didn't entirely agree with how Henry wanted to do it."

"How do you mean?"

"I don't know," she said, blushing a little I think, "I thought we should probably have talked to you about it all, early on. But Henry said that would have freaked you out, especially after what had just happened with you and Katie. He just wanted me to get to know you, flirt with you, see how you responded, and then maybe... something would happen."

"'Something would happen'?" I raised my eyebrows at that. "What, so maybe I'd think it okay to cheat on my friend with his wife?"

She shrugged, "I guess he thought that if he gave you enough obvious signals, got you to take me out on enough dates on our own... you know, you'd start feeling maybe he would be all right with you fooling around with me a little."

Boy did that make me feel a little like an idiot. They'd been hurling signals at me all summer, and I'd been duly dodging every single one of them. It also made me feel a little crushed—that if I'd only been more aware of what was really going on around me, I might have been allowed to fool around with this gorgeous brunette a little.

"So it didn't really happen, huh?" I stated the obvious.

She smiled, actually seeming impressed at me. "You were too much of a gentleman," she said, and the way she looked at me just then, with real affection in her eyes, sent a pulse of heat through my heart. "Oh, you flirted with me a little, but any time something more might have happened... well, you were respectful of your friendship with Henry, I guess."

"You know I would have wanted more...?"

She nodded, "I got that impression. Henry wanted to make sure you were really interested in me, so we started doing a few things so... well, so you might accidentally see us, you know?"

"I saw you alright," it was my turn to blush now, I think.

The way she looked at me made me wonder if she wasn't thinking about those times, when I'd seen her making love to her husband. When I'd watched her thinking that I was unobserved.

She said, "We were only meant to do it once, to check how you'd take it... I guess it was kind of exciting to know you were watching."

"So you did it a few more times?"

"Uh-huh. And then I told Henry, look, it's really time we talked to Sean about all this. If we're really wanting to go ahead with it."

"And that's when you moved into a hotel room?" I asked.

Another slight nod. "We needed to really talk it through. You know, this was a huge step for us. We thought it wouldn't be, that we might just fall into it, try it out, and if we weren't happy back out again, no big deal. Only it is a big deal."

"It's your marriage," I nodded.

We paid the bill, splitting everything 50-50 in the easiest way possible.

Then I found myself feeling a little nervous.

"So what's next?" I asked her, and really didn't know what to expect.

"Well, Henry assumed we'd just talk for a little while, and then we'd maybe see how we feel about moving things to the next level."

"Okay..."

"And for Henry, I think the next level means sleeping together," she smiled, but as we stood up ready to depart the restaurant, it wasn't difficult to sense that she probably thought sleeping with me right now might be a somewhat sizable jump from where we were.

Stepping out on to the High Road, which was beginning to fill with the lunch crowd, I said, "You're of the view that we should probably take things a little more slowly, huh?"

She nodded, but the way she took my hand in hers as we strolled off in the direction of our apartment felt somehow different to the way we'd been before, even on our walk over to the restaurant prior to our meal.

"I told Henry maybe you'd need some time to think about it," she said. "I mean, we knew you like me, you get on with me, you seemed to want to watch me with Henry..."

"You two!" I laughed. "I should feel manipulated. You're like undercover detectives trying to set me up for some kind of sting."

She shared my laugh. "Kind of," she said. "Only, I figured it would be a little unreasonable for me to spring all this on you, and suddenly expect you to decide one way or another instantly before moving on."

I squeezed her hand, and she looked into my eyes. "You know I'm interested," I said.

She smiled, a faint pink flush in her cheeks. She looked unbelievable in the bright sunlight. All curves and smooth skin, flowing cocoa hair, big blue eyes. And she looked a little giddy, somehow, that we were walking along hand in hand, talking about moving our relationship to the next level.

Some of it had to be the fact that she'd been a married

woman for five years, and committed only to her husband. Poly or not, she hadn't ever really expected to know the thrill of dating a new man again.

It was kind of thrilling to be that unlikely new man for her. Yet as I walked with her on our way home, I found my thoughts did jump to Katie, understanding how tempting it might be for her to seek out this kind of thrill after our own passion had fallen so flat for so long.

Did she feel a little giddy like this, when she first went out with Grant after our separation? Did she look as beautiful as this, knowing that after so long, she had the chance to experience the intense heat of a new romance all over again?

Jesus, I even felt happy for Katie, I even hoped that she had felt like this, that it had been wonderful for her to be with someone new.

"I probably do have a few things to think about," I added, not wanting her to imagine I was so vacuous that I'd jump into bed with my best friend's wife the moment she offered herself to me. I mean, I was that vacuous, but I didn't want her to think I was.

She nodded. "And you have to sleep," she insisted.

God, sleep was the last thing on my mind.

"I suppose it's that time of day. But you've taken the day off..."

"To meet you for a long lunch—which I've done," she said. "We can go out again once you've slept—and you'll feel so much better."

"I guess so."

I was quivering all over. It seemed to me like we were doing this. That this was happening. That as much as we both felt obligated to talk about it all, discuss until we were blue in the face the ramifications, the issues involved, the possible repercussions, nothing had yet been said that meant anything other than a continuation of our journey towards sleeping together.

How could I sleep feeling that was happening?

I was tired, though. It was getting late for my usual sleep shift. It was wonderful to think we could go out this evening, almost like a normal couple, and pick up where we'd left off only with me being fully rested. That would be a heck of a night off.

Only something was niggling at me a little from all this. I couldn't quite work out what it was. Maybe sleep and a little time to think would help me untangle it.

As we walked, Michelle retrieved her mobile phone and started tapping out a text message.

"Henry said anything to you since we came out?" I asked her.

"No, not yet," she said.

I pictured him hanging out in whatever hotel it was they'd booked into. What was he thinking right now? In what state of mind was he now that this year-long fantasy of his was stepping over the line into reality? I think I might be going crazy wanting to know what was going on.

I guess I was affected by how Katie had approached our marriage. Deep down, I knew the pain of an unexpected marital break-up, knew that it could flare up with zero notice. Henry trusted Michelle completely, and they'd talked about all this at length, all year. He couldn't imagine there was any risk that Michelle would seduce me and then decide she no longer wanted to be married to him.

Still, it was his fantasy coming to life, he had to want to know what was going on, if only because it would turn him on to know Michelle was in the process of engineering her sexual liberation.

"I'm just telling him we're on our way back to the

apartment after lunch," she explained of her text message. "And that I'm going to let you sleep."

I could detect a hint of excitement in her voice that hadn't been there before our meal together. It was probably related to the fact that she wasn't quite as nervous, wasn't afraid of my disapproval now that we were over that potentially awkward conversation.

There was undoubtedly a new spring in her step, though, and I flattered myself to think it was because she had the impression that I would willingly share her with her husband.

It made me feel like a million dollars that she might be excited to actually date me.

As we arrived back at the apartment building, and stepped into the elevator in the lobby, her perfume filled my chest again. God, I could see a little way down her dress as we stood there side-by-side. It shouldn't have hit me so much, I'd seen much of her bare body before thanks to her misadventures with Henry. But it was somehow different this time, because there was the very strong possibility that I would get to be with her.

On our way up in the elevator, the thing that had been niggling at the edges of my consciousness suddenly became clear. Thinking back to my relationship with Eddie Dorlen, he had had exactly the same calm demeanor as Henry had, when I'd first seen him after starting to date Magda. He hadn't seemed particularly annoyed with me, he was almost gracious about it.

Only, he hadn't really talked to me about Magda, not once. And then without telling me of any negative feelings he had, he had just quietly stopped spending time with me, and after a while it seemed that we were strangers.

What if the same happened with Henry? He might seem supportive of all this on the surface, but what if he didn't feel that way deep down? If he was still doing all this because he thought his wife was polyamorous, that she needed this, not because he himself wanted this.

"Do you think Henry's really going to be all right with all this?" I asked her as the slow elevator neared our floor.

She looked up at me and seemed thankful that I'd raised this particular point. "I think so," she said. "But you never know."

"Do you think he's going crazy right now, thinking that we're coming back to the apartment to sleep together?"

She smiled, "Maybe. But maybe it's good for him to think that way for a little bit. And if he's horrified, and he wishes we didn't sleep together, he'll have some time to tell us."

I nodded. "How long are you going to make him think we've slept together when we haven't?"

"Well, I'm not going to lie to him," she said, "but maybe while he's staying in that hotel room, I'll make him think it could happen any time."

"But really, we'll just take things slowly?"

"Right. You don't mind, do you?"

We had arrived at our front door. Even if she was talking about taking things slowly, my heart was pounding just then. If she was a single girl, and somebody asked, I'd be able to tell them I was now dating her. I was dating Michelle Robinson. I was dating my best friend's wife.

"I think it's the best way," I said, and slipped the key in the lock.

12

Sleeping together

*I*nside the door, she was checking her phone again as we went through into the living room.

"So, he's not freaking out yet as far as I know," she said, but seemed disappointed that Henry hadn't sent her any messages yet.

"He doesn't have anything to be freaked out about yet," I smiled, actually feeling a slight buzz that my friend might be imagining I was actually sleeping with Michelle right now—and I guess, because at some point, I might actually get to.

We slumped down on the couch, flipped on the television to one of the movie channels, which was playing an old black and white film that I could actually identify as Key Largo.

She said, "I think the hardest thing will be trying to work out exactly how he feels about all this. If he conceals how he really feels, it makes things difficult."

Michelle sat next to me, closer than she ever had before, it seemed. I felt my cock throbbing gently at her proximity, her fragrance.

"He wouldn't do that, would he?"

She shrugged. "It's not just his fantasy in his mind—he thinks I might need this. It might mean he hides it if it's difficult for him."

"We can go as slow as you want to," I said earnestly, since slow was probably good for me too, to get my head around all this, even though my body was crying out for hers.

"You know, some people I told about being polyamorous thought I did it because it was easier? I guess they thought it was easier not limiting myself to one guy."

"But really, it's probably pretty complicated," I observed. "If Henry can't handle it, you'd be happy to just go on being monogamous?"

She shrugged, "I think so. I promised him that when we married. I guess it's a balance between feeling that you're experiencing life, that you're missing out on love with some other special person, and desperately wanting to be with the man I know I love, I know I want to please more than anything."

A surge of electricity swamped my heart as she used the L-word. Was that what we were talking about here? Was she opening herself to the possibility of being in love with me, as well as Henry? Or was this purely about our physical attraction to each other?

"Have you talked to Henry about the possibility that you might fall for someone else?" I asked. "I mean, you know, the whole L-word."

She smiled, and snuggled into me. "I thought you needed to get some sleep?"

"I do," I said. "I guess the journalist inside me—who still exists, by the way—"

"Of course," she grinned.

"— Even though I just correct spelling and grammar

for a living." I couldn't help a little grin myself, and that moment right there was about the best I'd felt about my career since Henry and I had finished journalism school. "The journalist inside me is just naturally curious about all this."

She said, "We've talked about it. I think Henry's fantasy is mainly about the sex, but I think he understands the possibility—that as far as I'm concerned, love is not a limited quantity, that if I give some to someone else, I won't have any less to offer my husband. That's why he wanted to try this with you, I think."

I felt my ears burn. What if she did fall for me? What if I fell for her, and I couldn't handle her staying with Henry at the same time?

I found myself thinking about Katie again. About Alicia describing Grant as merely her fuck buddy. That had made me feel slightly better, I think. To believe that she wasn't in love with him, she was just having sex with him.

What if she met someone and fell in love with him? How would I feel about that? Hurt, probably. So how could Henry handle it?

"I'm not sure I'd ever love anyone else the same way I do Henry," she said, as though reading my hesitation a certain way.

"And if he wanted it to be just about sex, that you could play with other guys but not get attached?"

She smiled, "I guess I could bring myself to do that, if it was the right guy. Friends with benefits, I suppose. I don't think I would have been this way before I met Henry. Marriage does change you."

I could see Michelle partially reflected in the TV screen, and she really looked exquisite. Her long flowing locks, those incredible eyes. The rounded form of her breasts squeezed into that dress. She'd made a huge effort to prepare herself to see me, to seduce me. It seemed a shame that we intended to move things so slowly.

"What do you think about all this?" she asked. "I never really asked you. What do you think about my being polyamorous?"

I took a deep breath laced with her perfume. "I think I'm beginning to understand," I said. "I mean, it challenges the way I've always seen relationships. I'm trying to be open to it."

"You think you'd want to date me, knowing I'd still be with Henry?"

"Can't you tell?" I asked her, feeling my heart pounding like a kettledrum, the warm blood rushing to my face in a furious blush.

Her mouth curled up in a tender smile. She said softly, "I do hope Henry can handle all this."

She checked her phone again, and still there was nothing from Henry.

"I don't think he's ever really been the kind of guy who changes his mind about something," I said to reassure her. "And he definitely never regrets anything he's done."

"I guess you're right," she said.

I was so buzzed, my manhood so hard in my pants, there was no way I was ready for sleep. But I think if I sat there with her any more, I'd ruin all chances of sleep. Also, I figured the faster I got through my sleep shift now, the sooner we could go out on our first proper date.

I just had to tear myself away from my physical craving to be with her just then.

"Do you think he'll be angry if we make it seem like we're going all the way while he's staying at the hotel, but really we're not?" she asked.

I shook my head. "He'll understand why you want to do it that way, I'm sure. He'll probably find it hilarious."

"I guess."

"You don't have to completely lie. Just send him suggestive texts, you know, about how good you're feeling, how exciting it is, and so on."

She nodded, placed a hand on my thigh, grateful for my support. "You need some sleep," she said, turning her head and leaning down to nuzzle into my chest, breathing deeply as she pressed against my body.

"You smell nice," she said, a dreamy quality in her voice.

"Thank you," I replied, and lowered my face to touch very gently against her head, breathing in the clean scent of her hair. "So do you."

I thought briefly of the last time I'd been on this couch, breathing in the dark, forbidden aroma from her forgotten underwear. The thought made my heart skip all kinds of beats.

Michelle gasped. She pulled away from me and turned to look at my face. "Did I just do that?"

"What?" I was a little horrified. What had I done?

"That..." she said, and her hand gently touched down in my lap, her fingers tracing over the bulge straining in my pants for just a moment.

Now it was my turn to catch my breath. Michelle quickly snatched her hand away. Nevertheless, she was now looking at me with a glint in her eye that suggested mischief was on her mind, but also a hint of surprise that I hoped meant she approved of what she had briefly felt between my thighs.

"That's going to drive me crazy," she said.

"Crazy?"

"Knowing that's there." she shivered.

"Well, fair's fair," I smiled. "You've been driving me crazy for a while."

"A while?" she gave me an expression that insisted on innocence.

"You know—sitting out here in just a t-shirt. And God, having sex with my roommate in our living room when you knew full well chances were I might come home and interrupt you."

She laughed. "I did want to see how you'd react. I guess I wanted to see how Henry would react, too. He'd been talking about it for so long."

"I should get some sleep," I said. "You're going to be okay if I do..."

"Of course," she said, standing up as I did. The way she stood there in that dress was an image I felt would stay with me until sleep finally claimed me, if it ever did that day. It seems to have shifted a little so more of her cleavage was visible. "I might have a cat nap myself."

"Sounds good."

She smiled, fluttered her eyelids a little in a mock-seductive way. "We could just sleep together—you know, we don't have to do anything."

My heart pulsed with raw heat. "I suppose then we could tell Henry we just slept together."

At that idea, she grinned, ear-to-ear.

So that's what happened. When I came out of the bathroom, having let her use it first, I found her lying in my bed, under the covers, wearing one of my old t-shirts this time, as though her usual night attire in our apartment, Henry's old t-shirts, would prove inappropriate for her first sojourn in my bed.

I was a little disappointed that she'd dressed down from her killer outfit, but how bad could I really feel about that? She was so cute, and she was in my bed.

"Look!" she was beaming as she held out her mobile phone, her face truly lit up.

She'd had text messages from Henry, then. That was a relief.

"What does he say?" I asked, feeling a few butterflies fluttering in my belly at the idea that my friend must have been chilling out in that hotel room thinking I was in the throes of passion with Michelle.

"Here," she said, handing me the phone.

The brief text conversation started with Henry's message:

Henry: Hope you guys are having fun together!

Reading it felt strangely reassuring. I mean, I trusted that Michelle hadn't been making any of this up, but not hearing directly from him before this, it was a relief to see he really did approve.

Michelle replied:

Michelle: We're having a lot of fun—how are you holding up, honey?

Henry: Great—nervous, but it's such a buzz thinking what you guys must be up to. Everything going well so far?

Michelle: I'm nervous too. We can always stop.

Henry: No, it's good nervous. You want to stop?

Michelle: Not if you don't. We had a nice lunch at Zizzi's, and talked about everything

Henry: And Sean's okay with the idea?

Michelle: Pretty sure he is. I'm lying in his bed right now :-)

With that, I saw that she'd sent Henry a picture of herself lying there in my bed, having removed her dress, but before she'd changed into her casual sleepwear. Wearing black lace lingerie and stockings, she looked incredible.

He must have had a heart attack seeing her like that, in another man's bed.

I felt a hint of regret that I wouldn't get to see her like that myself, at least not yet. I had to remind myself she was his wife.

"That picture's going to drive him insane," I said before reading on in the text conversation.

"It should test how he really feels about this," she nodded, and I could see how happy she was at the reaction I'd obviously had to the sight of that photo.

"He's definitely going to think we're going all the way here."

"Good," she smiled.

Henry: You look amazing. No matter what happens, I can't wait to see you again.

No matter what happens. My heart did a little somersault at that.

Michelle had replied:

Michelle: I can't wait to see you either—I must be the luckiest girl in the world to have a husband like you.

Henry: I think I must be the luckiest husband, to have a wife as beautiful and adventurous as you. What are you guys up to tonight?

Michelle: We'll probably go out. Dance the night away, have a little more fun when we get home.

Henry: Don't tire him out too much, he has to go back to work eventually!

Michelle: I'll try not to.

Henry: Okay, don't keep him waiting. keep me posted xxx

I looked at her, and couldn't help but notice how hard her nipples were, straining against that t-shirt.

"He seems to be encouraging us to go for it," I said.

"Doesn't he?"

It took some serious self-control for me not to pounce on her, and Michelle looked to me as though she was fighting against her own instincts to jump me.

Were we insane to want to take things so slowly, and

apparently not do anything over the next few days, when Henry had all but ordered us to go all the way? Well, we had to be sure he was going to cope with all this.

We had to be sure I could cope with all this.

Trying to breathe normally and get on with the process of going to bed, I stripped down to my boxer shorts, acting as though there wasn't a gorgeous brunette in my bed waiting for me.

"You're just trying to make it difficult for me, aren't you?" she said, appraising my semi-nudity before I climbed in beside her.

"I'll never be able to sleep otherwise," I said.

I switched out the light, and even though I had a decent enough Queen-sized bed, Michelle quickly took the opportunity to nuzzle up to me. We were spooning in the darkness, her fragrance all around me, her warmth, her soft skin, clean hair. I had to be careful to keep my stiffness to myself.

"Thank you, Sean," she said in the darkness.

"You don't have to thank me."

"You've been very understanding about all this. About the possibility of going through with it... and my need to wait."

"Of course. It's no problem." I leaned forward and kissed her on the top of the head gently. "We need to be sure about all this."

"Yes," she agreed, sounding a touch sad. The last thing she said before we eventually did manage to drift off to sleep was: "I'll be dreaming of you tonight."

13

Testing the waters

J'm surprised how quickly I did actually fall asleep. Usually, any kind of change to my routine disturbs me out of slipping off to sleep, but I suppose once I'd calmed down a little, the enormous feeling of wellbeing from lying next to Michelle helped me relax.

Waking up, I actually felt a small amount of regret that I'd succumbed so easily, missing out on all those hours of being close to her, of the possibility that we'd both see through our logic and give in to the physical urge, to hell with the consequences.

I woke to find her still wedged against me, her legs reaching back to intertwine with mine - her skin so irresistibly soft, her flesh giving off such warmth, her scent so alluring to me. My arm was around her waist, whether I'd put it there or she had, and during the late afternoon her t-shirt had shifted upwards so that her midriff was bare.

I couldn't help but have morning wood, and it wasn't long before I found she was awake, and aware of what was going on between my legs, pressing her behind backwards against it.

I apologized for my rather non-platonic response to her presence.

"Mmm..." she said, "No, I like waking up like this."

The alarm clock said 6.30pm - we'd slept a long while. It had been good sleep, though - surprisingly, I felt rested.

Michelle reached forward to the bedside table on her side, grabbing her cell phone. As she stretched over, I was awarded a glimpse of her behind, in only a little pair of pale pink panties. I winced, and my erection throbbed.

"So, we're going out?" I asked, trying to find distraction from the sexual longing within me.

"Of course!" she said, lying back against the pillow to check her phone. There must have been a message, as she giggled, then held it to me to read.

Henry: Sorry, fell asleep. So what happened with you guys after you got home from lunch?

Henry, of course, was on the same time schedule as I was. He must have been staying awake hoping to hear something from Michelle, but while she fell asleep in my bed, he had also fallen asleep in his hotel room.

"He doesn't seem to regret letting us get together," I said.

"He doesn't. What should I tell him?"

"You still want to test his resolve?"

"Sure."

"Tell him we came home, talked some more and then... I don't know... say we fooled around a little..."

"Do you think Henry is thinking we were really bad today?" she asked innocently as she began texting her husband.

My cock throbbed between my thighs, I said: "I

imagine he believes something more than kissing was involved."

"More than kissing?"

I smiled at her expression of mock outrage. "I should think he will assume I peeled off your clothes, touched you."

"Touched me? Where?"

"Your breasts. Between your thighs."

"And you think he assumes I tore off your clothes at some point? And maybe fooled around a little with your beautifully hard cock?"

"It's probably safe to assume he assumes that," I joked.

She gave a shiver that may have been half involuntary, but she exaggerated its affects. "I think he probably thinks we were fucking like rabbits all day," she gave me a devilish glare. "And he seems okay with it according to this."

"Kind of makes you feel we missed out, huh? If he changes his mind tonight, tomorrow..."

She sighed, and I felt a little bad for breaking the mood.

"I should get in the shower," she said. "We should get going."

Now she slowly peeled off the covers, and at first, I didn't think anything of it, my mind distracted by the news that Henry was still okay with us sleeping together. When she paused for a long moment, though, I saw that she was gazing at my morning erection, albeit through my boxer shorts.

Then she cheekily snuck a finger in the waistband of my underwear and pulled it down for a quick peek, too quick for me to react quite in time to protect my dignity.

"Hey!"

She giggled, saying: "No harm in looking, is there?"

I rolled my eyes a little. "I guess not."

She quietly moaned, in frustration as well as lust, finally tearing her eyes off my stiffness to climb out of bed. Then she walked to the doorway, and as she did so, she pulled her t-shirt up and over her head to reveal her shapely behind, her smooth back, dropping the garment to the floor.

"Fair's fair," she said, turning to give me a look at her bare breasts. The sight of her standing there in just her panties took my breath away.

Then she hooked two fingers into the waistband of her underwear, and they dropped to the floor as well.

"Just for you," she smiled, and was gone.

I couldn't help picking up her phone, taking a glance at what she'd texted Henry.

Henry: Sorry, fell asleep. So what happened with you guys after you got home from lunch?

Michelle: We got home, talked some more, fooled around a little...

Henry: You still like him?

Michelle: God, yes. He makes me feel amazing.

Henry: Wonderful. So how far did you go?

Michelle: Well, we saved a few things for tonight.

Henry: You didn't go all the way?

Michelle: Not until after our date tonight.

Henry: Very exciting. So tonight—dinner, dancing?

Michelle: Something like that. You do know your wife is single again and going out to get laid?

Henry: It's going to be fantastic.

I had to agree with Henry about that.

---

*W*hen she came out of the bathroom, Michelle went into her and Henry's room to get ready for going out. I heard her talking on the phone—presumably with Henry. It made me feel nervous. Was he still supportive? Was she talking him down from a ledge?

It was also kind of exciting to think that she was in there dolling herself up for a night out with me.

I put on a nice shirt, a decent pair of pants, but had no idea what Michelle would be wearing.

When she finally emerged, half an hour later, you could have knocked me down with a feather. She looked sensational in a thin dark blue dress that had a sheen of satin about it that made it almost look as though it was a nightie. It came down to mid-thigh, her legs bare for a warm summer evening.

Her dress was so thin I couldn't imagine she was wearing anything underneath.

"Wow," was all I could say.

She smiled, gave me a twirl. Still no sign of underwear.

"Am I underdressed here?" I asked her, and made her laugh.

"No, you look perfect," she said, her eyes appreciating me enough to make me feel almost confident about my appearance.

She took my hand in hers as we walked up to the High Road to better our chances of getting a taxi, and perhaps because of the darkness, because of our progress, there was a new edge to the feeling of connection with her, a new wicked sense of excitement.

Confirming as it was that we were dating.

"How does it feel, taking the next step?" I asked her as we waited for a cab, another couple stealing the one we thought we might get.

"I'm a little nervous," she admitted, surprising me.

"But you've done this before."

"Not while I've been married. And not with a friend, and a friend of my husband's at that. Are you nervous?"

"Terrified." At her double-take, I added: "In a good way."

"If there is such a thing," she laughed.

"I guess we've gone out together before, we just have to relax and see it like that."

It was funny to think that Henry's long attempt at getting me comfortable with Michelle—having us all go out together, sending me out on platonic dates with her—had all been intended, potentially, to set us up for this kind of situation.

But this wasn't the same as one of our previous dates.

She'd been flirtatious before, but now she acted in a slightly different way—turning it on to a higher degree, stepping up her femininity somehow, flashing me the kind of glances that weren't just amused or mischievous, but outright lustful and daring.

Then there was the way she'd presented herself: before, we'd only ever gone out in casual clothes, jeans and so on. Tonight, I'd made a little more of an effort but Michelle looked dazzling.

The way she occasionally touched me, all through the evening date, in the taxi, the restaurant, the bars, the club —it wasn't just her coquettish nature now, it seemed more like foreplay.

It was so exciting to be on a date at all, particularly after being rejected by Katie in such a fashion. But it felt unlike any date I'd had before in my life. For one, it wasn't just us on the date—there was the constant, quiet presence of Henry with us all the way.

Not least since from the initial taxi journey, Michelle was in fairly constant text contact with him, but also because our conversation kept coming back to this strange situation we found ourselves in. Of course it would—that was the big new thing for both of us.

"It's like I'm a slightly different person with you than when I'm with Henry," she said. "It's just the natural way I am, I respond differently to each of you, I behave slightly differently—I probably think differently, see things differently."

"Because you're married to him, and not to me?"

"Partly, but I always was this way with guys. Different guys bring out different aspects of my personality. I like it."

"So if you dated more guys as well, you'd get to see more aspects of your personality?"

She smiled, and inside, I received a little tickle of fear that she'd consider dating other guys as well. I guess she would. There was something exciting about that, as well as frightening. Was this how Henry felt about me dating her?

"Why not date a different guy every day of the week?" I joked.

"Because that would be exhausting. I don't need to see every possible aspect of my personality."

"How's he doing?" I nodded at her mobile phone, which had just gone dark now that she'd finished tapping out her message.

"Okay, I think. I just told him we're in a taxi, a little nervous. He's pretty nervous too."

"Understandable."

The restaurant was up in Holborn, recommended by one of Michelle's business school buddies. It seemed a touch pretentious, but suited our needs I suppose. The menu was a little limited, a little expensive, but then food was the last thing on my mind that night.

Michelle handed me the wine list to peruse while she texted Henry again.

I wonder if I'd been some other guy on a date with her, if I wouldn't have been a little bothered by her texting Henry so frequently—but I actually found it added to the buzz surrounding this whole thing. It offered a constant reminder at what an experience this was, for Henry too.

She apologized almost every time, and I told her there was no need. She also felt no qualms about showing me what was being said.

Michelle: At the restaurant. It's a little over the top, but I guess tonight's special.

Henry: It is. Very special.

Michelle: Sean looks cute. I might have to make out with him soon ;-)

Henry: They might kick you out of the restaurant :-P

Michelle: Then we'll have to hurry up and eat our food ;-)

She'd drop little hints in her messages about how she was perceiving me, what she'd like to be doing with me, and it only turned me on more. She wasn't texting Henry too frequently, though. All through the meal, I even started wondering if he'd start feeling she was leaving him hanging.

"So in the future, you think you might want to see other guys?"

"I've been fine about committing myself to Henry," she said, "but if he's really interested in going down the rabbit hole, and someone else came along who caught my eye—who knows what might happen?"

"Right."

"As long as Henry's okay with it..."

It was a good chance for me to get my head around this strange situation. I did feel a touch of jealousy that Michelle might want to see other guys, it burned inside of me. But the thought of her being so wild and free was also a thrill, and made her seem more desirable, if that was possible. It made me think that whatever she wanted, whoever she wanted in the future, for now she wanted me —and that made me feel special.

And more than once during that meal, I found myself trying to imagine how I might feel if Katie were here in Michelle's stead, and I had allowed her to date some other guy. Undoubtedly I'd feel this kind of jealousy—more so, even. But would I also feel the excitement? And as Henry was feeling it?

Part of me longed to find out. Part of me just throbbed with pain when I thought about Katie, so the rest of me attempted to stifle those particular mental wanderings.

"Was it like this when you were dating more than one guy at college?"

"Not really. It was just... well, it was just dating."

"And this isn't?"

"I don't know... maybe because I've been interested in you for a while... because I know you so well already... or because I haven't been with anyone but Henry for so long..."

It wasn't just the cool air that meant I could see the pinpoints of her nipples pushing against the thin material of her dress. It made me feel all fizzy inside to think that she was having dirty thoughts about me, about us.

"And how does it feel?"

"Weird. Because we did this before so many times, only without... without the intent."

"Good weird, though?"

Under the table, I felt her bare foot stroking my leg, "Definitely good-weird," she smiled, something I could never resist. "Because this time we can really... you know... can't we?"

"When you're ready."

"Kind of exciting, isn't it?"

We finished our meal in record time—the waiter must have been disappointed in our ordering, although we both had glasses of wine to accompany our entrees, and none of

147

those meal options were cheap. In some ways we probably did him a favor, vacating the table quickly so he could fill it with diners who had more potential to give a larger tip.

We were soon in one of Soho's crowded bars, where we had to nearly shout to be heard, but where we could stand closer together, almost as though we were dancing. And in the darkness, where Michelle could stretch up on tiptoes, sling an arm around my neck and kiss me, igniting fireworks inside me.

Oh Jesus, she was so sweet, like partaking of the most incredible dessert.

As soon as she made her move, it was like some kind of damn bursting between us. All conversation stopped for a long while as we just pressed ourselves together, locked lips, gazed in each other's eyes. If we were worried about how it would feel, whether we would have chemistry after being friends, after having a whole marriage out there between us, this completely dispelled such fears.

Electricity flowed between us as we gently sucked on each others' lips, tentatively delved tongues inside mouths, breathed each other in.

"I wasn't expecting that," I said eventually, when Michelle finally allowed us enough space to actually take another sip of our neglected beverages.

She grinned. "I told Henry I was going to, didn't I?" she said innocently. "So he had plenty of time to stop me if he started feeling bad about it."

"I suppose so."

I felt a little dazed, shaken up. She was the first person I had kissed, other than Katie, for a long while. It was an incredible experience, but as well as giving me a huge buzz, made me appreciate how I'd let things slide with my wife. When was the last time we'd kissed like that?

Michelle slipped away to the restroom, I suspect to

either call or text Henry about what had just happened, and then we were away to the next bar, where I started wondering what was the point of even waiting to get served drinks if much the same thing was going to happen —we spent most of our time in that dark, crowded place in a corner exploring each others' lips.

This time, at least, there was a suitable ledge at hand where we could put our drinks while we fumbled like star-crossed teenagers.

It meant our hands could wander a little more, and I could sweep mine all over that sensational dress, feeling how soft and smooth it was clinging to her curves, her hot flesh responding to my touch.

I ran my fingers down her back, and over her shapely behind, and even then it wasn't entirely easy to tell if she was wearing anything underneath.

"Checking for underwear?" Michelle grinned as she busted me.

I shrugged, "You look incredible in that dress. A guy's always going to be a little curious about the engineering involved..."

She laughed, "And what would you most prefer? If I did, or if I didn't?"

"I don't know, I think there's benefits both ways."

Michelle held my gaze in hers, then seemed to wriggle, her hands moving by her hips. I half-thought she was starting some kind of surreptitious dance to the bar's overly loud music, though we could easily have just moved on to a club if she was in the mood for dancing.

Then she tucked something in my pants pocket. Fishing them out, I could tell what they were by touch. Soft satin, softer even than her dress, they were slightly damp and still warm from her body.

God.

"Well, now you know," she flashed her eyes at me.

Her nipples pushed at her dress like bullets. She was as turned on by all this as I was. Only, she had nothing but a thin dress to cover her nudity now. That was going to drive me crazy.

It must have been getting late, as the volume of the music was suddenly bumped up again, making it completely impossible to hold any kind of conversation. The bar was catering to the clubbing crowd now, trying to keep those hankering after a nightclub as long as possible by imitating the conditions.

"Let's go dancing!" Michelle cried over the booming, and still stunned by the fact she'd removed her panties right in front of me, in public, I complied with her wish, allowing her to drag me out of the place by the hand.

Outside, she continued to lead me, through the warren of lively, neon-lit streets at the heart of Soho.

Michelle was somehow managing to type text messages into her phone while also navigating a path through the crowded streets to her chosen nightclub. I was a little concerned as we went, but she seemed to see well enough with half an eye on the way ahead.

She seemed very amused by their text conversation, and as we progressed a few streets over, she passed her phone over for me to see.

Henry: Hope you guys are having fun together!

Michelle: We're having a lot of fun together. Of course we are, Sean is very good at kissing ;-)

Henry: Naughty girl. You still at the restaurant?

Michelle: At a bar. Think I'm going to take him dancing.

Henry: Dirty dancing ;-)

Michelle: Maybe!

Henry: You want real dirty dancing? Sans culotte, honey...

Michelle: One step ahead of you ;-)

Henry: Wicked, wicked girl. Now don't let Sean get too drunk or there won't be any dessert.

Wow. He really was egging her on, there was no doubting his intentions. It felt a little funny to me, but the more I thought about it, and perhaps the more alcohol I consumed that evening, the more exhilarating it seemed to me: these guys were actively plotting for this exquisite little pixie to take me to her bed and open up like a flower.

Even looking at her, holding her hand, breathing in her perfume made me tremble. And she was actively teasing her husband about her flirting, about her dirty thoughts about me, about the prospect that we would go back to the apartment in the small hours and ride each other until we collapsed.

Michelle grabbed the phone from me, and tapped in a final message as we arrived at the club, which she briefly showed me before we went in:

Michelle: He's switching to water.

---

*W*e both drank water while we were at that nightclub, but then we'd already hit that sweet spot in the evening's dose of booze where we'd taken the edges of our inhibitions without yet significantly impacting our motor skills.

The club was not one I'd been in, but Michelle said she occasionally went there with her university friends.

The music actually seemed quieter than it had been in the bar, with the music slower than Michelle's usual choice of club.

"It gets livelier," she grinned, noticing my response to our environment as she put her arms around me again.

"I don't mind a little slow dancing," I said, my hands

slipping down her back again, finding their natural positions cupping her delectable rear.

She kissed me, her own hands reaching to cradle my head as she swayed in my arms, moaning quietly as I held her, and as she pressed herself against the hardness stowed away in my pants.

"I could get used to this," I said as we eventually broke apart.

"We're supposed to be going slow, right?" she giggled. "It's kind of hard to do that with you."

"I don't see Henry showing any signs of regretting all this."

"No," she said, and flashed me a flirtatious warning glance as she felt my fingers slowly teasing the hem of her dress up her thighs, threatening to reveal her lack of underwear.

"When you were doing this at college, were your boyfriends comfortable with you dating other guys as well?"

She shrugged, "Some didn't care. Some did."

"But it wasn't ever like this?"

She shook her head. "Even if they didn't mind it, they didn't want to hear about it. Didn't really want to know. They knew when I was out with someone else, they just ignored it. And when I was with them, it was as though I was only with them."

Michelle was enjoying my reaction to her, enjoying how hard I was, enjoying pressing herself against me.

"I think the worst thing," she said, "was when a guy started out okay about it all, and then later on decided he didn't like it. I'd get all invested in him, and then it would just turn sour."

"It's a difficult thing to handle for guys, I guess," I said.

She nodded. "But I think some guys just want to sleep

with you, and so in the beginning they don't care that you're not exclusive with them. I guess mono girls have that problem too."

That made me chuckle. "'Mono girls'—I'm guessing you never call them that to their faces!"

After that, the music started picking up, in volume and intensity, with a little throwback pop falling into the mix to liven everything up.

It was getting difficult to keep cool bumping up against Michelle like that, knowing that beneath that skin-tight dress, she had absolutely nothing on. I wasn't complaining, though.

In the slower numbers, I could hold her and in the darkness of a somewhat crowded dance floor, I could slip my hands up her dress, which made her melt a little in my arms, though I kept it relatively clean. We were supposed to be going slowly, after all.

Simply knowing that her bare sex was right there, inches from my touch, drove us both wild.

I was so buzzed when it finally came time to call it quits. We were going well into the small hours—I was used to being awake at this time of night, and Michelle had no limit to her supply of energy, it seemed.

We caught the N9 night bus back to Chiswick, and Michelle appeared as giddy as I was at our evening, and what this was potentially heading toward.

"We are still taking things slowly, right?" Thought I'd better check.

"We're supposed to be," she smiled, snuggling up against me on the seat, trying to pull her dress further down, although the bus was nearly empty.

It felt as though I was in some magical little world, my chest filled with her sexy floral scent, the warmth of her body pressing against mine. It was difficult not to just start kissing her again, as we had for some time while waiting for the bus to turn up.

"So how did you start these kind of relationships before?" I asked her.

"I told you, it's different every time," she smiled cryptically. "I think in my freshman year, everything was so fluid, I just dated a few guys and never told anyone I was going steady with them, or committing to them or anything. Everyone just dated each other."

I widened my eyes. "I think things were different in my day. Or maybe just in my circles." Actually, I made myself feel like some kind of social leper with that.

She gave me one of those semi-patronizing "aww" pity sounds. "From what you've told me, you had your fair share of tail at college, right?"

I smiled, shook my head a little. "I was a geek before it was fashionable," I said, though I dutifully highlighted a few of my key dating successes, which mostly had occurred during my university years.

"If I was with you when you were at college, there's no way I'd be able to keep my hands off you," she said, flattering me more than a little. "Geek or not."

How time flew when I was with Michelle. Even the journey back to our little corner of West London seemed to take hardly any time at all.

We talked, and I felt emboldened by the alcohol and our honest conversation. I spoke more than I ever had about Katie, and what it felt like knowing she was now with Grant.

"You feel 'strange' about it?" she asked as I tried to put into words how I felt.

"Yeah," I said. "I guess I still love her, so... it's complicated."

"You know, part of this whole thing..." she indicated ourselves, with a quick flick of the wrist to indicate Henry away in some far-off place, "is to know that you can handle it, too?"

"Oh, I know. And I can handle it."

"You're sure? When you know I'm with Henry..."

"I've handled it so far, haven't I? Knowing you're with him. Hearing you. Seeing you sometimes."

She blushed at that, visible even in the artificial light of the night bus. "But it might be different after you've... been with me..."

I shrugged. "I can see that. But I think I'm different now."

"Different? To when you were with Katie?"

"I think so. I've probably wanted you ever since I laid eyes on you," it was my turn to blush, confessing all. "But knowing you were with Henry—being so close to you two —I suppose I've found a mental strategy to deal with it."

"The same kind of mental strategy that Henry's developed to cope with the idea of me as polyamorous?"

"Possibly."

"Interesting. Well if we're going to do this, you have to be able to deal with... well, sharing me."

"I do."

"This is why you feel strange about Katie, because of how you're feeling about us?" she said, impressing me with her perception, although I might have been signaling the way my conversation was going. I nodded. She said, "So that's the 'complicated' part."

"I'm probably just confused," I said. "This is all a little new to me."

"You still love her. If she'd come to you back then, and

155

said she wanted to see someone else as well—even just for the sex—do you think you would have let her?"

I sighed. "I think back then it would probably have been a bit of a shock. I guess I would have jumped to the conclusion our marriage was over."

"But if it happened now, with what you know now, with what you feel now..."

I had to search inside myself, seeking out the darker reaches of my feelings, since I was certain it simply wasn't worth hiding anything from Michelle, not about this.

"Well, I wouldn't want to lose her," I said. "I'd want her to be happy, to have fun even if she couldn't with me because of our schedules..."

"So you'd let her..."

"I guess I would." My heart was all fluttery even thinking about it. Oh, I'd swept it all under the rug in my brain, but just then, I seriously missed Katie, I felt a huge hole inside my chest start to burn.

"And how would you react if she'd gone for it? Knowing she was out with another guy, sleeping with another guy?"

I tried to imagine it: picture myself sitting at that desk at the Daily News fiddling with the words on the screen while I knew that Katie was back home lying with a big strong blond guy bearing a colossal prick. Knowing that she was getting the buzz from getting physical with a new man, a different man. That she was being naughty and sexy and that she was going to be satisfied and cheerful when I next saw her.

That she might want to jump my bones the next time we had five minutes together, because she was so happy now, and because she needed me as well as that other guy. And that I'd want to consume her with every ounce of my being—reclaim her, experience her new insatiable streak, indulge in her newfound confidence brought on by dating someone who wasn't obligated to compliment her.

"I think it would probably be quite exciting to know she was fooling around with someone else," I said, feeling as though I was in some kind of confession booth in a Catholic church, talking through a grate to a priest instead of this pretty brunette.

Michelle nodded, giving me a knowing look. "You should talk to her," she said.

*I*nside the apartment, the front door closed behind us, and while I rounded into the living room, Michelle ducked into her bedroom, as though checking to ensure we were alone.

Then she ran into the living room and leapt up to pounce on me. I was knocked down onto the couch, but then we were kissing, and the pure sweetness of it took away the jolt of surprise on losing my balance.

She sat on my lap, and tucked her hair back around her ear, smiling as we continued to kiss.

We were allowed to do this. In fact, Henry had directed that we should be fully sleeping together, and was no doubt in the belief that we were right at this moment, if not too far hence, while he remained at work. And yet kissing Michelle—holding her, her hands reaching gently behind my neck, mine slipping up to cup her breasts—felt so much like indulging in forbidden fruit.

She was not mine, she was my friend's, and the ring on her finger said as much.

How must Henry be feeling? Was he blocking it all out, as I had been surprisingly good at doing with Katie in the arms of Grant?

But I couldn't think about Henry just then. My world was full of this little vixen, and the delicate way in which she sucked on my bottom lip, closing her pretty blue eyes as she experienced this connection. She was sitting in my lap, wearing that dress, and nothing else.

My whole body felt as though it was on fire. Had it ever been like this with Katie?

I kissed her back, trying to match her passion, her intensity, her tenderness. It was as though she was teaching me how to kiss a girl, as though I had to learn from scratch. It did seem to me that I was experiencing something entirely new—I did have lessons to learn from her.

We seemed to kiss forever, time came to a halt in our honor. There was just our deep breathing, the occasional quiet moan, and the soft sounds of the city outside the apartment.

I guess neither of us had a game plan, we didn't know where this was headed, so the kissing just continued. We locked lips, tangled tongues, gazed into each other's eyes, as though what we could do with our mouths had to take the place of what we might have done were we both ready to engage in full contact.

It took a while before I realized that Michelle's pressing down on my lap was more than just her supporting herself on me. She was stirring her hips gently, grinding herself against me—she could feel my hardness, and though she was holding herself back from using it fully, she was experiencing it in her subtle way. Now her moans took on a slightly different meaning, she was getting off on rubbing herself over me. Grazing her little pussy against my cock, even though my clothes stood in the way.

After a while, she slowed her movement, and broke away from our kiss, looking at me with humor in her eyes and a quiet giggle on her lips.

She lifted off me, and stepped back, and standing up in front of me, slipped the straps of her dress over her shoulders to leave her as nature intended.

She took my breath away.

"Well you've already seen me in the nude," she said.

"We are taking things slowly, right?"

"Of course."

She sat down on the couch again, at the opposite end to me. I made to move toward her, desperate to hold her, to touch those incredible smooth, trim legs, those pert breasts, her smooth hairless mound.

The last time I'd seen her naked, I seemed to recall she hadn't been shaved down there. Or at least, she'd had a landing strip. Was this part of her seduction of me?

She stopped me with a teasing foot on my chest, grinning as she held me back, amused at the transparent lust in my face.

"Slowly, right?" she said.

I groaned, but took my place on the couch, wondering what she meant to do sitting there like that.

She faced me, her legs running down the couch, her feet touching my leg. She gave me a seductive, naughty look, her hands running down her thighs, and then sweeping slowly up over her shapely stomach.

"Show me," she said, the amusement leaching out of her face to be replaced by raw desire. She nodded over to me, her eyes signaling that her focus was firmly on my loins.

Then she parted her thighs, opened her legs to show herself to me. Her right hand gently brushed over her calf, and then she was stroking it over her mound, over her pussy.

She moaned, and I saw her fingers sliding into the glistening pinkness of her little pussy.

"If it turns out that Henry comes to see this all as a mistake, you think he'll be okay about us seeing each other like this?" I asked her.

I swear, I could already detect the slight mustiness in the air from her arousal. It caused little ripples of energy to surge through my body.

"You've seen a naked girl before—it's no big deal, right?"

"I guess."

"And you've seen me having sex with Henry, so it's even less of a big deal than that."

"Sure."

Her thighs wide, her hands gliding over her sex, it was the most I'd ever seen of her before. Eye-opening.

"You like it?" she smiled, her eyes indicating her sex. "Henry helped me shave it."

"He did?"

"Does that make you feel weird?"

"I don't think so."

"I never shaved it all off before. It gives him a buzz, if he helps me get ready for a date. I guess he sees what he's giving away. He gets me all beautiful, and he won't get to enjoy me. Or at least, not until... after."

It seemed a little odd to me until I suddenly thought of Katie. How it would feel if Katie was going on a date with another man, as part of our arrangement to keep our marriage going considering her need for sex, and my growing fantasy of sharing her.

"He helped pick out your outfit?" I asked Michelle, wondering if that was what they'd been talking about on the phone while she got ready.

"Exactly."

I imagined how it might feel to prepare Katie for a date with someone else—it would feel so wrong. Picking out sexy lingerie for her to wear, and she wouldn't be wearing it for me. Helping her shave her pussy for the first time, and I wouldn't be the one enjoying it.

It fed into the strange mix of jealousy and excitement that could threaten to overwhelm me.

With her fingers Michelle spread her moisture all over her smooth mound. Oh, how I wanted to taste her. Yet we weren't ready for that just yet.

Still, I had light at the end of the tunnel—as soon as we had breakfast with Henry, we would see how he had really taken all this.

Then, he'd have a little time until our next date to deal with his feelings. And then we'd be free to do as we wanted.

I watched Michelle quiver a little, and wondered if she was having a minor orgasm, but then she surprised me by sitting up, leaning over to me. She looked as though she was about to kiss me, only then she was gently slipping two fingers inside my mouth, two fingers that were wet and slippery with her juices.

I tasted her. Salty, creamy, tangy, divine. She whispered: "We can't get in trouble for a little kissing, for fingers in mouths..."

She kissed me, pressing her nose into mine, sucking on my lower lip. She was so soft, so beautiful. Enchanting.

But she didn't give me a taste for long. She lay back again in her corner of the couch, legs splayed, fingers reaching inside herself, hand holding her mound.

Writhing as she touched herself, her breathing sounding like silk moving on silk.

She smiled at me when she opened her eyes to find me so fixated on her, and as her fingers accelerated in the ministrations of her pussy, she placed her foot over my crotch, pressing against my hardness there.

"Show it to me," she said in barely more than a whisper, biting her lip. "I want to see."

I put my hands to my crotch, my own legs parting, and looked back over to her. She looked positively ravenous. Gave me a nod as I glanced at her, confirming that this was what she wanted me to do. I unzipped my fly, and retrieved my manhood from my pants.

She let out a little gasp, which did no end of good for my confidence as I felt the cool air on my exposed member, which emerged full and hard from my fly.

Then I was holding myself, fingers curled around my considerable size, harder than I'd been for a long while it seemed.

I watched as she got more and more into her own little zone, her body undulating as she took care of herself, and as she struggled for oxygen, her face strained from the power of the sensations flowing through her, her fingers reminding me of a concert violinist, fluttering over her pussy.

The sight of her climax hitting was sensational, the way she seemed to just let go, her body moving with the force of the orgasm, her plaintive cry sending shivers down my spine.

Should I have come with her? I guess I felt a little awkward sitting there, my manhood in hand, watching such an exquisite girl like that—it was probably the only reason I hadn't already exploded.

After a few moments to recover, however, Michelle picked herself up and came to kneel before me, and I guess I wasn't supposed to have gone with her.

"Can I touch it?" she asked me quietly, her smile broad, showing her teeth as she looked intently at my hardness.

Well, I wasn't going to remind her we were supposed to

be taking things slowly that night. I was happy enough for her to do as much as she wanted with me.

"Of course," I said.

As she knelt there in front of me, I was a little surprised that she put a hand between her legs, and when she pulled it out, it was glistening with her juices. And it was this hand with which she touched my hardness, before doing the same with her other hand, coating my shaft in her juices.

It seemed so very filthy.

She used both hands and her own lubrication to massage my hard cock. I could smell her sex, it was so invigorating.

She was very effective, seeming to know how to pace herself so that I didn't just blow immediately in her hands. She was exploring me, not just holding me firm in her palms to pump me, but using the tips of her fingers to trace around the little head, and over my shaft.

While she massaged me with one hand, she used the other to pull my shirt open, and with a little help from me, off completely, followed closely by my pants.

I was naked before this stunning brunette, and while I wasn't inside her, it felt so incredible, I'd never experienced anything like it before, even with Katie – it must have been the added excitement of knowing this was my best friend's wife, kneeling naked in front of me while stroking my cock.

We kissed, and it was so sweet. I thought the way she bit her lip meant she wanted to go further, but she held herself back.

Finally, her pumping accelerated to the point where I could no longer control myself. What was she going to do?

She just kept going, until I exploded everywhere, a jet shooting into the air, then streams of white come all over my chest, Michelle directing it well to keep it from escaping anywhere but on my skin. She wasn't squeamish, she rubbed it into my cock, and into my stomach, my chest.

Glorying in the feel of it, come from another man. The first time she'd felt it in years.

Her eyes seemed to blaze as she licked her fingers.

14

Henry's view

$\mathcal{M}$ichelle crashed out almost immediately when we got into bed, leaving me to simply lie there in something of a haze.

It was the middle of my usual night shift at the Daily News, so I wasn't sleepy. I lay with Michelle a while, transfixed with her beauty and the fact that this was all happening.

At some point I got up to fix myself some food, watch some TV, but I kept wandering back in there to see her, almost to make myself believe it was really happening, this girl was in my bed. Henry's gorgeous wife.

I tried reading my Kindle, lying with her, breathing her in, but I was too buzzed to concentrate on the text. Eventually, I drifted off myself into what I suppose you would call an afternoon nap if I was a day-worker.

When I woke, Michelle was no longer in my bed. One look at a clock told me why—she had to be at work already. Yet when I opened my bedroom door, intending to fix myself a bite of dinner, my erstwhile sleeping companion was rushing around getting ready for work.

I just stood there in my doorway, watching as she flew this way and that, cleaning her teeth, applying her make-up, dressing in a one piece swimsuit that made me certain I'd never be able to focus on the exercise if ever I took one of her aqua aerobics classes, and then putting sweats on over it.

She did offer me the occasional kiss, but there wasn't time for much.

"So when do I get to see you again?" I asked her at one point.

"Tonight, when you're done sleeping," she said, making it sound obvious.

"I mean, when do I get to see-you see you?"

I felt my body craving hers, and it probably didn't help that I saw her in various states of undress wandering back and forth between her room and the bathroom,

"You'll have to wait until next time," she said with an alluring smile, apparently pleased I was hounding her for clues as to when I might get to be with her again.

"Well obviously," I sighed.

"You have to share me, so I can't always be with you," she said, giving me a waggle of her hips as she returned to the bathroom in her swimsuit.

I nodded, accepting that this wasn't just dating. She belonged to someone else. Maybe I'd get one evening with her a week, if this continued.

She kissed me long and hard before leaving, her hands falling to give my hardness a firm squeeze.

"Think of me while you sleep," she whispered as she withdrew, her eyes drinking in the sight of me standing there naked, before the front door closed between us.

I never saw Henry come in from work. He wasn't around before I turned in for my standard sleep shift, and that fed my paranoia that he was somehow unhappy with the way things were going, and what might have happened on my first true date with his wife.

Fatigue and the sweet memory of time spent with Michelle—assisted by the lingering scent of her perfume in my bed—lulled me to sleep despite the nap I'd taken with her before.

When I eventually got up for breakfast, however, he was sitting there in the living room, innocently watching Channel 4 News, and looking bright and sprightly as though everything was fine with the world.

"Morning, Squire."

"Morning yourself."

"Ready for another thrilling episode of the Daily News?" he smiled, a move that made me feel real relief.

"As ever," I returned his smile, sitting in the armchair with my bowl of cereal.

"Enjoyed yourself last night? You didn't miss much in the office."

"I didn't think about the office much."

"Me neither," he laughed, "and I was there."

"You survived, then?"

He nodded. "I think it probably helped that I spent that time preparing for it, and that I had work to distract me when I needed it. Still..."

In that moment, I saw Henry as I'd never seen him before. Emotion was imprinted in his face, even though he wasn't one to really show all his cards in that way.

"Any regrets?" I asked him, knowing that if there were any, I would cease all contact with Michelle.

My heart was actually pounding in my chest in those moments, before he shook his head.

"None at all," he said. "It was the most incredible experience—and sounds like it was for Michelle, too."

Had she called him? Texted him? It was one of her nights at business school, I knew that much, so she wasn't around right now. It warmed me that she'd told him that she'd had a good time.

I said: "We never really talked about it, did we? Before it happened. Before you sent her over to ask me out."

"No, we didn't," he gave a nod. "I didn't want to freak you out—pretty weird situation, right?"

"And you thought it would be easier coming from Michelle?"

He smiled, "I've seen the way you look at her, old man. Pretty face sets the heart all aflutter—thought you'd probably end up accepting any bizarre arrangement we cared to float."

I couldn't help smiling, not least because he was probably right. Michelle could probably have come and asked me to invade the lion's enclosure at London Zoo and I would have considered doing it.

Henry pulled himself up from the couch, grabbing his keys from the side table. "Fancy a drive into work ce soir?" he said.

"Sure. Just let me run under the shower first."

"I suppose you must think me some kind of Caligula," Henry said once we were on the road.

"I thought Caligula slept with other people's wives..."

He shrugged off my attempt to lighten the mood. "I honestly never thought this would ever cross the line, you know? Become reality. Thought my fantasy was just a temporary phase, that it would pass."

"Michelle said you've been talking about it a while."

"Talking about it," he nodded. "Took a while to get it out there—it's not the easiest thing, to open up to your wife about your dirty little thoughts, you know?"

I laughed, but there was no humor in my laugh. "I was never able to do it with Katie," I said. "Perhaps that was what went wrong."

Henry slowed for a traffic light just as we came into Hammersmith. "Plenty of couples never even hint to each other how they really think. I guess you have to spend the rest of your life together, so you don't want to risk losing your partner's respect straight up."

"But Michelle told you she's polyamorous. Are you saying you had thoughts about... about her dating other guys, before she told you that?"

"I think so," he said, taking the opportunity of being held at the lights to reach over my knees for the glovebox, to retrieve a pack of cigarettes he'd hidden inside. "I might not have had my thoughts fully formed when she told me. But I think there was already an interest there. Who knows how these things form? Everything's supposed to come from your childhood, right? That's what the shrinks all like to believe. My childhood was about as harmless as anyone's could be."

"Perhaps it's a reaction to a harmless childhood."

Henry chuckled. "Maybe. I mean, Michelle's always been a bit of a flirt... you know, when we were out with her friends from college, and so on. Even after we were married. I guess it all stems from that."

"She ever think about dating any of those guys?"

"I guess we would have considered one of them, if you

hadn't come along when you did," he said. "Or if you hadn't caught her interest like you did."

I felt a little flutter inside my stomach at that.

"I always trusted her, I never felt she'd cheat on me," he said. "I saw her with those guys—and it was so obvious that if she made a move on one of them, they'd go for her like a shot—I saw her with them, and it made me feel a little funny inside. But not in the way I expected it to."

I thought of the odd feelings I had, imagining Katie with Grant or some other man. I guess they had been there, in some shape or form, ever since I'd seen her with him.

"Turned on?" I suggested.

"Something like that." Henry was fumbling with the cigarette packet, pulling one out. I could tell he wanted something more, but you didn't want to go into work reeking of illicit substances.

Lips locked around a Silk Cut, he said: "Kind of frightening, to begin with. I still felt jealous, you see. I was afraid of losing her to one of them. That had always been there, in the background. From when I met her."

"Are you afraid of losing her to me, now?"

He smiled, but it may have been because a brief scramble through his pockets had come up with a Zippo. He managed to light up while pulling away from the traffic light as it turned green, and while winding his window down.

"You, old man, I trust you as much as any man could trust another. Besides, you still want Katie."

I felt a sharp stabbing pain in my chest merely to hear it from his lips. Sometimes, it did seem that Henry just blundered into sensitive subjects, but on this occasion, amongst the hurt that his accurate statement inflicted on me, it also perhaps brought some catharsis. I was impressed at his insight, thinking I must have revealed more to him than I'd thought.

To some degree, it made me feel better to admit that yes, I wanted Katie back. To admit that I would forgive her if given half a chance at reconciliation. But the pain was still there from the knowledge that I didn't have that chance.

Henry patted me on the shoulder, shaking me a little, but I guess comforting. "You have to talk to her, squire."

I nodded, but I didn't want to talk about it.

I said: "Michelle's friends—when she's out with them, and we're stuck at work, you're still afraid she might want to go with one of them?"

He smiled, breathing out a plume of smoke in the direction of the open window. "Hopeful, these days. I don't know. I'm different now. Years of marriage have settled me. I still get that slight sense that we're taking a risk here, that things could progress with another guy to the point where she falls for him—but even then, I have to feel she won't stop loving me."

"She's polyamorous."

"Exactly. If anything, it should give me comfort. A strictly monogamous girl might decide she loves another man, and jump to the conclusion that she has to jump ship to be with him. My only issue is if she decides she's in love with a guy I really can't stand."

A District Line train soared over our heads as we swung left and dipped under the bridge through the Hammersmith one-way system. It probably took longer to drive into work, but whenever Henry drove us in, even in this battered old Austin, it felt like cheating to miss out on the usual tedium of the Tube.

It put me in good spirits, despite the reminder that I still had a hole inside me from the loss of my wife.

"So you actually thought about her... being with another guy... before she told you she was poly?" I asked him. It might have seemed like a grilling, but he didn't object. We were journalists, we hadn't chosen to get stuck in subediting. And this was interesting to both of us.

Plus, it almost felt like therapy. Getting our thoughts out there, dealing with the fact that we were sharing the same girl.

"I'm not sure I recognized it at the time," he said. "They were just vague reactions to her being with those guys. We got into one of our drunken conversations, and I pointed out that we'd never really talked much about our romantic history before we met. And we just got talking about that—"

"So she mentioned that she was polyamorous?"

"'Was' being the prevailing sentiment. I mean, it was a surprise, I'll admit that. She swore it didn't change anything to do with her commitment to me—made it seem like it was all in the past. But when she told me what it all meant, that she didn't believe a person had to limit them-selves to loving one person, it sounded as though she still believed it."

"Sounded to me like that," I piped up.

He nodded. "Oh, she was very sensitive to the fact that I'm just boring old middle-of-the-road Henry, as conven-tional as conventions can be—she didn't want to offend me. That felt quite reassuring, but it also felt like she was repressing part of her nature."

"But polyamory isn't just about sex, is it?" I asked him. "It's not just about letting her date other guys."

He shook his head, "No, it's not."

"You think you'd be okay with it if she did fall for someone else?"

"I have to think so. We've talked about it a lot. She's

not looking for it, particularly, but if it happens, it happens. I'd want her to enjoy that, too. And in the mean time we can enjoy the fun stuff—the sex, the dating."

"Did you tell her you'd been thinking about sharing her even before she first told you about the polyamory?"

"I did. I'm not sure she believed me. She imagines I only started thinking about this because I think it'll make her happy to feel we're open to her polyamory."

"I guess it doesn't matter any more."

"No. It was fairly obvious when we were in bed, and we talked about her being with someone else, how I felt about it all," Henry laughed, "Actually, she was a little surprised how attractive the idea was to me."

"And this was a whole year before I came along, and you guys thought about me being with her?"

He shrugged, "It was just a fantasy to begin with—she never thought I'd ever really be able to handle it, and I didn't expect that she would ever get out from the shadow of our marriage vows. We both just enjoyed imagining it. Thought it would always be like that."

"And that changed when I came along?"

"I didn't want to freak you out, old man," he said, and for a moment or two paused our conversation to negotiate a little traffic through Kensington. "It wasn't as though I invited you to stay because I thought you might be someone for Michelle. But it was fairly obvious early on that she was into you."

God, I was such an egotist. It felt so warm and melty inside whenever he reminded me that Michelle wanted me.

Henry continued, "She flirted with you, and then at some point when we were in bed imagining her being naughty, I dropped your name into the scenario, and it turned her on like nothing before."

I felt my ears burn a little, that I had been the star of their role-playing.

"And you didn't feel jealous at all?" I said.

"There's always going to be a little jealousy," he said. "It's only natural. The male body's natural response to seeing his mate making eyes at a rival male. Biological. But for guys like us, the brain can supersede that. Even find it all adding to the thrill ride..."

Talking about this, I felt the cogs in my own brain slotting into gear as I began to understand some of my feelings about Katie.

"...and then she comes to me one night and says: 'you really want me to do this, don't you?' and no matter how much I protested that I didn't want her to do anything she didn't want to do herself, she pressed the point: 'you want me to do this, so if that's what you really want, I'm ready.' God, my heart nearly jumped out of my chest."

I found I actually envied Henry, envied the fact that he had discovered how he felt about Michelle at a point when they could still do something about it.

Katie, oh Katie. If I'd even suspected that I might be open to the idea of sharing you, would I have lost you?

"Talk to her," Henry said, seeing right through me. "You need to talk to her."

"Yes," I nodded, "I do."

15

Proximity alert

$\mathcal{T}$he next time we went out, Henry and I had our day off together, so all three of us hit the bars.

Things started out as they'd been before—perhaps Michelle was a little more flirtatious, a little more overt in her approach toward me, but still respectful that her husband was there.

Yet as the alcohol flowed, and Henry's quiet encouragement continued, the public displays of affection grew steadily more apparent.

It seemed like another test, exposing Henry to his wife's attention on me.

He seemed to enjoy it, I could see my voyeur roommate appreciating the beauty of his wife from this strange new perspective, and instead of being irritated by her the way she flaunted her connection with me in front of him, he seemed to be genuinely thrilled by her excitement at playing with a new man.

Michelle eased into things through the evening, as though prodding her husband, checking what he could handle. From the outset there was a lot of touching, brushing against me, gazing into my eyes with increasingly unconcealed lust. Then there were the little displays of affection, from her fingers brushing my hair, to a brief shoulder massage or perhaps the holding of my hand as we progressed to another bar.

Henry didn't isolate himself: Michelle was just as affectionate with him, something I realized was supposed to be a test for my coping mechanism.

But he really did enjoy the sight of her being with me.

It impressed me. While I'd been having thoughts about Katie, about how I might have done what Henry was doing in order to save our marriage, that evening I found myself wondering whether if I had had the chance to do all this with my wife, I'd be able to cope with such proximity to Katie being with another man. Somehow, that edgy feeling I got imagining it held some appeal.

"You two really do have great chemistry together," Henry said as we were walking down Dean Street debating whether to hit another bar or find some place for a little dancing.

"Don't we?" Michelle giggled, squeezing my arm as she walked by my side.

"You can never tell how it's going to work out," Henry said, so casually. "You can never guarantee the chemistry."

Michelle said, "We kind of knew there was chemistry before we started this, though."

She stopped me in the street, and took me rather by surprise with a full-on kiss. I felt awkward, though she was a great kisser, of course. This was right in front of her husband, my friend.

But breaking apart briefly, Henry had a dazed smile on his face, enchanted by this display, it seemed. Happy that

Michelle was having so much fun. So I got more into it, indulging in her sweetness, the passion flaring up a little as our arms encircled each other and our kiss stepped up to full intensity.

In all this, I don't think I'd considered anything happening in Henry's presence before. I warmed to it, though, as Michelle continued kissing me and showering me with affection after we arrived at the club and found the dance floor.

There was something sweet about it, about the way they looked at each other while Michelle was being wicked with me. Without even saying anything she could display her excitement about all this, her gratitude to him for letting her play, while teasing him that he had to wait his turn to enjoy her like this.

I felt certain when we got home that Henry would want to drag Michelle off to his cave and reclaim her after our display on the dance floor—and in the taxi afterward.

But getting out of the taxi, I heard Henry whisper to his wife: "Go with him tonight."

"Are you sure?" she replied quietly.

"Absolutely." Then he looked at me, said a little more loudly: "Take care of her, my friend. She's a little wound up."

"Sure," I said, a little surprised, but thinking that since all this was so new, Henry was simply wanting to appreciate the experience a little more.

It wasn't until we were climbing the stairs toward our apartment that I realized this would mean there being only a thin wall between Henry and I while I was with Michelle. He'd hear everything. Would he be able to handle that?

More to the point, perhaps, would he figure out that Michelle and I were not yet having full sex with each other, as he expected?

Michelle wasn't thinking about such things, it seemed. In celebratory mood, she grabbed my hand to drag me upstairs.

A last glance over my shoulder at him as I disappeared off with her, and Henry gave me an amused look, his eyebrows waggling suggestively, and I have to admit it was strangely erotic to know he was inferring that I should go and sleep with her with his approval.

Upstairs, we went straight into my room, grabbing each other for a long slow kiss before the front door even finished closing.

Sealed in my room, we didn't hear Henry enter the apartment, couldn't tell where he'd be in the apartment when he got up here—his bedroom, the living room, or even the kitchen. But we whispered to each other as though he might be at our door, crouched to listen through the keyhole.

"He can hear us."

"Not that well."

"I could hear you with him when you were with him. So he can hear us."

"So we'd better make it a good show."

Her thin top had fiddly buttons pulling together the front part, which I was fumbling with as I kissed her. She leaned back from me, looked down as though ordering me to go through with it if I was going to mess around with those buttons.

I unfastened them, gaining a brief flash of bare breasts as her top opened before she giggled and folded her arms over her chest coyly.

"You know we only need to sound as though we're having sex," she whispered, teasing me, though we'd both seen each other naked, both seen each other touching ourselves, both seen each other come, though our own touching had been limited.

"I'm not that good an actor," I said, sweeping my hand down the smooth, smooth skin of her chest to find one of her breasts, her nipple already hard.

"Hmm," she said, trying not to react to my fondling caresses, though she was clearly quite seriously in need of some real attention. "Maybe we'll have to do a little more to seem authentic then, this time."

She pushed me back, her smile broadening, and I sat down abruptly on the corner of my bed. I pulled her to me, my hands moving to the fly of her jeans, flicking it open, since it was right there in front of me.

She did not object, even kinked her hips to help me slide the denim down her thighs, revealing a simple turquoise thong underneath.

Strange how powerfully aroused I was, as though I was a teenager again experiencing a girl for the first time. Because she'd controlled my access to her so rigidly, granting me only a small progression each time I slept with her, this promise she now gave me that we would go further, possibly significantly further, was such a thrill.

She leaned over me to kiss my mouth as my hands cupped her soft warm behind. She tasted of warm Baileys, her silky hair hanging around my face as we kissed to add the fruity scent of her shampoo.

Then I was pulling aside her top again, revealing her bare breasts, those stiff little buds that were crying out for a pair of lips to wrap around them.

She moaned quietly as I sucked on her, swirling my

tongue around her areolae, my fingers taking in the superlative shape of her cleavage.

But she pushed me away, said: "That's not going to be enough to make me sound... authentic."

I was puzzled a moment or two, but then she sat on the bed beside me, and tilted her head down, her eyes pointing the way to her sex.

I felt a jolt of burning heat shoot through my chest, and end in a tingle that had my manhood pushing to try and escape my underwear.

"Go ahead," she whispered.

I was down on my knees without further demands, and as she parted her thighs for me, revealing the scintillating shape of her womanhood for me, hidden only by the thin cotton and lace of her underwear, I simply did what I wanted.

For a while I only touched her, sweeping my hands over her soft skin, taking in the curves of her legs, the camber of her stomach, the heat of her flesh right up to the edge of her underwear.

It was hard to believe that my good friend could give this beauty to another man. But he had, it turned him on. I couldn't fully understand the nature of that relationship, because I was not married to Michelle.

I could appreciate, though, that I was beginning to enjoy knowing she went with Henry as well—that she was desired by him, that she was an incredible sexual creature who could not be satisfied by one man alone.

She loved the attention from two men, and I loved that she did. Her panties were already so wet when I came to press my hand against them.

Considering how I felt about Michelle, and about how Henry felt about her, it did make me curious as to what it might have been like with Katie, if she'd come forward to honestly tell me she needed more, she wanted another man.

I guess I was a different man back then, my eyes had not been open to the possibility that sharing a woman did not mean giving her up, did not necessarily mean threatening your relationship with her.

I eased forward and ran my mouth and nose gently along Michelle's inner thigh, up and over to her mound. Her perfume and that extra spice from her arousal strengthened as I neared her pussy, breathing her in deeply as I kissed the warm cotton directly over her sex.

Now she moaned a little louder than before. I kissed her, pressed my mouth to her, almost teasing myself by going so slowly. Was she going to stop me? Prevent me from going beneath the cotton?

I slipped my tongue out to lick along the join between her legs and her torso, and then I subtly edged back toward the center, nudging aside her panties, my tongue finding its way to the soft, smoldering flesh of her pussy itself, and then the groove that bore the wetness of her excitement.

She groaned as I tasted her briefly, as I inhaled her thick musk.

"This more authentic?" I asked her quietly.

"Uh-huh," she moaned.

With a grin, I grabbed her panties with my teeth, playfully pulling them up, so the thin band of turquoise split her labia, and pressed inside her. Pulling them aside, I dived in wholeheartedly, sucking on her lips, penetrating her with my tongue, enveloping her clit in the wet heat of my mouth.

I picked myself up to kiss her mouth once again, my fingers now finding their way to her slippery folds, and she didn't flinch from tasting herself on my lips and tongue.

"You're not giving up, are you?" she said with a smile. "I was just beginning to get the noises right."

"I haven't even started properly," I replied, stroking her with my middle finger, thinking how wonderful it would feel to be inside her, a hint of injustice in my head at the idea that Henry was already allowed that, while I was not.

Michelle lifted her hips and pulled off her panties, before opening her thighs for me again.

"Make me come, Sean," she said, loud enough that anyone in the apartment might have a fair chance of hearing. I half wondered if her demand referred to penetrating her, but then she was grabbing my head, pulling me to her.

I hauled her hips a little closer toward me, and sank onto her precious flower.

Feasting on her, engorging myself with her flavor, rubbing my face over her so that I coated myself in a mask of her wetness, I fully indulged in this new experience of her. As I licked her, she squeezed her breasts together, massaging them, fingering her nipples.

And how she moaned as I teased apart her pussy lips, thrust my tongue deep inside her, lapped up her copious juices.

Did it feel strange to be so intimate with her sweet shaven sex, knowing that another man enjoyed it from time to time? A little. I guess I could have ignored it, put it out of mind, even imagined to myself that she wasn't having regular sex with Henry, that she was all mine. But once something is in your head, it's difficult to shift, particularly if you're focussing on it.

I had that mischievous, dark little part of my mind constantly reminding me: this pussy is married, used, stretched by another man's cock.

The funny thing was, if anything, this thought made

me even more hungry for her, desperate to defy conventions.

Gently tugging on her pussy lips with my teeth, pressing my face against her, running my nose through her slippery folds, I reveled in her, reveled in the wrongness of this situation.

It was exciting in the way sex had been exciting when I had been first experiencing it: when, as a teenager, everything was a taboo because according to those around me, I shouldn't have been having sex.

Here, I was eating out a woman who continued to sleep with another man. It was all wrong.

And yet, so delicious.

Was this wrongness something that Henry felt? Something to disrupt the staid stability of an established marriage?

I ate her, and the taboo nature of what I was doing lent me a passion that I think I'd never had before, not with Katie, not with any woman.

At first, Michelle had been enhancing her moans and her cries, wanting to put on a show for a husband who believed her to be having full penetrative sex on a regular basis with another man. By the end, though, she had no need to amplify anything, she was on fire, pulling my head against her, locking me in between her thighs, wailing as her trembling, shuddering, quaking orgasm rocked her entire body.

"*T*hat was incredible," she said, breathless, as she lay back and I rose to lie next to her, spooning against her, my hard cock pressing against her thigh through my pants.

"For me too," I said, loving that I could still taste her tangy, salty flavor on my lips.

"There's no way Henry can doubt we're into each other."

"You think he heard?" I asked, knowing there was no way he couldn't have.

"He heard."

"He could've been listening to music or something."

"With his wife sleeping with his friend in the next room? He wasn't listening to music."

I felt her cool fingers wandering over my hardness. "Do you really think he likes listening to it?" I asked.

"I think so," she leaned into me, kissed my lips, so that she had to be tasting herself on them, too. After a moment or two, she leaned back, saying: "This is new for me, too."

"New?"

"Before Henry, when I was with more than one boyfriend at a time, they were reluctantly accepting of me being that way. Each one kind of wanted to deny that I was with anyone else, act as though I was only with them, that the other boyfriends were just friends."

"So you never did it with more than one boyfriend under the same roof at a time?"

"No."

"And you never talked about other boyfriends with any of those guys, what happened with them?"

"No. But Henry wants to know everything."

"Everything?"

She looked at me, a touch concerned, "That is the deal, here, you know?"

I nodded, reassuring her. I'd worked it out. I didn't have real privacy rights when I was lying with another man's wife with that man's consent. This wasn't hard-and-fast adultery.

"But you never tell me about him, about what you do with him," I pointed out.

She looked at me, one eye raised. "You want me to?"

A shrug—did I? When I got the opportunity, I listened to her sleeping with him. While I was at work, knowing that Henry was out with her, or home with her, I pictured them making love. And now I felt envious of what she had with him, how she teased him about being with me, how she drove him wild with her stories of being a sexy, insatiable wife.

"I guess," I said. "I mean, I live with you guys, I can't really help but hear you when you're with him. I can't really detach myself from your other relationship when I'm not with you."

She nodded. "I'm sorry, I guess... I'm used to treating boyfriends a certain way, hiding things, not opening up."

Recovered a little, Michelle picked herself up and pulled my pants down and off my legs before straddling me, kissing my mouth, her weight over me, her soft skin sliding over my burning, pulsing, rigid cock.

"You like listening to me being with Henry?" she asked, her mouth curling up into a naughty smile.

"I'm not sure I did in the beginning," I said. "But I think I do, yes. It's strange. It's kind of sexy, knowing that you're enjoying yourself, being wicked, and that when the time comes, I'll get to be with you."

She kissed her way slowly down my upper chest, her hair in my face, wafting the fresh smell of her shampoo.

"Maybe you want to watch us some time," she said, moving slowly down, my cock lodged between the smooth hot flesh of her breasts.

"I'm not sure how I'd feel about that now that I'm with you too," I said, but a glimmer of something inside me was drawn to the idea.

"Henry's interested in watching. He won't, though, unless you're okay about it."

I guess I had to realize that Henry might want to watch some time. He was getting off on her being with another man, he would want to see how she enjoyed it.

I found myself wanting to be there when those two enjoyed the moment of Michelle being shared. See how they looked at each other, how Michelle showed off for him with me, how they both responded to each other in such a strange, sensual situation.

And perhaps, I found myself wanting to know how it might have been with Katie.

"I might be okay with it," I said, as she touched her lips to the tip of my cock.

Plus, I hadn't yet gone all the way with her, so I was willing to say anything to make sure that happened.

"That's good to know," she said, her fingers squeezing my manhood, her head sinking onto it to engulf it in the hot wetness of her mouth.

I felt suddenly quite Machiavellian, that I could use this particular bargaining chip to get what I wanted. As she slowly bobbed up and down on my hardness, I said: "For him to watch us kind of implies that we're all accepting that this is really happening, that we're all three happy with me sharing you."

"Uh-huh," was all she said, her mouth full of my cock.

It felt like I had a free pass right now to get whatever I wanted.

"For him to watch us, we couldn't have any limitations," I said.

Without stopping, she tilted her head to look up at my face, flames in her eyes. "Uh-huh."

"So you think we'll be able to try that soon?"

She slipped me out of her mouth, and gave me a long slow lick up my shaft. "Very soon," she said.

Holding her hair out of her face, I was coming in no time at all after that, and Michelle was happy to take my cream in her mouth, swallowing and relishing it, apparently fired up that a man who was not her husband was shooting his emissions down her throat.

16

Just plain wrong

I was awake when Michelle finally drifted off to sleep around 3am, since even on my nights off, I tended to be awake at that time. While it was very late for ordinary people, for us night workers it was like shortly before lunchtime.

I watched her sleeping, distracted from the book I was halfway through on my Kindle. She was so sweet. If I was Henry, would I ever risk losing her by bringing another man into our relationship? But then, Henry was under the impression that their relationship was so solid, it wasn't even remotely a risk.

And, of course, his view was that since she was polyamorous, if he attempted to stifle her and confine her to monogamy, their relationship might be under even more of a threat.

There was something magical about her, beyond the prettiness of her face, the exercise-toned curves of her body. I couldn't quite put my finger on what it was.

As I increasingly contemplated this mysterious creature lying beside me, rather than the latest tome of the Song of

Fire and Ice series on my e-book reader, inevitably the recollection of her lips wrapped around my hard cock came back to mind, or my lips pressed up against her sweet pussy.

I could still smell the earthiness in the air from her arousal, it made me tingle a little as I lay there.

Was Henry really going to watch us having sex? Would I really want to watch her make love to her husband? The thought seemed to corrupt my mental images, so that the recollections passing through my head turned into Michelle wrapping her lips around Henry's cock, Henry's mouth lodged up against his wife's dripping pussy.

My manhood stiffened at the thought—it really did turn me on. To think of Michelle with him, to think that I might lose access to her, since her sex life with her husband was being so well re-energized. The risk, the jealousy, the pain made the accompanying arousal feel more powerful.

After a while, I came to see that the special quality I saw in her, beyond her looks, her sparkling personality—it was her insatiability, her need for sex, and her openness to engage with more than just her husband.

It was different, it was interesting, it was sexy.

I had to try to calm myself, since she was sleeping. I guess I was a little tired myself, too. So even though it was effectively mid-afternoon for me, I did drift off into an afternoon nap.

---

*W*hen I awoke, my bed was empty. Was she awake? What time was it? 7am, about the time Henry and I returned to the apartment after work on a normal night. Michelle would be getting up, ready to go to work.

I assumed she was in the shower, or having breakfast, or getting dressed for whatever her schedule was for that day.

Yet emerging from my room in a pair of boxers, rolling into the bathroom to relieve the pressure on my bladder, there was no sign of Michelle. Maybe she'd gone out already, maybe she had an early morning errand to run.

I felt a little foolish for having napped so long. It might disrupt my timetable, might mean that when it came to 11am or so, and I really did have to be getting to bed, I might find it difficult to sleep.

Shuffling into the kitchen with the vague thoughts of scraping together something for dinner, I heard the sound of Michelle moaning—or at least, the stifled sound. It was as though she'd buried her head in a pillow.

Jesus.

I felt a sudden pulse of intense heat spark inside my stomach. There it was again: Michelle, crying, moaning, whimpering, the noises blurred by a pillow or whatever else she was using to try to conceal herself from detection.

She was with Henry.

I stood there in the kitchen, motionless. Listening to the unmistakable sound of Michelle going through the final stages of an orgasm. And there was the low groan of Henry along with her.

Well, they were married. And yet, I felt wronged somehow—I was supposed to be with her tonight, Henry had urged me to be with her. She'd waited until I was asleep, and then snuck out to be with her husband.

I felt a little stupid at my negative feelings, at the jealousy coursing through my veins—no one had ever said I had sole custody of her when I got to spend the night with her. I had to accept it. It was just a surprise, that's all. That she would make love to him quite so soon after being with me.

Perhaps it was part of the thrill for him.

I knew that part of the annoyance I felt was because Michelle wasn't allowing me the full experience with her, while her husband could fuck her whenever he wanted. I had to chill, it would come when she was ready.

I went back into my room, switched on the bedside lamp, got back into my Kindle book, though I could hardly concentrate on the events unfolding in the Seven Kingdoms of Westeros. I waited, not wanting to go out into the living room or kitchen if she or Henry might be there, since I could feel myself irritated, and did not want any threat of confrontation.

But then my door opened quietly, and Michelle slipped inside.

"You're awake," she said, and I saw her blushing a little. She was carrying a glass of her chocolate milk—an energy drink she usually had before her morning run instead of proper breakfast.

"I am," I said, holding my Kindle as though I'd been awake for ages, sweeping my finger across the screen to turn a page as though I was really into this story, and she was only secondary in my thoughts.

"I guess I woke a little earlier than usual," she said, slowly wondering over to the bed. She was still wearing those turquoise panties, though now sported one of my work shirts, tied to expose her midriff. Had she been wearing that while Henry had fucked her?

She stood by the end of the bed, sipped her chocolate milk, looking at me with a calculating expression as though trying to work out whether I'd heard her with Henry, whether I knew she'd snuck out, how I felt about such behavior.

This was new to her, after all, sleeping with two guys living under the same roof. She didn't really know how we felt about it.

"You felt the need of a little hubby time?" I said, trying to sound a touch disapproving, though not surprised or weak.

She bit her lip. "You heard?"

"Hard not to."

"I'm sorry," she said. "He needed it."

"He needed to reclaim you."

"Something like that. Are you jealous?"

"I guess so. You planning on sneaking out of his bed for a little Sean time after you've been with him?"

She stepped back, and I saw a flicker of desire in her eyes. She bit her lip again, signaling her arousal openly.

"If that's what you wanted," she said, casually leaning back against a desk that I used only to hold piles of books, sipping her drink. "I figured you'd want separation between you and him."

"Separation?"

She smiled. "I get quite hot and sweaty after I've slept with someone. If I take a shower, I wake him up. That's no way to sneak out of his bed."

"You didn't shower when you crept out of my bed for him."

"He likes me dirty."

She was jigging one of her legs, as though fighting to control her libido. I felt things fizzing down below, my blood pumping into my manhood. Knowing that she had just been with Henry, that attempting to sneak back into my bed to make me think she'd never left, she hadn't had a shower.

She was dirty, dirty after being with another man.

She thought to shock me, perhaps enough that I'd tell

her to go, to get in the shower, to have her little interludes with Henry at the end of my nights with her. To make me feel so secondary.

But I wanted her now, and if she was offering me a taste on Henry's nights, I wanted that too.

Dirty, sexy girl. Insatiable wife, unable to control her desires.

She made my blood pump twice as fast as any woman I'd ever met, and it was because this wasn't just me taking somebody else's ex, this was me taking a girl engaged in a live relationship, interspersing sex with me with sex with somebody else.

She was standing there, dirty, and it was so wrong. I had to have her.

"You think I'm squeamish, is that it?" I asked, pulling myself to the edge of the bed, surprising her a little at my new direction.

She shrugged, "Are you?"

As she stood there, propped up on the edge of the desk, she casually lifted one foot, placing it on the nearest corner of the bed, opening her thighs to me.

I felt my heart pounding in my chest, my eyes drawn to the large wet patch evident at the centre of her panties. Dampness caused by another man, as well as me.

A little tickle of lust broke out inside my chest, igniting a warm pulse of raw arousal that shot down to my thickening cock.

I approached her slowly, hungry, curious. Sure, I was a little squeamish, perhaps, but I was never going to admit it. I was a little weirded out by the surefire fact that she'd just fucked another man, mere minutes previously. The thing was, as with the jealousy enhancing my arousal when I knew Michelle was with Henry, this weird feeling also seemed to spur me on, drive me to challenge it, to take her there and then.

It was biological, I was sure of it. The need for a male to take a female his instinct believes will fall pregnant by another, if I did not challenge it.

I think as I perched on the corner of the bed, prizing apart her legs further with the clutch of my foot, I started to feel that I could blame that biological drive for whatever I now got into. It was safe to do that. I wasn't a bad person for wanting Michelle so much right now.

She smiled down at me, which seemed to both dare me on, and take delight from my doing this, from the fact that I was confronting my boundaries head-on, trying to be fully open-minded about this whole thing—and desperately craving her sex.

I paused, not out of reluctance, but not quite knowing where to begin. I couldn't just drive inside her, we hadn't progressed that far in our exploration. It was for her to lead us in that respect.

She saw me pause, but didn't complain, didn't tease me. She was ultra relaxed, and as ever, her confidence was so sexy. The offer in her eyes: take it or leave it, it's up to you.

She took a huge gulp of her drink, and a tiny bit escaped the corner of her mouth, dribbling down her chin. I reached up to kiss her, licking up the sweet, cool liquid as I sucked on her lower lip.

Jesus, this felt so very depraved, something I think I'd never be able to admit to anyone. I thought about where these sweet lips might have just been, and it elicited a little thrill in me.

Her mouth tasted only of her chocolate milk, though as I kissed her, my hands cupping her breasts, I could definitely detect a hint of Henry's cologne on her. It emphasized to me just how filthy, how wicked this beautiful woman was, which was beyond exciting.

After a while, I pulled back, checking out her expression, defiant at proving myself.

Michelle pursed her lips and nodded, wryly appreciating my boldness.

Then she put the glass of chocolate milk up to her lips again, and this time as she drank, she purposefully allowed it to spill out, to dribble down her chest, the shirt, and down her stomach until the liquid soaked into her panties, a small amount pooling between her thighs on the desk.

Now she gazed into my eyes to fire a fresh challenge my way.

Wow. Tentatively, though trying to conceal my reticence, I reached forward, touched the dampness of her underwear, checking out the immense heat underneath. Could I really handle this? To reconnect with her womanhood after she'd been so intimate with another man, my friend?

I stroked her pussy, trying to seem calm, collected, cool. Michelle smiled, delighted.

Little trickles of milk continued to run down from her stomach, and as I pressed my fingers against her panties, some squeezed out of the saturated cotton. I eased her underwear aside to reveal her rosy pussy lips, so flushed with blood, wet with more than just the chocolate milk. Used.

Michelle sipped her drink and allowed more to escape over her chin and pour down her body, really soaking the shirt, my shirt, which she'd put on before sneaking out of this room specifically to give Henry that little thrill reminding him she was with me that night.

She leaned forward to kiss me, her hand tilting up my jaw to meet her wet chocolatey kiss.

"It doesn't put you off that I've just been with him?" she asked, stoking the fires inside me.

I purposefully slipped my tongue into her mouth, showing her that I wasn't repulsed knowing she'd most likely taken another man's cock between just these pretty lips not so long ago.

She grinned, but I felt it was not sufficient yet.

I untied the knot she'd made in my now saturated shirt and pushed it up, revealing her breasts, made shiny and brown with the chocolate milk, her skin mottled by goose pimples and her nipples hard as though she'd been swimming in cold, muddy river water.

But still, swirling my tongue around her breasts, lapping up the sweetness of the milk and the lingering traces of saltiness from her recent exertions, it didn't seem enough for me.

I ducked down between her thighs, and now touched my lips to her womanhood.

Inhaling the strong scent of sex, of a woman who had lain with two men tonight, I tasted her, feeling somehow so alive as I pressed my mouth to her, sampling the strange cocktail lent sweetness by the chocolate milk.

I tasted her own juices, the tangy flavor I recognized from before, though it seemed somehow enhanced now, by the knowledge that this beautiful flower had been stretched by another man's obscene hardness.

It was wrong, it was so very wrong, but it was such a thrill. Knowing how devilish this woman was.

Michelle poured more of the milk over her mound, forcing me to lick in order to avoid more spillage on their carpet.

She moaned as I lapped at her, and I wondered how she felt about this, about sharing herself with two men in one night. It didn't seem to bother me, in fact, it drove me on, I liked that she'd just been with Henry. It was that taboo factor, that made this seem naughty, wrong, and therefore so much better.

We moved to the bed, kissing and rolling around, Michelle dispensing with her clothes, the remaining traces of the chocolate milk making our skins sticky, though sweet.

Though the signs were covered up by the milk, I could definitely tell she'd been with someone else, could detect the occasional scent of him, and the musty saltiness of her recent lovemaking.

It was so dirty, it became animalistic between us. I respected our continuing limitations, but the force between us was still ferocious, like some kind of whirlwind as we locked mouths, grazed our bodies together, pressing my hardness between us in order to drive us both wild with the restrictions we had set in place ourselves.

Sweaty, sticky, indecent, we wrestled.

I ultimately allowed Michelle to win out, ending up on top of me, taking my hardness in her mouth as I pulled her slit into position over my head, so that I might taste that strange exotic flavor of her well-used pussy until we both came explosively in each other's mouths.

---

*A*fter that, it seemed that I felt less inhibited about sharing Michelle, and sharing her more directly.

It meant that on Henry's nights with her, if I got home on time from my shift and Michelle didn't have to be at work early, I might have a little time with her before I ate supper and slowed down before bed.

On our combined night out, it didn't seem to matter who Michelle chose to go with when we returned home, we all seemed to know that she'd be slipping out during the night to keep us both in the manner to which we'd become accustomed.

I'd listen to her making love to her husband, and know that it wouldn't be too long before she joined me. Even though I did not have penetration privileges yet, it was a real thrill for her to come bounding in, pouncing on me, perhaps riding my mouth, or perhaps filling hers with my already rock-hard cock.

It rather naturally made us both assume that Henry was well beyond mere acceptance that I was sleeping with his wife. There was nothing left for us to fear from him.

17

A city for lovers

*I*t did seem a little ridiculous that Henry was so obviously au fait with what was happening between Michelle and I, and we were reluctant to take things to their full conclusion in bed.

Waiting for it, as we had, seemed to turn it into this huge occasion that deserved some kind of ceremony to celebrate when it did actually arrive.

Perhaps as some kind of prompt for her, one evening I suggested a weekend away, just the two of us. I didn't really care where we went, but judging by how Michelle was taking things, I thought somewhere a little romantic might help to seal the deal.

"Paris! Oh my God that would be so wonderful!" she said to my first suggestion.

"I haven't said anything about it to Henry, though. I suppose he might not want to lose you for a whole weekend."

"No, we've talked about a weekend away," she said, already bouncing around the apartment in glee at the idea.

"It's something that'll really push those weird buttons of his."

And she was right about that. Both Henry and I seemed a little giddy in the days leading up to the mini-break.

Naturally, I was buzzing at the thought of finally going all the way with Michelle, and the idea that I'd get a weekend with her alone to do little but make love.

Henry seemed more excited than me, however, and in the quiet moments in the dead of night, when we were supposed to be arranging the dullest of dull business stories on a newspaper page, it was rather apparent.

He liked the idea of his wife going away for a dirty weekend, that she would spend a lot of time indulging in sexual pleasure, perhaps teasing him along the way with hints at what was going on.

"But you must be feeling crazy about her being away from you for so long?" I asked.

"Absolutely. I mean, it feels like I'm jumping off a cliff here—my subconscious is telling me you two will bond like mad, that you'll have all that sexual and romantic bliss together. And in Paris, for Heaven's sake!"

"You're torturing yourself."

"I can't help it. Jesus, I'm hard as a rock the whole time," Henry said under his breath. It might have seemed an odd thing for two guys to talk about—but then we were both sharing the same married woman. It was all odd.

"So you're enjoying it, then?"

"Weird, huh? I think of you two having such a great time—of Michelle being so naughty, and getting so much excitement from it—and I can't help but enjoy it. I mean, I know plain enough that it's crazy to send my wife off with her boyfriend like this, and I have all these butterflies in my stomach making me feel it's dangerous..."

"But you know she'll be coming right back to you on the Monday."

"Of course—I trust her implicitly. But the heart feels no guarantees, right? The paranoia. Yet somehow that fear is part of the turn-on."

"You're a crazy, crazy man, Henry Robinson," I said, but deep down I envied him. He looked so damn alive. This was an extreme sport, and he was a champion, king of the thrill rides.

It was interesting to me to have a running commentary from Henry on what he was going through, and how everything was playing out prior to the weekend away.

"She's asked me to go shopping with her for under-wear," he'd tell me, for example. "You are in for a great weekend, my friend."

Or he'd tell me something like:

"I keep asking her what you guys will get up to on your weekend, and she won't tell me until after it happens."

The day before we were due to leave for Paris, Henry sacrificed some of his sleep to take his wife to have her hair and nails done, a facial and full body treatment, and by the time I woke for my final night shift before the weekend, he was finding it difficult to contain his excitement.

I was surprised that Michelle hadn't told him that we hadn't actually had full sex yet, since he was so obviously into this, so clearly enjoying the sharing of his wife.

When I'd asked her about it, she said after this week-end, she'd be telling him everything. She didn't like secrets, even though this was like the opposite of cheating—we were not fucking, while making him believe we were.

"You think he'll be angry at the deception?" I asked her.

She shrugged, "Hopefully not. By then, we will have

201

caught up to his expectations, right? We just needed to go our own pace."

Nevertheless, I could tell that she was a touch nervous about what might happen when it came time to reveal all. I guess I was a little nervous too. It wasn't necessarily that Henry would be angry with either of us, more that it might upset him.

---

*T*he issue of what would happen after our dirty weekend was in the backs of our minds as soon we set foot on the Eurostar train at St Pancras station, bound for Paris. I guess we wanted to ignore it, pretend it wasn't there. It would be, though, constantly.

It was a fairly late train, departing just past seven in the evening, to arrive well past 10 o'clock. It made it easy enough for Henry to come see us off and not disrupt his sleep cycle.

There on the platform, Henry seemed as excited as Michelle and I were that this was all happening. And she was jumping up and down with glee at this little vacation of ours. The glint I caught in her eye— suggesting that at least some of her joy was from the prospect that for the first time this weekend she would finally have me inside her —was seriously hot.

Despite the public setting, as Henry handed Michelle over to me, wearing a cute blouse that showed off more than a touch of cleavage, she kissed me long and slow, right in front of her husband.

I could see how it was eating at him, that I was taking her, that she was mine for the weekend—but at the same time, he was enjoying the conflicted feelings.

"He's so amazing, isn't he?" Michelle said as the train

finally pulled slowly away, sending a waving Henry backwards away from us.

"I'd have to say 'yes'."

"He's done everything—booked our train tickets, our hotel, even a restaurant for our big date tomorrow."

"Big date?" I raised an eyebrow, and it was enough to ask the question as to whether Henry knew how important it was for us.

"I haven't told him," she said. "He just thinks tomorrow we're going to have a big Paris experience, topped off by a very romantic date."

"Uh-huh. Well, he's enjoyed preparing for all this, from what he's told me."

Michelle giggled, then said quietly so that no one else in the carriage could overhear, "You should have seen him when we bought all that new lingerie. He didn't know whether to blush or gasp or smile."

"He liked picking it out for you to wear for somebody else?"

"God, and when I was getting my spa treatment..." she rolled her eyes, "I could see how hard he was."

"I bet he was feeling all kinds of messed up by all that."

"Part of the whole thing, isn't it?" she shrugged. "Preparing me for my date with another man. Teasing himself by knowing exactly what I'll wear while I'm unfaithful to him."

"You're hardly unfaithful."

She smiled. "You remember your wedding vows?"

"Only too well."

Then she leaned over and whispered into my ear: "I think I've come up with a plan to make it easier to tell him we only just had our first time."

"Oh?"

She gave a shifty glance to some of the other passengers in the carriage, hardly being subtle. Then put her lips to my ear again, and said: "We video ourselves during our first time... then he gets to see it."

Her eyes were wide with amusement at how surprised I looked, but after the initial reaction, the idea kind of sank in—and seemed a logical possibility for placating an angry or upset Henry.

We might have deceived him a little, but if he got to witness Michelle's first time going all the way out of wedlock, it had to be a thrill to compensate any injury.

I'd just have to deal with the thought of being watched.

"We can check the footage after we've filmed it," Michelle said, as though knowing exactly what I was afraid of from the anxiety on my face. "You know, make sure we're happy with it."

Well, if Henry was going to watch—and after knowing how easily it was to listen to sex in our flat, it bothered me less than I would have thought—it would be better knowing that we could perhaps edit parts that looked less... artistic... than we would want.

"We can try it," I said, and knew that the important thing as far as my thought process was concerned was first and foremost getting to the sex part.

After that, we relaxed a little on our train journey—I guess, having a plan to deal with Henry once we got back was a good reassurance at least.

It was so nice sitting with her during the train ride. Just sitting with her, breathing her in, appreciating her like a Christmas present sitting under the tree, ready to unwrap as soon as the right time arrived—it was my own little torture.

From time to time she'd send Henry a text, and even took the occasional selfie. I did manage to glimpse some of her text messaging—she wasn't hiding it from me—

and it was clear she was having fun winding her husband up.

Michelle: You doing okay without me?

>Have this strange ache, hard to describe. A little queasy, but somehow it's good at the same time. Makes me feel alive. Makes me realize how unimportant anything else is in my life compared to you.

Michelle: You're the sweetest. You need to find some distractions while I'm away

Henry: Doing lots of chores! The apartment will be clean as a whistle when you get home. So does it feel good going away with your boyfriend for the weekend? ;-)

Michelle: Exciting! He smells so good, just sitting next to him, leaning up against him, I'm tingling all over

Henry: Bet you can't wait to get to the hotel

Michelle: My panties are already wet thinking about what he's going to do to me ;-)

What wasn't so clear was something Henry touched on in his replies, along the lines of:

Henry: Are you going to talk to him?

And Michelle responded to these kind of mystery references with equally vague answers:

Michelle: I'll talk to him, just have to do it the right way.

What did Henry want her to talk to me about? It was something sensitive, perhaps. Were they thinking that it was time I left their happy household? Worried that romantic bonds were forming between Michelle and I, above and beyond the friend-on-friend sexual connection we had?

I felt a little flutter of butterflies in my stomach at the thought of suddenly losing Michelle. I guess I had to accept that at some point it would be time to move on, though.

In the mean time, I had a weekend away with her to enjoy.

It was late when we arrived at Gare Du Nord, then transferred in a taxi to our hotel, a nice little place on in the Latin Quarter, the Rive Gauche. I might have been fully awake since my normal schedule would have me just about starting work at this time, but Michelle was ready for some sleep.

The plan was for me to take a sleeping pill, then try to get some sleep during the night, so that we would be fresh for some sight-seeing in the morning—and of course, the big date in the evening. It would mess me about when we got back to London and our normal schedules, but I wasn't about to complain.

Checked in, I ordered us some room service to fill the holes in our stomachs, while Michelle slipped away to the bathroom.

She was in there a while before I heard the quiet laughing, and realized she had to be talking with Henry. The room service even came while she was still in there, and mine was gone by the time she returned.

———

*S*he came out of the bathroom wearing a long-sleeved black lace bodysuit and black nylon hold-ups that reached mid-thigh.

"I thought we were just going to sleep tonight," I said, trying not to let my jaw drop too much as she twirled to show me the whole outfit, revealing that her bodysuit was backless other than a little triangle of lace that shot between her buttocks like a thong.

"We are," she said. "I thought I'd give you a little taster before we do. Help you sleep."

She looked devilish, and yet elegant, particularly with her crystal drop earrings, and the way her hair was tied up.

She tossed over her smartphone to where I was sitting on the couch, and I looked at her, confused.

"Will you take a picture of me?" she asked.

I raised an eyebrow. "One for the scrapbook? I'm not sure Facebook would allow it..."

She rolled her eyes, said: "For Henry. To show him what he's missing out on."

I held up the phone as she started posing, and flicked through to the camera app. I felt a strange envy, despite the fact that I would be enjoying Michelle entirely uncensored this weekend, I could actually imagine the strange thrill that Henry would get as his wife sent little teasing text messages back to him, and photos of herself in revealing clothing.

"You want your food?" I asked.

She shrugged. "It can wait," she said, bending like some kind of gymnast to touch her toes, and provide a superlative view of her legs and her tight behind in the process.

Then as I watched her, and took a few more snaps, she said: "You think maybe we should have a strategy for how we should do it tomorrow?"

"Strategy?" I laughed, "Is this some idea that came out of your business school?"

She straightened up, and looked at me seductively over a shoulder. "Well, like do I give you a nice show before we get down to it... a little dancing..."

She turned to face me and jigged her hips playfully. Oh my God, she looked incredible. That lace all over her front and arms just seemed to flaunt every curve of her body, from her shoulders to her breasts, and that toned stomach, down to the tight, narrow triangle that covered her sex.

Her nipples were straining against the lace. I dropped the smartphone.

"You know..." she walked to me, or perhaps I should say prowled, then stood there just a few feet away, lifting her leg to place her foot delicately on the back of the couch, "...tease you a little..."

She ran her hands all over her body, one sweeping down to glide over her mound and her sex. I just watched, stunned.

The bodysuit opened at the bottom with snaps, allowing her to just pull at it, and show me that sweet, sweet pussy.

"I think Henry would like it, don't you?" she said, smiling at my open mouth and wide eyes.

"Of course," I managed to say.

She was touching herself, right in front of me. Her fingers stroking her smooth, soft pussy, slipping inside her, glistening as they came out.

"A little planning might provide him the best possible experience when he does see it, right?" she said, then slipped her dripping fingers in my mouth.

I closed my eyes and sucked on her fingers, craving that wonderful, tangy flavor. When I opened them again, she was peering at me, delighted. Loving how I adored her taste so much.

"You don't think he'll have a good experience even if we just go with the flow?" I asked her.

She smiled, "Oh, I'm sure he would. But I want this to be really special."

"Well if we're putting a script together, I don't think your show should go on for too long," I said, pulling myself up onto my feet before reaching for her, as though I was about to dance with her.

She squealed as I pushed her down on the couch instead.

"Well," she grinned, "I guess I would primarily be teasing you, so I can't be too cruel..."

I swung my hips a little, gently mocking her own little dance, "You don't think he'd like it if I gave you a little show?"

That made her laugh. Coy, she toyed with her hair, smiling up at me, bit her lip. Was she nervous about this weekend? I guess it was the point of no return: up to this point if Henry had taken a dislike to the arrangements, she could turn around and tell him she hadn't actually cheated on him yet. Not by the White House definition, anyway.

"I'd like you to," she said, and her laugh was sexy but possibly trying to conceal her nerves. "But I don't think my husband would care for it so much."

I took my jacket off, and then my tie, and that would have been it for my little jokey strip show—except that she sat there on the couch, her legs wide, and one finger was stroking up and down her wet pussy.

I took off my shirt, continuing the silent swaying of my hips just so I could watch her, teasing her clit, twirling circles around her flushed pussy lips, her breathing getting deeper as she got going.

Her eyelids dropped, and it seemed to me that my dancing was not really the major turn-on for her here, so I fell to my knees, my gaze focused on those two fingers of hers sinking inside her. I held her nearest foot, ran my hands over her nylon-clad leg, besotted by her beauty.

She had a silver anklet around her ankle, which seemed sophisticated and yet a trifle decadent. Naughty.

"This is nice," I said, "something from Henry?"

She smiled, "He gave it to me a long while ago, when we were just beginning to talk about all this. Before you came along."

"I've never seen you wear it before."

She laughed, "When we went dancing, sometimes he would let me dance with other men. It was quite fun, when we were talking about this strange compulsion he had about my sexual past, about the fact that I used to see more than one guy at a time...

"...well, I guess it started with me trying to show him that he'd get jealous if I did actually go back to my poly ways. Only he didn't get jealous... or if he did, it just seemed to excite him..."

As she spoke, the scent of her arousal in the air was getting too much for me, drawing me in like some kind of magic love potion, to kiss my way up her fine calf, her knee and her thigh on my way to heaven.

"...then I wore that anklet to a nightclub one time, and suddenly the number of men coming up to me asking me to dance skyrocketed."

"Oh, right?"

"Toward the end of the night, this couple came to ask us if we were in the lifestyle, and when we looked totally confused, they explained to me that my anklet signified that I was a wife free to date other men."

She bit her lip and dropped her hands as my kisses reached her inner thigh, and then the upper limits of her leg.

I touched the flat of my tongue against her hot pussy lips, and made her gasp.

I chuckled, "Did Henry know about this stuff when he bought it?"

"He swears he didn't. I went online, and I guess it's true in some circles, but in a lot of places nobody knows anything about it."

She curled a hand around the back of my head, encouraging me as I began to lap at her, each brush of my tongue teasing out another little moan from her.

"Did you stop wearing it when you found out what it was?" I asked her.

She gave me a wicked smile, "We wore it a few times when we were going dancing. Well—it made the game easier from my point of view. The only thing that stopped us was when you came along."

"But you're wearing it now."

"Henry thought it might be nice."

I nodded. Strangely, it appealed to me to take Michelle out wearing that little delicate silver chain around her ankle. To have other men want her, while I got to finally take her myself that weekend.

"So I take it you two are talking about the idea of you having a little fun with someone other than me and Henry some time?" I asked.

She gave me that wicked smile again. "Would you think that an awful idea?"

I felt a little out of the loop—but had to remember I wasn't part of the marital component of this unconventional arrangement. I was finding it most appealing to my version of the fantasy to think of Michelle as my wife, too, when she was going to Henry. So shouldn't I enjoy experiencing the art of Michelle flirting with other guys, perhaps with strangers?

"Not entirely."

"I think Henry likes the idea of me being free in the dating world—as if I were a single woman. But we wouldn't want to do anything you weren't happy with."

"You want to do something like that this weekend?"

She said, "I'm supposed to broach the subject with you this weekend. Find out what you think."

I paused, and had to accept that this was inevitable. Henry wanted his wife to be entirely liberated, not simply bedding his best friend.

"I think it would be an interesting experience," I said, and she positively beamed at that.

Almost as though punishing her for her wicked thoughts, I pushed myself up on my elbows and then thrust two fingers deep inside her, making her suddenly gasp.

I draped my other hand over her mound, and began focusing it on her clit, massaging her around that sensitive little button while I fucked her with my other hand. She bucked and writhed under me, gasping for breath before starting to pant. Primed by my tongue, she was ready for climax.

With my fingers vibrating over her clit, while others filled her, perhaps anticipating the moment when she finally allowed my cock inside her, her orgasm was a quick, trembling one. As it erupted through her quivering body, I replaced my fingers over her clit with my hot mouth, enveloping it with my wet tongue to finish off her little peak.

She pressed her hands to my head as I enjoyed her flavor once more, but then after a few moments, she was pushing me over and up, kissing me, tasting herself on my lips her hands sprawling all over my torso.

I thought, for a moment, she was tempted to take me.

But then she resisted, and while she shoved me in one corner of the couch, she now backed away to the other, lying so that her legs overlapped mine, some distance between her sex and my raging hard-on.

"I can't wait for tomorrow," she said.

"So don't," I shrugged.

She shook her head. "It's going to be special. And we have to get the cameras rolling, don't we?"

I smiled, "You don't want to practice it? Get the strategy right?"

Another shake of her head. She lifted her foot, started rubbing it over my crotch, feeling out the shape of my erection. "You're a bad boy underneath, Sean," she grinned. "You think you're this nice, quiet, unassuming boy. But really, you're just a big bad wolf."

I chuckled at that, but something in what she said was definitely nice to hear.

She bit her lip, and though it was a little playfully overdone, it was clear she was having a hard time keeping to her self-imposed strategy. It flattered my ego that such a beautiful woman, who could have any man in the world—her husband in full approval—really wanted me.

I guess there was something I could actually do quite well in this world. I might not be much of a journalist, but...

Michelle pitched forward, kneeling between my thighs, her hands sweeping up my torso—which her own exercise classes and constant prodding had toned into a shape it had never been before. She touched her nose to mine, swamping me with her scent, and offered a flirtatious smirk before dipping to kiss under my jaw, and then slowly lick her way down my bare chest, her hand pressing at my hardness.

"Would you feel bad about me fooling around with another guy?" she asked me.

She grabbed my shaft through my pants with her teeth, playing at being a predator, with an accompanying jokey roar.

"I don't think so," I said. "It isn't really up to me, is it?"

She looked up at me, a touch serious, rubbing my cock more suggestively now through my pants. "But you have a stake in this," she said.

I gave her an understanding nod. "I think it's just

something I have to get used to. Like I had to get used to you going back to Henry after you seduced me."

Unfastening my fly, she looked up and flashed a smile, "You had to get used to me going back to Henry?"

"Of course." I laughed as she pulled my big, hard cock out of my pants. "In a normal world, we would have been having an affair, right? I probably would have tried to encourage you to stop doing anything with your husband, and go exclusive with me."

"I suppose in a normal affair you would."

She licked me slowly from base to tip.

"But you don't hate that I see Henry as well?"

I groaned as she squeezed me and pumped me, her hand tight around my shaft.

"No, not at all. I knew from the start that would happen, didn't I? You were clear enough."

"Doesn't mean you have to like it."

She licked her lips, and then the underside of my cock head, before opening her mouth wide to take me inside.

"I think... I wanted to like it..." I said. "I like Henry so much, I wanted to like it because he liked the idea of you going with me. I wanted to understand him."

Michelle was holding her feet up as she lay on her front between my thighs, sucking increasingly ferociously on my cock, and the way she kicked her feet back and forth in the air seemed a touch girlish, playful, but perhaps revealed her real enjoyment of this.

"And do you? Understand him?" she said, snatching a breath before resuming her bobbing up and down on my pole.

I really had to control myself: someone as good at this as Michelle made it very difficult not to just lie back and come in her mouth in mere moments.

"I think so." Conversation helping me pace myself

sexually. "I have to think of you as mine, and then I can begin to know what he'd be going through."

A grin as she licked me for a moment or two. "You think of me as yours?"

"Sometimes."

"When I'm with you, I am yours."

"Right, but when you're with him, I think of you as mine, too."

"And you're jealous? Angry?"

I groaned as she took me deeper, using both hands to squeeze the base of my shaft. "Jealous, but not angry. I'd have no right to be angry. Plus... Henry's right. When you look at jealousy in the right light... there's something exciting about it. I don't know why..."

I reached down beside me and found Michelle's smartphone—and as though to prove my courage to her, I held it up to take a picture, or a few pictures, of her pretty face sinking on my shaft.

She was a little startled when she first saw what I was doing. Then she gave me a sultry pose with her lips stretched around my cock, getting into the idea of sending Henry something to shock him that night.

Well, I had to get used to the idea that Henry would see our performance the next night, even if it was recorded rather than in person.

Michelle slowly withdrew my cock from her mouth, and the self-satisfied look on her face told me she knew I was about to blow if she didn't.

She brushed her rogue strands of hair out of her face, then pulled herself up to kiss my mouth. She was so pretty. God, and I got to be with her. It never stopped surprising me. Her lips tasted a little of my cock. It wasn't disturbing to me in the way it might have been as a young man.

"You know I'm yours as long as you want me, don't you?" she said.

I pulled away from her, off the couch, so that I could kneel on the floor and appreciate her laid out before me. Run my hands all over her incredible figure.

"So if I was to... you know... look at another man..." she said, "You'd be angry at that? Because it wouldn't be Henry..."

I paused, circling my hand around the sweet contours of her bottom, the stiffness between my legs crying out for the chance to sink between those cheeks and fill her pussy.

There was definitely something very attractive about Michelle being a liberated woman, free to date whoever she chose. But while I could probably tolerate it as one of the men she saw, the only way to actively enjoy it in my mind was to imagine possession of her. To feel that little spicy kick of jealousy that she would seduce and sleep with another man. A stranger, perhaps. But knowing she'd come back to me to share details of her adventure.

The thought of her coming back after a date with another man was fascinating to me, but to truly appreciate the arousing potential of such taboo behavior I almost had to imagine she was my wife.

"I wouldn't be angry at all," I was certain about that. "I think it would be interesting. Maybe I'd feel the same way Henry does."

I lay over her, and now it was my turn to tease her, perhaps. I pressed my hard cock against her firm ass and held her as though I was about to penetrate her. Only, as I nuzzled my face against her cheek, breathing in the clean scent of her hair, and the exhilarating whiff of her perfume, I refrained from blowing her strategy out of the water.

She sighed and groaned as I gently rubbed my hardness against her, coursing it through the hot valley between her cheeks, her curved body tilting her behind up, so that my cock might brush against her pussy.

It was slow, gentle, tender. Affectionate, perhaps, as I breathed her in and kissed her cheek.

"Oh God Sean..." she breathed, "...fuck me, please, fuck me..."

I'm not sure whether she meant it, or just said it to get me going. It was tempting.

My hands slipped around her chest, cupping her breasts, my hips stirring a little more forcefully, and it seemed to me that Michelle was going with this, too. I didn't even need to be inside her, it felt so incredible.

I came, spurting my stickiness between us, all over her back. What did we care about the mess? We had the whole weekend to ourselves. We could hold each other as long as we wanted, indulging in our closeness, then when we were ready, just hop in the shower together, and resume the wonderful exploration of each others' bodies. We didn't need to rush. We could sleep when we wanted. And soon enough, I would be inside her, experiencing her completely.

Henry had to be going crazy waiting for us at home.

18

The big date

I woke to the sound of our hotel room door clicking shut, and bleary-eyed, I pushed myself up on my elbows to see Michelle coming in from a run, all fresh-faced and bushy tail in her skin-tight gray leggings and figure-hugging white tank top.

"Hey sleepyhead," she beamed, pulling off her sneakers.

"Hey," I said. "What time is it?"

"Ten. I let you sleep in since it's vacation time."

She looked irresistible in her workout gear, as usual, and definitely flaunted it as she skipped over to the door of our en suite.

"You getting up?" she asked, and might have meant it as a double entendre. If she had, she was entirely correct at my physical response to her in that outfit.

Even more so when she went into the bathroom and slowly peeled off her top, her sports bra and then her leggings to leave her in a simple yet sexy plain white thong as she reached in to switch on the shower.

"I guess so," I said, peeling back the bed sheet to reveal my morning wood, which made her giggle.

"Care to join me?"

She stooped briefly to slip her panties off her hips and allow them to fall to the floor before stepping into the shower. The benefits of a dirty weekend, huh.

Turning to me again, she ducked her head back under the stream of water, presenting me with a scintillating view of her trim body.

I jumped out of bed, but sauntered into the bathroom, enjoying watching her soaping herself, and the way the glistening water danced all over her tight curves.

When I stepped into the large shower stall with her, though, and ran my hand up from her upper thigh, over her cute behind and the curve of her lower back, she said: "Don't expect too much, sir."

"Too much?"

As my hands reached up and around to cup her slippery breasts, she pressed her body back so that my hardness was crushed against her behind.

"You're saving that for our date night, right?" she asked, turning around now to curl her fingers around my shaft.

"Is that in your strategy?"

She stepped back from me, pushed me away with a smile. "Of course," she said, running her fingers through her hair, and then over her body. "We want you in peak condition, don't we? So no touching."

My eyes followed her hands as they slid down between her legs. I grabbed her and snatched a kiss, but then gently yet firmly she pushed me away again.

"I'm not kidding," she said, but was clearly amused and delighted by my obvious desire. "You behave."

"Yes, Ma'am."

Her hands continued flowing all over her body, fondling her breasts and then sinking around her bare mound, teasing me while pleasuring herself. I wasn't going to stop her.

"So what's the plan for today?" I asked.

"We're going to have a nice day seeing the sights, and then we'll change for dinner."

"Sounds nice."

I found myself a comfortable place on the tiled bench installed on the opposite side of the stall to the shower head, which seemed designed for this kind of arrangement. Her hands were focusing on her pussy now, the fingers on one slipping inside her as the steamy water continued to pour all over her.

"You'll change for dinner first," she said, shaking her hair out of her face, "and then you'll go, and let me get ready in peace."

"With Henry watching you?"

She grinned, "I told you: it's part of his treat. And then we'll meet at the restaurant."

This wasn't just a show: her breathing was heavy, she was shaking a little at times as she touched herself, her eyes closing, head tilting back. She'd lost any signs of amusement—this was a serious business.

It was beautiful to watch, and perhaps even instructional in how she liked to be touched, although I'd had plenty of instruction already since she'd been forbidding me full sex so far.

"How's Henry doing? Have you heard from him?" I asked.

"Of course. He's doing good. He's got what he wanted."

"A sexy wife in another country, fucking another man all weekend?"

Her fingers coursed through her slit and danced around her clit, her hips gently rocking as she drew out her pleasure right in front of me.

"I guess he's nervous that we're forming a stronger attachment—but at the same time he swears that fear is pleasurable to him."

"You don't believe him?"

"Not about the fear." She cried out briefly, her jaw dropping as she struggled to suck in enough oxygen. "I don't know... I guess I'll never be able to entirely understand him. But I believe when he says he enjoys the jealousy, the fear... it's really just because they're so tangled with the feelings of excitement he gets from thinking about me being naughty and having sex with someone else."

"I guess they are tangled in there, not like you can separate out the feelings."

"No."

"So how do you feel about it?"

She shrugged, "I guess I'm nervous about it, too. I get mixed feelings, but they're a little different, I think."

"How so?"

I was finding it difficult to abide by her no-touching rule. She was so tempting, standing there writhing under her own touch.

She said: "Well of course the independent woman in me just loves the idea of having my husband let me have fun with other guys."

"Of course."

"And going away for the weekend with my husband's best friend, with full permission to do as I like, fuck his brains out, or whatever..."

She lifted one of her feet, propping it up on a small ledge running around the tiled wall, opening up her pussy to my gaze while she continued stroking it.

"...and sure, I love the fact that it all seems to turn my husband on like nothing else... only there is that guilt inside me that I'm enjoying it too much... that while he's so turned on, he is hurting a little inside."

"I'm sure he's not. Not really."

"He is. A little. But the dilemma is that he gets that little crushed feeling inside, but he also gets a serious erection, and apparently does truly like the idea of me completely breaking the rules and getting satisfaction from another man..."

Her little cries became constant as she pushed back, leaning against the wall, putting everything into her exquisite masturbation, and it killed our conversation. I didn't mind.

After a while, she had to sit on the tiled floor to continue, glancing briefly up at me to check I was still watching—or perhaps that I was refraining from touching myself in response—before penetrating herself once more with her fingers, the heal of her hand pressing against her clit.

Wives should touch themselves for their husbands on a regular basis, as far as I was concerned. It was so beautiful to watch. Did Michelle do this for Henry? I couldn't help but wish I could have seen Katie in such a manner.

The breathless sighs, those plaintive cries, the way her chest heaved as she panted for air, the pleasure in her face so intense it almost resembled pain... so bewitching, so captivating.

Then she was whimpering and shaking and blushing, and it was so powerfully personal and deeply intimate it felt an honor to witness.

And of course, I was left with the warm feeling that despite my lack of input, this beautiful creature had her sexual satisfaction—no need for fakery when she was making herself feel good.

---

*B*oth showered and dressed casually, and one of us at least sexually satisfied for a while, we went out into the clear Parisian winter air to enjoy the sights of the city.

I hadn't been to France since I was a teenager, but it seemed a lot nicer than I remembered. The tourist crowds were sparse since we were out of peak, but the street cafes were humming, and the bookstalls along the Seine lively as we checked out some of the hotspots from Notre-Dame cathedral and a walk around the atmospheric Ile Saint-Louis. We window shopped down the Rue Saint-Honoré before an overly hasty tour around the Louvre. And of course we visited the Eiffel Tower.

We had this feeling that we weren't really in town to be tourists, and that cut out the pressure we might have felt to stick to a busy site-seeing schedule. We saw things, things we wouldn't ordinarily see, and that was wonderful. But the enjoyment for me came in simply Michelle hanging off my arm while we soaked up the atmosphere of this romantic city—a breath of her perfume here, an earful of her laughter there and the occasional kiss.

The day seemed to fly by.

Michelle kept Henry up to date with regular text messages and selfies, making a point to show herself having fun—and that she was having fun with me, with selfies that showed us as a couple, rather than just friends, our poses and expressions revealing affection and even romance, flaunting Henry's idea that we were in Paris as lovers, not simply touring companions.

From his replies, he was loving every minute of it.

---

*D*inner was at the Georges, an upscale restaurant on the top floor of the Centre Pompidou, that wild tangle of steel that looks permanently clad in scaffolding, which houses various exhibitions, a large public information library and the national museum of modern art, which I was able to slouch around while waiting for our appointed meeting time at the restaurant.

The restaurant itself was a huge cavern of a place highlighting the industrial-style architecture of the building around it. The place seemed hardly intimate on first glance, so open-plan, so many tables—but the atmosphere was given class by the furnishings, the lighting, and the incredible views over the twilit city.

Quite a place, though not quite enough to draw the eye from Michelle, who looked unbelievable in a short sleeveless white dress, her hair bound up by some kind of band or tiara that gave her the princess look. With her legs covered in white nylon, and her feet propped up on matching high heels, the effect was almost bridal—or perhaps, virginal.

"Wow, you look incredible," I said as she stepped out of the elevator with a beaming smile.

"Thank you."

She leaned up to me to kiss me on the cheek, and I detected a slight tremor in her—nerves? It was cute, sexy. This was a big night for her, too.

"Henry must have enjoyed watching you get ready," I spoke quietly as I slipped an arm in hers to escort her into the restaurant itself.

"He did. He looked ready to blow by the time I left our room."

We were shown to our table, Michelle assisted with her chair by the attentive maitre d', and by accident or design we were seated by the windows and the panoramic view over Paris.

Still, however, during our meal it was hard to take our eyes off each other.

"Are you nervous?" I came right out and said it over our starters. Just getting it out there seemed to deflate some of the tension between us, the anxiety.

She nodded.

I guess I was nervous too, but for the usual guy reasons of worrying about my performance, whether when all was said and done it would feel good for her when we got to the evening's main course. By this time, I no longer had to worry that Henry might change his mind, and come to find the thought of our union distressing.

"Excited, too," she said, offering me a faltering smile. "I've wanted this for such a long time."

"But you still feel a little... uncertain about this?"

She shrugged, "I don't know. Henry's proven that he wants this. And I want this—God I want this. I want you. But... I guess part of me..."

"Can't quite let go of the guilt?"

A small nod.

She gave a small smile—so pretty, but so fraught with tension. "The thing is," she said softly, "I think I'm beginning to understand why he wants this, but I still feel if I'm doing this, he should be out there enjoying himself too."

"But none of this is about Henry seeing another woman."

"I know. It's supposed to be about me being polyamorous, and about whether Henry can handle that."

"It's not just about him handling it, though. It's about you handling it, too. And to do that you have to let go of the guilt."

"I know."

I thought of Katie, automatically, as I tried to put myself in Henry's shoes. I don't think I'd ever be able to get out of that shadow, that great influence of my failed marriage. But the strong feelings I had at least let me understand Henry.

"You have to accept that he really does enjoy the feelings all this gives him. He's not just handling it, he's loving it."

"I guess so."

She nodded, and seemed to relax a little.

"You know it's funny," she said, "when I was in college, when I was the little self-righteous poly girl, I didn't let my boyfriends complain that I wasn't exclusive with them. If they didn't like it, they didn't get to have me at all. I guess the theory was that any of them could go out and see any other girl, too. But none of them did. I didn't even really think about it."

"You were having too much fun."

"But what if one of them did?" she was serious. "If one of them had started dating someone else? I think about it now, and I can't help but think I might not have liked it. I might have wanted them to stop seeing the other woman—and that would have made me a complete hypocrite, wouldn't it?"

I sipped my wine. "I don't know about that. I think it might have meant you weren't really polyamorous, or not fully polyamorous. I can't say I'm an expert in the jargon."

"Polyandrous, I suppose—a woman who has intimate relationships with more than one man. But still, hardly fair," she said. "When I was doing it, it was all about being liberated, completely free to love whoever I wanted—but I think my mindset was that anybody should be free to love who they wanted, without restriction."

I put down my glass, "I'm not sure you can entirely judge how you would have been in college, based on how you are now."

"I guess."

"If Henry did want to see other women, you think you'd let him?"

She nodded. "He hasn't said anything to you, about—"

"No, he hasn't. Just hypothetically."

"I'd let him," she said. "Of course I'd let him. If I believe a person shouldn't have to close themselves off from enjoying other people, that shouldn't just refer to me."

"No."

"I'm not sure I'd be the same as him, though. I'm not sure I'd be interested in all the details. I'm not sure I'd find any jealousy that happens... you know... exciting."

"But you might."

She smiled, shrugged.

"I guess I never thought enough about how my boyfriends in college might feel while I was seeing other guys. I just thought they had to deal with it."

"Maybe they enjoyed it, some of them."

"Maybe. I guess no one would have said if they did. We kept my relationships all nicely separate, each guy ignoring the existence of the others. If one of them liked the thought of me sleeping with other guys, they might have worried that I'd think badly of them."

"They'd think you might doubt their manhood. And that's so important in college."

She smiled, "Thank God that's over, huh?"

"I don't know... I wouldn't mind another run at my

college years, knowing what I do now," I laughed. "So—you're feeling a little happier about tonight?"

She gave me a mock-seductive Marilyn Monroe look that despite being semi-humorous was actually smoldering hot, particularly when he subtly pushed up her breasts to emphasize her cleavage in that low-cut dress. "I've always been happy about tonight," she said. "Can't you tell?"

"And your guilt?"

A shrug, "I'll deal with it. This has definitely helped—thank you."

I smiled. "You and Henry seem to have it all worked out—I mean, you tell each other everything."

She raised one eyebrow, "Excepting that one little thing..."

"Which we're putting right tonight, aren't we?"

"Yes, definitely." A grin. I felt myself thicken slightly in anticipation.

I said: "I wish Katie and I could have been like you guys in talking everything through."

Michelle paused before taking a sip of her Chablis. "You know, you guys still could."

I sighed, "I'm not sure if the opportunity's still there."

She shook her head. "You still have feelings for her, Sean. And you've changed. You think of her differently now, don't you?"

I nodded.

Michelle was so sharp. She said: "You've been thinking of me as yours, so when I'm with Henry you can experience the pleasurable side of my absence—but I'll bet you've had thoughts about Katie that way, haven't you? Of sharing her..."

"I guess Henry's influence has rubbed off on me... or else it's just my way of dealing with the fact that she's been seeing other guys since we separated."

She took a big gulp of wine. "You need to talk to her, Sean. She didn't stop loving you. She left you because your sex life died, but not just that. It's pretty obvious you had communication issues. You might have rediscovered your sexual mojo, but if you still want her, you need to work on your communication."

"I suppose so."

"I'm sure plenty of women—Katie included—would kill to have a husband who loved them, and who would let them date other guys if they wanted. But you have to learn to talk to her again."

I nodded. Perhaps she had a point.

*W*e spent a long time over dinner. I didn't see Michelle send any texts to Henry until we were ready to leave—he must have been wondering what was going on.

We just talked and talked, getting through a few bottles of wine.

"He's okay?" I asked her as we finally left, arm in arm, walking slowly to the elevator.

"He's nervous about whether we had the talk."

"And did we?" I smirked. "I guess we did."

"Do you feel possessive about me?" she asked as we stepped into the elevator. Another couple stood to the side, and we arrogantly and probably stupidly assumed they wouldn't understand our English. Maybe we also just didn't care – we were in Paris, about to embark on what others would definitely class as an extramarital affair – the thought that another couple might hear our personal conversation only added to the illicit appeal of that evening.

"A little."

"You imagine I'm your wife. Sometimes."

"Sometimes."

"And when you imagine your real wife, nowadays you feel a certain interest in her... being with other guys."

"Call it a survival mechanism." I was teasing her. Sue me.

"You're curious, at least?"

"I am."

"So you could try it out with me, right? See how you feel when you're imagining I'm your wife, and I start dating other guys."

"You're already seeing another guy, aren't you? Your husband?"

She giggled, "I don't think Henry entirely counts in your eyes any more, he's not a challenge to you. You can happily share me with him, right? It's anyone else who would make you feel... uncomfortable."

I took a deep breath. I could feel Michelle slipping away from me, somehow. My status as just another of her boyfriends, rather than one of the two men in her life making me feel that tickle of danger.

Wasn't that, really, what it would be like sharing my wife?

"Okay," I said.

"Okay we had the talk?"

"Okay, when you're ready, I'd like to try it."

She smiled brilliantly. "I'm glad we had the talk."

As the painfully slow elevator came to a halt at the ground floor, and we stepped toward the door, I heard the other woman in there giggle, and whisper something to her partner.

When we stepped out through the opening doors, I glanced back to see her standing a little in front of him, her hand squeezing his crotch subtly but so that I could see. There was a ring on her finger. While he was trying to look as though he hadn't noticed me looking back at them, his wife looked me straight in the eyes with an unmistakable expression of lust.

Stepping out onto the street, I silently conceded that they had understood every word we'd said in that elevator.

---

*S*he was texting him on the way back toward the hotel in the taxi, though there was no selfie this time.

"He's doing a lot of pacing back and forth apparently," she said.

"Even though he's of the opinion that we've had full sex before, countless times?"

"Oh, it doesn't matter how many times it happens. Each time he feels crazy. Every time it happens, it's me crossing the line, stepping outside our marital monogamy."

I nodded. Perhaps when I thought about Katie, I didn't quite appreciate how it might be to really share a spouse long-term. Thinking that it got easier once you were past the first time, and yet it probably didn't.

"Well," she sighed, "he's not been sending me many texts, so I guess he can't be suffering too much."

She seemed almost disappointed. I said, "He just doesn't want to get in your way. Of course he wants constant updates, but what he wants most is for you to enjoy your evening."

She smiled. "You know, I think it helps me as much as it helps him to keep sending him text messages," she said.

"You need to know he's still happy, it's perfectly natural."

As we neared the hotel, Michelle leaned forward and asked the driver: "You know somewhere we could go dancing around her?"

The driver had enough English to understand her, responding: "Of course."

---

*I*t was the Rive Gauche, so there were probably plenty of places around there. It was small, intimate, crowded enough to provide a lively atmosphere without becoming intimidating.

As we found a quick drink and then a place on the dance floor, I did feel a little old among the passionate twenty-somethings moving about around us. But I guess Michelle put me back in touch with my more carefree twenties again.

She was smiling so broadly as we eventually found our place, and held each other while we danced to some acid jazz numbers, that I knew I'd do whatever she asked of me, go wherever she wanted, drink as much as I needed to keep up.

It was heavenly to have her clinging close to me all night, pressing herself to my body as we moved to the music, pulling me in for the occasional kiss, allowing my hands to drift up to caress her pert behind as we swayed to the slow numbers, while just about holding on to my hands as we threw ourselves about to the faster numbers.

Just knowing that there were no limits on our closeness now, that we were going all the way, made me appreciate every moment in a new light.

By the end of a long night of dancing and drinking, I was feeling invigorated, horny as never before, and also now fully appreciative of exactly why Henry had come to the conclusion that he alone could not keep up with this delightful nymph of ours.

Yet while I might ordinarily be in danger of collapse after such exertion, I was on such a high I felt I could coast on through on the buzz alone. I was so exhilarated to be dancing with this beautiful girl - and the fact that at the end of it, I would get to sleep with her. It was just strange feeling that she was from a slightly different generation than me, a generation still into clubbing, and a generation that perhaps didn't see relationships in quite the traditional way that I did.

When we were heading back into the hotel, Michelle said to me: "Okay. The next time I text him will be the first time after I've gone all the way with a man who is not my husband."

It sent a shiver through my body, and left me feeling suddenly sober and alert.

19

Completion

*J*n public, in the hotel, we had to keep calm.

We walked in silence to the elevator, and then while we waited for it to arrive, Michelle leaned up to whisper in my ear: "I'm going to fuck you until you pass out."

Her words were shocking and thrilling to me, setting my heart racing, the blood rushing straight to my cock.

I can't wait," I said, kissing her briefly. She was like some kind of incredibly sweet and creamy liqueur to sip slowly at the end of an evening, with that slight bite of dangerous hard liquor underneath.

Inside the elevator, she grabbed my hand and pushed it up under her dress, so that my fingers were brushing against the rough lace of her panties, which appeared to be soaked already.

Then I was following her down the hallway to our room, my eyes trailing down her shapely form presented so well in that dress, her slender shoulders, her neck visible despite the loose tendrils of her hair falling from her loose bun.

Admiring the way she moved with her hips gently swaying, like a catwalk model, and how her butt squeezed into that dress.

She gave me a coy look before slotting the key card into the lock to open the door to our room—silently asking me if I was ready for this.

Boy, was I ready for this.

I stepped inside the room. She turned, pulled me to her, her hand reaching up for the back of my neck as I closed in for a sweet, sweet kiss.

My heart was thumping so hard as I sucked on her full lips. We were whirling around on our feet as though dancing, unable to keep from each others' lips, perhaps because finally we knew we were free to go as far as we wanted to now.

She pushed me back against the wall, pressed her hands up against my chest, stroking the muscles her training regime had given me before reaching up to slip my jacket off my shoulders and away.

"I've waited for this for so long..." she whispered as we finally allowed ourselves a breathless but very brief pause. "And now I get to finally have you."

"You're so beautiful," I breathed, kissing my way down her neck. "I'm a lucky guy."

"God, I want you so badly," she said, her hands immediately moving to fumble with my tie.

I wasn't going to object to her urgency.

Her excitement, her impatience were thrilling to me.

She smiled as she saw in my face how amused I was at her sudden desperation, and kissed me again while her fingers struggled with the buttons of my shirt, as though trying to stifle any dissent I might care to express.

I helped her with my shirt, a few of the buttons probably coming off as I tore the rest of it from my back.

She wasn't going to stop—she was at my belt, pulling it open, forcing my pants down my legs. Kissing her way down my chest. My whole body was on fire, even though we'd already gone this far. Just the fact that this was headed all the way made me feel a new burst of energy.

"You look amazing," she breathed, her hands running all over my back as she kissed my stomach. "All that exercise paying off, right?"

I laughed, "You know I was only doing that to impress you."

"You definitely impress me," her hand briefly brushed over the hardness straining against my boxer shorts.

I guess my joining Michelle's fitness classes had helped with the tone to some extent—I don't think I'd ever looked like this.

She dragged my underwear down my thighs, and her hand was around my shaft, squeezing, pumping, wasting no time before enveloping it with her mouth.

"Oh God..." I groaned, trying not to overreact to the sight of her lips stretching around the head of my cock, sinking down on my pole, her eyes closed, hand pumping me at the base.

The way she withdrew me until my cock was resting on her tongue, her eyes opening to look up at me and gauge my response, her little purring revealing her joy at having the freedom to savor a cock that was not her husband's.

I placed my hand gently on her head, appreciating her, perhaps encouraging her, perhaps ready to force her away if things became a little too wonderful.

My hand slipped under her chin, and then as things did get a little too intense, I pressed on her jaw, ushered her back up to her feet. We kissed, our tongues touching, exploring, dancing with each other, never mind that my cock had been filling her mouth.

I turned her, pushed her gently back against the wall, my hand brushing the inside of her legs as I pushed up her dress, feeling the nylon and the lace of her stockings give way to the bare flesh of her upper thighs before my fingers reached the wet fabric of her panties and the heat of her mound underneath.

For a few moments I touched her there, loving how wet she was, while I kissed her velvet neck, breathing her in, moaning as her fingers curled around my shaft to continue pumping me.

Then I sank slowly to my knees, pushing up her dress to reveal dainty white lace panties, the underwear of a pure bride about to be despoiled, and her bare stomach, which I could have kissed for hours on end and never tired of it.

As I kissed my way along the waistband of her panties, breathing that thickening scent of her arousal in the air, she reached up and behind her shoulders with both hands, then found the zip to unfasten her dress.

I helped her pull it down her body so she could step out of it, then she was reaching behind her back again to unfasten her strapless white bra.

I rose to take her hard little nipples in my mouth, and explore her pert breasts with my kisses, indulging in the softness of her flesh, the sweetness of her fragrance.

What an honor to be able to appreciate such a woman —a woman that society insisted should be completely off-limits to me, and every other man save her husband.

Michelle was breathing quite deeply now, those deep blue eyes gazing down on me saturated by unconcealed lust.

"Were you angry I didn't allow this from the beginning?" she asked. "When Henry said we could?"

I stroked my nose along each side of her underwear,

inhaling that exhilarating blend of her perfume and the underlying scent of her arousal.

"Of course not," I said. "It was important you took it the pace you wanted to."

"You've been very patient."

"Well, I never expected to be able to do anything with you—even kissing you seemed like a bonus to me."

"You're sweet."

"I can be sweeter," I said, and now I was running my mouth and nose gently over the moist lace of her panties, breathing in that strong aroma of female desire, glorying in the heat coming through the thin fabric, more than a little awe-struck that I was nudging into the most intimate area of such a beautiful woman.

She let out a long sultry moan as I started to kiss her through the lace, pressing my lips and tongue to her hot flesh, tasting her arousal.

"You know, you're very different to Henry," she said.

I was a little surprised that she might be talking to me about Henry's qualities as a lover. I guess we'd never set any boundaries on what we could talk about while we were together.

"Is that a good thing or a bad thing?" I asked.

It made me wonder what she talked about with Henry while they were intimate together. I guess as husband and wife they'd have no secrets, but I had always thought Henry might be the kind of guy who would not want to know too much detail about his wife's experiences with his friend, even though he was allowing it all to happen.

"Well, Henry always thought it would be pointless for me to take another lover if he was exactly the same as him."

"I'm not going to ask you who you prefer," I said. And I didn't want to know. To think I was the better man for her might make me feel sorry for Henry, and to think he was the better man... well, I guess I could put it down to the fact she'd married him, but it might not be so great for my confidence.

"Oh no, I'm not sure I do," she said. "Vive la difference, right?"

"Right."

I dragged her panties down her thighs and past her knees, letting them drop. Her legs opened to present me with the exquisite sight of her bare pussy, with its delightful little pink petals.

She had one hand already on my head as I tilted my face up to spread my lips over her exquisite flower.

The moan she emitted as my tongue coursed through her searing, soaking slit made me shiver with desire. She tasted so good, she smelled so fragrant and yet so wicked, I was in heaven as much as she, sucking gently on her sensitive little bud, my fingers teasing open her lips to aid my tongue in penetrating her.

She looked down on me, seemingly incredulous at how I was making her feel, while I looked up at her and smiled, appreciating the superb view up her toned form, and how she was writhing in response to me.

"He's rougher than you are. And he wants things his way," she said.

"You're saying I don't take you my way?" I grinned, but wasn't taking offense. Resuming my little kisses along the top edge of her inner thighs again, just breathing in her scent and building the momentum again before pouncing on her pussy once again. I was in heaven.

"You're softer, you take things more slowly," she said. I didn't say anything about the fact that I'd been forced to take things more slowly, by the denial of the full experience. "Henry's more like when you're really thirsty, and you just gulp down some ice cool water. With you, it's like sipping wine slowly over a whole evening."

"How slow do you really like it?"

But a brief glance up from between her legs, and I could see the urgency in those navy blue eyes gazing down on me, her firm stare ordering me to go on.

"Slow is nice, but sometimes a girl gets thirsty, too," she joked.

It was only as I slipped a thumb inside her, to feel just how tight and wet she was inside, that we were reminded of our plan to include her husband in the evening's performance.

"Wait..." she said, breathless.

"The cameras," I said for her, and took a few last laps of her juicy slit as she nodded confirmation that we had to do this, had to film this for Henry.

We moved on through into the bedroom proper, and while I went to switch on the iPhone and Henry's iPad, then the little camcorder that Michelle had positioned while she got ready earlier, I saw her stopping to put her panties and dress back on.

"Take two, huh?" I joked.

"I'm going to give him a show," she insisted. "Hey don't complain, you get to have it, too."

"Oh, it's fine with me."

A double check on the video equipment, and she had me sit on the bed, my underwear and pants back on, feeling a little like an actor might, trying to make this second take appear like the first time we were starting out our carnal explorations of the night.

She went to the window, facing it, letting me feast my eyes on her firm ass showcased by the form-fitting dress as she unfastened her hair and shook it out over her shoulders. Her dress rode up on her thighs just high enough to provide a glimpse of the white lace tops of her stay-ups.

She moved slowly, sensually, turning to face me, teasing her dress further up her legs, and then over her hips to expose the tops of her stockings and those sexy white lace panties of hers again, along with her taut midriff.

Her smile was a little nervous, coy, fitting with the virginal white of her clothes to portray to me a wife about to stray from the path of righteousness for the first time.

She was enjoying how I looked at her, how I lusted after her. She toyed with her panties, stretching them this way and that, pulling them away and down from her mound to tease me—and no doubt, her husband later on.

She turned to bend over the windowsill, flaunting her bare behind, covered by only the flimsiest strands of white lace. Then I watched her strip off her dress and dance for me like some exotic, devilish creature trying to entrap me. She brushed her hands through her long brown hair, and came to sit in my lap facing away from me, teasing me with the gyration of her hips over my hard cock, but directing a fair amount of her performance to the camera facing us.

Lap-dancing with me, for her husband.

I didn't mind that he was in her mind. She reached behind for me, kissed me. How could I mind anything? I was about to take her, to have her as fully as I'd ever wanted.

She rolled off me, and I moved up the bed, as though getting her to chase me, though she only needed to crawl up my body to reach my available kiss, straddle my hips to possess me, her silky hair flowing all over me as we locked lips.

She sighed as she began grazing her sex over my hardness, her underwear and my clothes providing the only barrier.

This was her scene. She was the wife crossing the line, the lover producing a show for her husband to enjoy. I let her direct us.

Kneeing up above my chest, she hooked her thumbs in the waistband of her panties and pulled them down over her thighs, revealing the full glory of her smooth pussy again. I could still taste her from before, and craved more. She lifted one leg, and then the other to remove her underwear, leaving her in nothing but those white lace-topped stockings.

I was so hard as she kissed me, at how close I was to her unprotected sex.

She kissed my lips again, and one of her hands swept down from my head to between her legs, and then reached inside my pants and boxers to grasp hold of my hardness.

She was looking so intently into my eyes as she pumped my cock mere inches from her bare pussy, the atmosphere was just electric.

I struggled a little underneath her to pull off my pants and underwear, but Michelle was still in the teasing mood. She sat up on me, nipples so hard, still stroking her hand up and down my shaft, her legs parted, the lips of her sex almost close enough to brush against my cock as she played with it.

She was teasing me, she was teasing her husband, since the iPhone was poised above us, looking down from the top of the bedstead. I think she was teasing herself, too. Delaying the moment she stepped over that line, enjoying her freedom to do so, marveling that this big, hard cock in her hands could be inside her, and all three of us in this strange relationship would take pleasure in it.

"I'm so lucky I get to have it," she said softly. "It's so beautiful, Sean. So big. And I get to have it inside me."

I smiled. I'd seen Grant, I knew I was little more than

average size, but Michelle's flattery never failed to stroke the male ego inside me.

"Whenever you're ready," I said. "I can't wait."

"You'll have to," she grinned, leaned forward, and then lifted one knee, and then the other, and then up on her feet she turned over me, giving me a wonderful view as she sank down, knees either side of my face.

I'd been expecting something more: to record our first time for Henry, there was no way it would just be a quickie.

I held her by the thighs, my hands spreading over the rough lace of her stocking tops, as she settled down over my face, facing my feet and my perpendicular prick, her soaking wet sex covering my mouth and nose.

I could only imagine how hot it would be to see her, probably from the iPad filming us from the foot of the bed, riding my face while I did my best to lap at her savory juices.

Her knees were far enough apart that her thighs did not enclose my ears—I could hear her heavy breathing as she waggled her hips over me, circling her pussy around my lips and my attentive tongue.

I reached to grab her buttocks, squeezing her pleasing roundness as I ate her like a ravenous beast, and for a while she just enjoyed the ride.

Then she leaned slowly forward, her hands initially supporting herself on my chest, before she lay over me, fingers taking up the base of my shaft, my tip swamped by the heat of her mouth.

She was so good at sucking cock, I knew that well enough. In the weeks she'd been doing it, though, when I'd known she'd want to finish that way, I never had to really hold myself back against the glorious sensations of her hot mouth on my staff. This time, though, I had to pace myself.

I managed, just barely.

I guess if I'd exploded in her mouth, we could have waited and done the scene again. Hell, we still could try it over and over again, even if we succeeded the first time. Edit together the most incredible half hour of footage drawn from the whole night. But she stopped, and I felt her rolling the cool latex of a condom down on my length. Where had she been keeping that? The only solution I could think of was that she'd had it tucked into the top of her stay-up stockings.

She pulled herself off me, and off the bed, dancing around it in those stockings. This was the Big Moment, both of us could feel it, even if I hadn't been left lying there with my cock sheathed.

I pulled myself up after her, wanting to know what she was up to, but as she stood there at the foot of the bed, it was clear how she wanted to go.

Michelle leaned over the edge of the tall bed, her hands flat on the mattress, and pushed her butt back toward me as I stood behind her.

"I'm all yours, Sean," she said, looking over her shoulder at me. "Take me."

I stepped up to her, my hand sliding over her rump to hold her hip. She turned to face the camcorder we had at the side of the room, sitting on the small dining table, and lifted her nearest leg to that little cold black eye, sliding her knee onto the edge of the mattress. Opening herself up to Henry's view as I approached her, guiding the tip of my formidable hardness to her slick entrance.

If Henry was going to see this moment, it was going to be exquisite and excruciating for him in broadly equal measures, I was certain. So it was going to be slow as slow could be. I felt the heat of her pussy lips through the thin condom as my tip touched so very gently against her.

Then I edged gradually forward, entering her half-inch by half-inch, Michelle moaning in time with each move forward.

I thrust into her the last inch or so, completely filling her, perhaps even stretching her a little. She closed her eyes, opened her mouth and moaned long and hard, little dimples appearing between her eyebrows as the strain and pleasure of taking my full length showed.

Finally, after all that waiting, I was inside Mrs Robinson.

My God, her ass was perfect. Her body was perfect. I could hardly believe it that I got to see her like that, let alone have my big hard cock inside her, splitting her cheeks, making her gasp for breath as I slowly stirred inside her.

"Oh Jesus..."

She seemed almost to be in mourning, the way her face appeared in response to my slow pumping into her, so intense it was. Was she in pain? Was she grieving for her marital fidelity? My heart, my breathing seemed to pause for a moment or two as I feared that she was suddenly regretting this, that she was upset because she'd gone along with this whole plan, and now in her mind she might have betrayed her husband.

But then she said: "Oh, that feels incredible. I never felt anything like it..."

And it did not make me feel she wanted me to stop.

She was rocking back on my cock as I thrust into her, mirroring my moves, as much a part of this as I was in the culpability stakes.

Her nipples so hard underneath her, her pussy so wet around my shaft.

"You're so big..."

She seemed a little shocked, at how it felt finally to have

me inside her, at how good it was, or perhaps at the realization of what we'd done, the reality of crossing that line.

To me, it was a thrill beyond merely making love to a wincingly beautiful woman. In the back of my mind I knew how Henry must feel about it, the joy of a husband knowing his wife was experiencing such wicked delight, and it just amped up the whole thing for me, too.

"Jesus... Jesus... Jesus..."

She may have been playing up her response for the benefit of the camera—I was playing up the physicality of my plunging into her, I'm certain of it. As I guided her onto her back, and she turned to face me, there was no faking how hard her nipples were, how flushed she was with the perspiration beginning to break out on her brow —and of course, how wet she was.

Briefly as she parted her magnificent stocking-clad legs for me, revealing that gorgeous pink flower, I had to kneel and duck down to taste her again, forcing my tongue back inside her, sucking on her slippery folds, slurping at her tangy juices.

She groaned and lifted her head to watch me, her hands slipping around my scalp to press me to her.

Between her thighs it was almost as though she were a wonderful musical instrument, and I was a maestro performer, exploring the various tones and keys I could provoke in her sighs and moans as I touched her.

As I sucked with increasing vigor at her little button, my fingers slipping in and out of her glistening folds, her moans were soon becoming yells, and Michelle was clawing at the bedsheets, apparently having difficulty getting quite enough oxygen into her chest, though begging me not to stop.

And then her body was quivering around me, coming violently, her back arching, body twisting into what an outside observer might even have termed anguish had they not born witness to its cause.

She was gasping for breath as I pulled myself back onto my feet, to slide back inside her. Her eyes widened as I filled her, stretched her, my big hard cock rubbing up against every sensitive part of her tight channel.

"Oh, it feels amazing," she moaned as I held her calves and fucked her sweet married pussy.

Her hand slipped between her legs as I pulled them together, touching her clit while my bulging manhood pounded into her again and again, her chest heaving as she panted for breath, her whole body shaking with each thrust into her.

After a while, she grabbed me, and hauled me over like we were wrestling, so she could climb on top.

Michelle was such a beautiful sight over me, her forceful, almost plaintive moans so stirring to the very deepest essence inside me, that I clearly forgot about our complete lack of privacy for a while.

Holding her by the hips, timing my own gyrations to hers, it felt so perfect inside her, making me wonder if this was truly as good as it got.

How graceful she was, arching her back, thrusting out her breasts, those stiff nipples so straight out in front. She leaned back, supporting herself on her hands behind her to offer me a gloriously filthy view of her pussy as she writhed on top of me.

She certainly didn't hold back in vocalizing her own response to the exhilarating sensations of our congress, uttering increasingly loud cries in between her breathless panting. All good for her husband's enjoyment at some later time.

It seemed strange to me that I wasn't bothered by the thought of Henry seeing this. I guess his focus would be on her anyway, I was just some guy. I think it even drove me on to enjoy this more, thinking about how this might please my friend.

Michelle now turned around, and with my cock firmly inside her, lay back against me, her head resting on my shoulder. Sweeping my hands over her luxuriously smooth skin, I coaxed her breasts and squeezed her nipples between thumb and forefingers

"God you feel so good inside me," she breathed.

"Everything you were hoping for?" I asked.

"And more."

I slipped a hand down between her legs, sopping up some of her moisture with a finger or two through her soaking groove, and then I was trailing her wetness around her clit even while we still writhed together, my cock thrusting into her hot pussy.

"Oh God..." she wailed as I started massaging the flesh immediately around her clit, and turned to suck my earlobe into her mouth, her hips accelerating the motion on my hardness, encouraging me in my pursuit of her little button.

"I've been fantasizing about this ever since I first saw you," I breathed into her ear, making her smile like the Cheshire Cat.

I turned her again, with what little energy I had left for the evening, straddling her once she lay on her front, sliding inside her from behind while her legs were still together.

So tight, so hot inside her.

She was gripping the bedsheets with every ounce of her strength as I shoved into her, her yells now stifled by the pillows, though still audible. She pushed up her pert little butt to meet the force of my pounding full on, and it wasn't long before she was shuddering as though caught in an earthquake.

And I was shuddering with her, pumping my hot fluid inside her, though it was caught by our thin latex barrier. The first time any man had done so for years, other than her husband.

20

Confirmation

I woke late in the morning again, but then it was supposed to be a vacation. The other side of the bed was empty, so I supposed Michelle to be on her usual morning run, though it was probably late for that, too.

After a few moments relaxing, trying to get my head around such an incredibly carnal night in which I had fucked my best friend's wife time and time again, I heard her voice out in the living room part of the suite.

"It was lovely, really special."

She was trying to keep quiet, but failing since this time on a Sunday saw the street outside our hotel window even more quiet.

And there was another familiar voice, though quieter, not so clear. Henry.

I pulled myself out of bed and went to the doorway. Peered around the corner to see her sitting there on the floor with her laptop, cross-legged, still in her little blue skin-tight crop-top and yoga shorts from her run, her hair neatly tied back in a ponytail, her freckled face all aglow from the run—and perhaps from memories of the previous night.

"So after the restaurant we went dancing in this place in the Rive Gauche..."

"That must have been fun," came Henry's voice through the laptop.

"It was kind of jazzy stuff, you know, the kind that's good for holding someone close, feeling their body against you..."

She giggled, rocking back and forth on her behind, clearly thrilled to be seeing her husband like this. I guess it reassured her about his contentment, as well as simply allowing her to reconnect with him overseas.

"And maybe a little kissing?"

"Yeah, we kissed a little... maybe a lot. He's a good kisser. Among other things."

I felt myself swelling inside with pride. She had no reason to lie, not to Henry. If anything if I was a little average she'd be able to flatter his ego, tell him I was nothing compared to him.

But, I suppose he wanted to hear that the man sleeping with her was good, was worth the angst, and that she was enjoying herself.

"So after the dancing?"

"Then I was dragging him back to the hotel, I couldn't stand it any more," she said. She pulled the hem of her crop top up to reveal her black sports bra to her husband, beaming with happiness at his reaction.

"I bet he couldn't either."

I guessed Henry must have been on his way to bed at this time of day. He'd be working again tonight, on our last night in Paris, and then he was scheduled to have the Monday and Tuesday nights off—no doubt when he could reclaim his wife.

For now, she was just teasing him, fondling her breasts, flaunting her toned figure.

"I was just buzzing all over... it was so wild. When we got in the room, I was dancing for him, it was so hot seeing how much he wanted me..."

"What were you wearing? Did he like it?"

She laughed, then lifted her hips briefly, and I watched her slowly rolling her yoga pants over her thighs, up over her knees, teasing Henry, revealing a tiny little black thong underneath.

"Yeah... the white one... lace... I'm pretty sure he liked it."

She was so beautiful, Henry must have been tearing his hair out watching her, knowing she was so far away, and that she was spending the entire evening sleeping with his friend. But I could imagine the pleasure he must be having, too. An extended version of that little tickle I felt when Michelle was sleeping with Henry, and I heard them.

Or that strange arousal I'd felt seeing my Katie in bed with Grant.

That particular thought shocked me, more than a little. That even before any of this with Michelle and Henry, I had had that feeling seeing Katie in bed with another.

I really adored being with Henry and Michelle, it was so incredible to be allowed access to the cute little brunette. But was I a man like Henry? The feelings I'd had about Katie that day—did that make me the kind of messed up husband who wanted to share his wife? Assuming I'd lost Katie, would the next time I got married find me feeling a deep-seated need to see my beloved wife enjoying herself with men other than just me?

It didn't distress me to think I might be that way. It just came as a surprise, I think, even after everything that had happened.

Would it be the kind of dark fantasy I'd have to keep a permanent secret from any woman I married, though? It was controversial. It wasn't for everyone. Plenty of women probably wouldn't understand it.

"Tell me what happened then."

Michelle briefly lay back and pulled her knees up to her chest as though stretching before more exercise, though watching her panties stretch over the sweet form of her pussy made it clear it was merely for the benefit of Henry's viewing pleasure.

Then she was back sitting cross-legged, grinning with delight.

"I was just all over him... he was so hard..."

"He's big, right? Bigger than me?"

"Yeah, I think he is bigger. It's just different, mainly... how he uses it..."

She pulled up her top and this time her sports bra too, to cup her bare breasts, to tease her stiff nipples for him. She was laughing, rolling back, sliding her hands over her thighs, even her sex.

"...From behind. To start with... it felt so good... Mmm..."

Then her top was gone. Sitting there in her underwear in front of that laptop—did she make the assumption that I would be sleeping a while longer? I was fairly messed up, schedule-wise.

"Take it off."

"Like this?" she reached behind to unclip her sports bra, then hauled the thing up over her head.

I was so hard watching her performing for him. After going all the way with her, I did feel a stronger bond with her. I could feel a little more jealousy of her spending time with Henry, with another man. But it was hard to beat the underlying knowledge that she was his wife.

"And the rest."

"Okay, okay..."

She peeled off her panties, revealing that perfect little pussy to her husband's gaze, all smooth and slick with arousal. She kneeled up to show him, and then sat back in her cross-legged position that probably showed him even more of that pink, flushed flower.

"Yeah, it's a little... tender. What do you think, huh, sweetie? He was inside here so many times last night... really stretched me..."

She giggled, then blew him a kiss.

Her hand slipped down between her thighs, fingers teasing apart her pussy lips, showing him how red she was, her used sex.

"God, I'm going to explode."

"No," she said with a sudden stern note, "I told you not to, didn't I? You've got to wait."

Now it was my turn to smile—was she forcing Henry to avoid touching himself during her show? That was cruel.

"You've been good so far on this trip, right? So you can be good another day."

That made me stifle a gasp. She'd forced him to go without any touching all weekend? Wow. He really was going to be a mess by the time we got home.

"You're cruel," was all he said.

And now she lay back, shoulders resting against the edge of the couch behind, her legs parted, her fingers stroking her pussy. Really cruel.

I was a little shocked how cruel she was to Henry as her caresses accelerated, her hands circling over her pussy lips and her clit, fingers diving inside her, her breathing deepening, body writhing. Her eyes closed, her quiet moans grew louder and louder, and she had to believe that doing this would wake me from my slumber even if I wasn't already awake.

She reached her peak, and trembled a little, her legs coming back together, knees raised as she seemed to want to pull herself into a little ball to deal with the force of her climax.

Only after a few moments did she open up again to the view of her husband, offering him a mischievous smile.

"I couldn't help it," she said. "The thought of you going crazy about all this... it's pretty hot..."

"I'll say."

A giggle, and then she was blowing him another kiss. "Go to bed, sweetie. You need to sleep."

"I suppose so."

A pause, and a little impish grin as she slipped a finger in her pussy again, just to tease.

And then she said, "Okay. I'll text you later. You sleep."

"Love you."

"Love you, too."

I watched her close the lid of the laptop and push it away, and then she was looking over toward me, knowing I was there.

"You going to join me?" she smiled.

I moved to her, sank to the floor, pushed her legs apart again and dropped onto her. For a few moments I gave into my base instincts and covered her glistening folds with my mouth, my tongue delving inside her, drawing out long sighs as I tasted her.

But after her show, I was impatient. I broke off to kneel up between her thighs and rub my hardness all over her smooth mound and her wet lips.

She once again produced a condom as though from

thin air. Had she stowed one in the couch? "How do you do that?" I laughed. "Always prepared."

She gave me a smirk. It was kind of hot that she'd been doing that show while talking to Henry on Skype, knowing that she'd wake me, that I'd be drawn to her and that I'd have to have her again.

"Go slow," she said as I slipped the tip of my sheathed cock inside her.

"Sore?"

She nodded, "A little."

As I filled her again, though, it seemed to me that she was so wet it wouldn't possibly hurt her. Thrusting into her as she groaned and fondled her breasts, there were no signs of pain. Only sheer, complete pleasure.

"Henry's good?" I asked her before kissing her deep.

"Mmm-hmm."

I knelt up again, appreciating the view of her stirring, heaving body, shaking her as I fucked her slowly.

"You're refusing to let him... take care of himself... this weekend?" I asked her.

She laughed, "It was something... I read somewhere... He did agree to try it... oh God... oh my God..."

The way she was moving, spurring me on, made it clear she wasn't put off by any soreness. Then she rolled us over, sat astride me cowgirl-style, and with all the control, she was certainly not taking it slowly any longer.

I just held onto her hips and tried to keep myself from finishing too early—no mean feat considering how she felt around me, and the view I had of her trim curves over me, her shapely breasts shaking with each rise and fall on my hardness.

She came, hard, and I got the impression she'd wanted it that way, that any subsequent soreness would have been a calculated risk.

But then she wasn't entirely done. Lying beside me, I was still inside her, still thrusting into her, slowly but surely, my hand between her legs stirring her clit in some vague attempt to put into practice what I'd just seen of her Skype performance.

"So how does it feel?" I asked her, "Being confirmed as an unfaithful wife."

She grinned, "I'm not sure I'd say I was unfaithful..."

"Not in spirit," I agreed. "But to the letter of the law."

She laughed, "It feels pretty damn wonderful, actually."

That made me laugh.

"I have two sexy guys on hand whenever I want," she said. "They both want me, and they both make me feel incredible whenever they have me."

"An enviable situation."

"Uh-huh. Feels kind of naughty, kind of selfish, but so wonderful," she smiled, and rolled over, presenting me with her behind. She laughed again, "I mean I have a husband who gets sexual satisfaction from my encounters with other guys. Doesn't that just sound ridiculously great?"

"Absolutely."

"I have sex with other guys, and he just wants me more."

I kissed her lower back, breathing in her scent, the scent of sex that surrounded us both. Michelle was on fire, I'd never seen her as vibrant and buzzed as I had on this trip—in her mind, everything was now confirmed, and as far as that confirmation was concerned, she had the perfect husband.

I was happy for her, I was happy for both of them. I was happy to enjoy this beautiful woman physically, too. I just envied them. I envied Henry for having someone who looked at him as the perfect husband.

"Well, we have one more day here," I said, "let's make him want you a little more, right?"

I entered her from behind.

"Oh God, right...."

And we became animals again.

21

Share and share alike

I was feeling like I needed a vacation on the way back from our vacation. It seemed as though we'd been away a lot longer than just a few days. We were changed by it, we were somehow different coming back. Michelle was a married woman who had had an affair—albeit with her husband's encouragement.

And I felt... well, better. I couldn't explain it completely. I guess I felt some kind of self-worth, because someone like Michelle had wanted me so badly, and I had consumed her.

I might not have a great job that was going places, I might not even have my own home, or prospects for getting one now that London was owned by the oligarchs and the landlords, with the government locking everybody else out of the housing market. But, I could make a woman feel great.

For someone with nothing else, it was something I could pin my self worth on.

And coming back from Paris, I felt a strange new inner resolve, which gave me a surprising sense of seeing light at the end of the tunnel. If there was any woman in the world I wanted to make feel great, it was Katie. She'd ended things between us because I wasn't inspired enough at the time to recognize what was at risk. On the train coming back from France, I felt certain that if I could somehow get Katie to see I'd changed, that I could give her the satisfaction she needed—not only through my own abilities, but by allowing her to see other men—perhaps she would take me back.

And if she didn't—well, at the very least I'd have some closure, I'd move on with my life.

I realized as we returned to London that if I wanted to win back my own life, either with Katie or independently, I'd have to move out of the shelter of Henry's wing, I'd have to strike out on my own.

I was a little uneasy about telling them, about clearing off after we'd all come to settle into this wonderful arrangement of ours.

I didn't see Michelle much on our return, not for a few days. Henry had his days off, and he spent them with her, reclaiming her.

I worked, of course, both nights.

Despite what I was certain I now felt for Katie, my body did cry out for Michelle. We'd formed that unassailable bond of two people who cared for each other and were now sexually engaged—the physical bond of the mating couple, which I'd always found affected me in the early days of sexual relationships whether or not true love was involved.

And so though I'd thought perhaps I wouldn't feel it

any more, I did feel the jealousy of being at work while Henry was with my new lover.

More and more, though, I felt myself drawing into alignment with my friend, in how he viewed Michelle, and marriage in general. The weekend in Paris had just confirmed that.

Perhaps if my grand plan of reconciliation with Katie didn't work out—it was certainly no easy task, particularly since she'd been the one to leave me, not vice versa—then maybe I would be happy staying with Michelle and Henry. If that was going to be the case, I'd have to accept that her dating would not limit itself to Henry and I.

Then that Wednesday evening, I saw Henry for what seemed like the first time in an age. He was beaming from ear to ear.

"Michelle tells me you guys have been pulling the wool over my eyes," he said as we both fetched our breakfast-for-dinner bowls of cereal. I sent an alarmed look to the back of his head, but then he chuckled: "Making me think you were on full throttle all that time. Tut-tut."

"She told you, then?"

Of course, I'd been expecting her to come clean during the past two nights. It was just such a paradigm shift for our relationship that it was all now out there, it took me a little by surprise that it had actually happened.

"And showed me the footage," Henry flashed his eyes as he passed me, bearing his fully-loaded cereal bowl out to the living room, while I finished up pouring my milk.

He was amused. It felt like an enormous relief to me, a load off my mind.

"We had to be 100 percent certain about your state of mind," I said when I came in after him, perching at the opposite end of the couch.

"I can understand that," he nodded. "Actually, I'm feeling kind of grateful you did it that way."

"Grateful?"

"Being able to actually witness your first time—her first time—crossing that barrier. That was a powerful experience, amigo."

"I'll bet."

"Being able to see the look on her face..." he shivered. "And to think that I just wanted you guys to rush it all through behind closed doors. No, hats off to your strategy."

"I'm glad. So it must've been a wild few nights for you after we got back. Well, I suppose during, too."

"Unbelievable. I'd say you have to try it, but..." He caught himself, believing that he was straying into inappropriate territory.

"...but I don't really have a wife to try it with," I nodded, finishing off his sentence, showing there were no hard feelings at all. "You know, I was thinking about that on the way home."

"Thinking about trying it?"

I shrugged, "Like maybe I should try to get Katie back, somehow. I don't know. Probably an impossible task, but maybe if I could talk to her some time..."

Henry smiled, "Tell her you want to be with her while letting her see other guys as well?"

"Something like that."

"Can't hurt to try. I'm sure there's plenty of women, plenty of wives out there who might be tempted at an offer like that."

I took a deep breath and decided to simply come clean: Henry had that kind of influence on you. "It would probably mean moving out again. You know, if I was successful.

And I probably wouldn't get to see Michelle again as I have been."

Henry nodded, "But it'll be worth it, won't it? If you get her back. That is what you need to hang on to, old man. It'll be a shame to see you go, but we'll be happy for you."

I was relieved to hear him say it. I don't think the assumption had ever been that the three of us would form some kind of permanent polyamorous family. But it had almost been feeling like that was happening.

"You'll see her at the wedding, won't you?" Henry asked. Perceptive, as ever.

"Alicia's wedding, right," I said.

"Well, there's your moment, my friend. You can talk to her then. Tell her everything."

I felt my heart lift. It would be an opportunity, certainly.

---

*T*he next time all three of us went out together felt like a breath of fresh air—because the little deception Michelle and I had enacted, making Henry believe we'd gone all the way on our first date, was now moot. We had gone all the way. I had fucked Henry's wife.

It was a relief not to have to drop in little white lies all evening.

It was also kind of hot to be out with the two of them, knowing that this hot girl had both of us sleeping with her, both of us able to lie between her trim thighs and slide inside her. It seemed to me that Michelle's flirting with us reflected the fact that we were both her lovers.

She'd kiss me with just as much intensity in front of

Henry as she kissed him in front of me, all night. And strangely, I felt a tingle of pleasure even when she was kissing my friend rather than me, since it was as though I was getting to see what she did with me, only from a fresh perspective.

We came home from our night out relatively early at 2am, after heating things up on the dance floor, Michelle moving so sensually between us, lapping up both of our attentions.

On the way up to our apartment, Michelle was giggling as Henry tried to pull up her dress to expose her underwear, and I was bringing up the rear.

I didn't even think to ask who Michelle was planning on sleeping with that night. It seemed plain that she would go with Henry, leaving me feeling a trifle disappointed after being teased seductively all night.

But then as we went inside, and Henry escorted Michelle to their room, he called out to me: "Grab us a bottle of something, old man."

"Sure, no problem."

I was a little surprised. But, I wasn't going to object to continuing the night of partying in their bedroom.

I came into the bedroom bearing an ice-cold bottle of Sauvignon Blanc, to find Henry and Michelle already on the bed, Henry sitting up against the headboard, his pretty wife straddling one thigh, gently kissing his lips.

They were so tender with each other, so affectionate, I felt a sharp pang of jealousy watching them together. They had a relationship I could never quite match with Michelle. I had such strong feelings for her now, it was hard to take, though I had to accept it.

Henry swept a hand gently up the back of her thigh, pushing up her dress to reveal her shapely derriere. Did he know I was back in the room? The two of them seemed so into each other, I suspected not.

It was fascinating to me, watching them together. Although I'd caught them being together a few times before Michelle had crossed the line and seduced me, this was the first time I'd really seen her with him properly, after I'd formed my strong connection with her.

It was so erotic to see them like that, the little soft touches between them, Michelle's hand stroking her husband's cheek, Henry tucking her cocoa strands behind an ear to keep her hair out of her face. My jealousy was simmering underneath, but somehow enhancing my attraction for Michelle, if that were possible, boosting my arousal considerably.

She was someone else's woman, my old weakness—and this scene playing out before me was certainly playing on my deep-seated weakness.

I wanted her so badly, wanted to make her my own, to have what shouldn't be mine.

They broke apart, smiling lovingly as they looked into each other's eyes. Saying things to each other so quietly that I couldn't determine their words.

Was this really going to happen? Michelle would be with both of us?

Could we handle such a thing? I had to guess that Henry could, after what he'd been through during our weekend in Paris, and the fact that he'd watched our first time going all the way. Could I handle Henry being in the same room? I'd handled the thought of him watching, but this was something different.

I felt sure that all of us being in the same room would see a step change in the challenge we faced, though.

Seeing them together made me wonder if actually, I would find it a thrill to see her with him. It might hurt, but that might elevate the excitement, too. I could see that now.

"So," Henry said to me, "you guys are really into each other, huh? From what I've seen."

His voice had turned stern—not like Henry at all. It turned my insides to ice. He turned his head to look at me, and I was quite frightened by the impassive nature of his features. The Henry I knew did not do impassive, did not do neutral. He was an open book, as far as his emotions went, and as far as his emotions went he rarely strayed away from happy and amused.

It was kind of shocking to see him like this. He hadn't mentioned any doubts, any real fears before.

Had Henry changed his mind about us, now that he'd witnessed us together? Now that we'd actually crossed the line so there was no taking it back?

I said, "I'm no threat to you, Henry. If you want me to back off—"

The only optimism I was offered was that Michelle remained there, on her hands and knees over her husband's lap, smiling at him, pure love and affection continuing to pass between them in their expressions toward each other.

Henry's eyebrows sank further as he glowered at me. Then, in an instant, his face suddenly brightened.

"You're very sweet, old man," he smiled, his voice back to its normal happy-go-lucky tone. "I'm just messing with you. But seriously: you are important to Michelle and me —whether you decide to pursue Katie again or not."

I felt a little warm glow inside me at that. "Thank you," I said.

Michelle chuckled at her husband's teasing of me. "Just tell him, Henry."

He nodded. "You guys talked about this. About the next step."

The penny dropped—I finally figured out what we

were talking about here. Michelle was going to start dating other guys.

I said, "It's for you to decide, Henry. You and Michelle."

He nodded. "It's worth a try, don't you think?"

Michelle was looking at me nervously, and it seemed almost to be my decision to make. "Let's see how it is," I said, feeling my hairs stand up on end.

Then Henry looked seriously at me, and at his wife, adding: "We need to be straight with all this, guys. No more deception of any kind. That will kill it."

Michelle said: "Of course."

I agreed. The tension in the air was electric. I felt a strange new bond with Henry just then. We were in this together now, sharing Michelle.

Michelle kissed her husband, a sudden sharpness in her tone, "Okay, but for tonight, I'm Sean's."

Henry looked up into her eyes, and I saw his eyebrow raised in question. Had he been expecting this?

Michelle gave him a mysterious smile, then ducked down over the side of the bed, reaching for something. I guessed that she had her bag down there.

When she sat back up, she had a coil of thin white rope in her hands and an impish grin on her pretty face.

"You saucy minx!" Henry exclaimed, a trifle breathless.

I felt my heart rate picking up. She was going to tie him up to watch us? Sure enough, she shuffled down on the bed, and kneeling at the end by his feet, she started wrapping the rope around his ankles.

"Just a little idea I had, ever since you said you wanted to watch," she said.

"You never told me you were into this kind of thing," Henry said.

She smiled sweetly, "You never asked."

It turned out that the coil of rope was really two coils of rope, the second of which she wrapped around his wrists, straddling his lap as she bound him fast.

"You like me taking control?" she asked, wiggling her hips as she pressed down in his lap. "Sure feels like you do."

Henry was gazing up at his wife as though he was having some kind of religious experience. "Feels like it," he said.

I didn't know where to look. It almost seemed as though I ought to slip out of there and leave them to explore this new idea for their relationship.

"Interesting," she said enigmatically. In that moment, I was so envious of Henry for having a wife like Michelle.

She pulled herself up from him once his hands were tightly bound in front of his chest, and Henry lay comfortably but immobile there on the edge of the expansive bed. Stepping onto the floor, she approached me, and I actually saw a hint of trepidation on Henry's face. Was he really as confident about this as he said he was? Maybe he had doubts about whether he could stand to watch this after all.

"Come here," Michelle told me, and I wondered if this new experiment in her control was going to extend to me.

She pulled me to her, but while I might have expected her to launch into a full kiss on the mouth, she surprised me a little by manhandling me quickly around before shoving me back to fall onto the bed beside Henry.

I heard Henry's little gasp as Michelle pounced on me, slinking up my body like a panther.

Kneeling between us, she placed a hand on my crotch, her fingers tracing out the shape of my hardness through my pants.

"You want my pussy, Sean?" she asked, taking both of

us gents a little aback by her sudden descent into risqué language.

"Uh-huh," I replied, feeling perhaps as nervous about this new persona of hers as Henry was.

"You want to fuck my brains out?" she said, leaning over me, her face so close to mine I could smell the Champagne on her breath.

"Uh-huh."

She kissed me, her hand tightening around my package.

A wicked smile actually reassured me, somehow. "Think my husband can handle it if you fuck me to oblivion?" she asked, and kissed me long and slow, before breaking off to look over and take in how she was affecting Henry.

The guy looked mesmerized. Sitting there statue-still, his mouth open, his eyes wide, his face openly betraying his fears and desires.

Michelle picked up my hands now, and placed them on her behind, hauling up her dress to emphasize that I was free to roam. Then she slipped her tongue inside my mouth, moaning quietly as she pressed her body against my hardness.

I just went with the flow, finding that the concerns about performing in front of another man leached away as she writhed on me, filling my every breath with her fragrance, firing up my taste buds with her sweet mouth.

It wasn't until she sat up on me, to strip her dress off over her head, that I could glance to the side and see how Henry was taking this.

He looked shocked, but more like someone who had just been told he'd won the lottery. The fear wasn't quite so clear in his features any more.

Michelle slipped off her bra to reveal her full breasts,

and the stiff little buds jutting out from them. So tempting. But then everything about her was so tempting. Was this what my life-long weakness for other men's girls had been leading me to try? Indulging in them while their men waited and watched?

Yet as I sat up to take those enticing dusky nipples into my mouth, a small but significant part of me envied Henry this experience. I'd formed a strong attachment to Michelle, I'd heard her making love to him. I'd been restricted from fully satisfying my needs with her—it had been a powerful experience.

Michelle had changed me, from a man who apparently got off on taking women from other men, to someone who could understand the attraction of sharing my woman with somebody else.

"Oh, that feels good," she said now, tucking her rogue strands of hair back behind her ear, before stroking my head while she looked across at how Henry was taking this.

Was it me making her feel good by touching her, by sucking on her breasts? It seemed to me that she was talking about more than that, of performing for her husband, of driving him crazy.

She pushed me back down so that my head hit the pillows, then wrestled to unfasten the buttons from my shirt, dragging the thing off my body.

"I'm so wet right now," she said, speaking to her husband. "Are you sure you can handle me doing this with him?"

Henry nodded, but remained silent.

"You do remember our safe word, right?"

She shuffled a little further up my body, so that I felt the hot smooth flesh of her thighs on my stomach.

"I do," Henry said, almost seeming to mock the

wedding vows which he and Michelle were now bending if not outright breaking.

"Good," she grinned, and now shuffled further up my chest so that her sex was just inches from my face. God, she was beautiful. "I trust you won't use it."

Was it strange of me to feel envious of Henry, that he had a safe word with Michelle, whereas I did not? It was testament to the difference in our relationships, and I guess deep down I hankered after the kind of relationship Henry had with her.

She glanced down at me, snatching back my full attention as she said: "You hungry for me, Seanie?

"Very," I said, flashing my eyes at her.

She lifted one foot over my shoulder, and eased over my face, her toned body easily maneuvered into the position she wanted, so that she could set herself down over my mouth.

I was her willing servant, holding her supportively in place with one arm, while my other hand slipped aside her drenched panties so that I could taste her sweet pussy.

Michelle let out a long moan, which was probably a little dramatized for the benefit of her audience, but I wasn't complaining. I was hungry, ravenous, addicted to this exquisite pussy, my nose crushing her clit as I thrust my tongue inside her.

I guess the long drawn-out foreplay we'd enjoyed over the past few weeks before my first real penetration had certainly given me a taste for this heavenly creature's nectar.

The way she rode my face, flaunting her use of me both in how she forced herself down on me, how she held my head in her hands, and also in how she vocalized her response to my feverish assault on her soaking pussy, made me believe she was teaching her husband something of a lesson.

She enjoyed this, and she didn't get enough from Henry, perhaps.

Had she purposefully expressed concerns about how her husband would take her consensual infidelity in order to develop the expansive foreplay in our repertoire? I did wonder.

I'm fairly sure she came before her dismount—though her amplified performance might have opened her up to accusations of fakery, I'd experienced enough of her genuine orgasms with my face lodged between her thighs to feel confident this was no fake.

She also needed a little time to recover, taking things slowly with a little tender kissing, tasting herself on my lips and tongue, showing me real affection with her caresses and quiet moans, which must have spurred Henry's jealousy.

Her breath regained, she lifted up in order to drag my pants down my thighs, and my underwear with them, to expose me fully. She seemed almost to be purring as she settled between my thighs, tucking her hair back behind her ears before taking my stiff shaft in her hands.

I didn't feel I could look at Henry to gauge his reaction with his wife stretching her lips around my cock, then sinking down on me. Staring down at her pretty face, I could see how hard her nipples were, just as I could see the excitement in her cool blue eyes at sampling another man's cock right in front of her husband.

I could see the effect in her at having two men adore her, two men focus their attention on her, two men making her feel so beautiful, so desired, so powerful.

It made me wish I was the husband who had given her this gift, who was ultimately responsible for these feelings she was experiencing. So while I sympathized with Henry for witnessing his stunning wife being so obscene with another man right there next to him, having removed his control, I also felt how satisfied he must feel having his wife do this.

As she licked me, her tongue slurping around my head and along my shaft, and as she bobbed up and down on my pole, I found myself imagining it was Katie doing this, with me witnessing her debauchery with Grant.

It did make me feel different, picturing my own wife in this kind of situation. It did tweak my curiosity, my desire. It very nearly made me lose control of myself.

As though to pull my thoughts back to her, Michelle pulled herself up, and now slipped off her panties. She crawled up to Henry, and held her sodden underwear up to him, stroking the wet cotton over his face.

"You see how wet he makes me?" she said, her tone not really cruel, but rather grateful that her husband had given this experience to her.

Henry moaned, inhaling her scent.

She didn't give him more than that, but reached again for her bag. This time, she retrieved a little silvery packet that made her husband draw in his breath.

"Safety first, huh?" she giggled, and returned to me for a brief taste of my cock again before she removed the condom from its packet, and rolled the cold latex down my shaft.

"You remember when we bought these?" she said, throwing the unwanted packet over to land on her husband's lap. "You were so excited. It was like taking a little kid to buy a puppy at the pet store."

Henry smiled, and wriggled a little, perhaps feeling the urge to touch himself.

Straddling me, Michelle crushed my hardness under

her, swamping my sensitive staff with the intense heat of her body, though she did not yet take me inside.

"Oh, I love how big you are," she said, and while everything I'd seen up to that point indicated that I wasn't much different from her husband, the way she glanced over to him on saying those words suggested this was part of their fantasy play. Henry liked to think his wife was enjoying the benefits of a cock larger than his own.

I felt flickers of jealousy inside my stomach, that Michelle was still really thinking of her husband's fantasy while riding me.

I also checked myself: wasn't this how it ought to be? Though I selfishly harbored something for Michelle, I was merely their plaything, I had to accept my role in this. I wasn't here to break up their marriage, but to strengthen it.

I tried to play along, said: "You're not used to it, are you, sweetheart? It feels so tight when I'm inside you."

She smiled, "Mmm... you totally stretch me, you fill me like I've never been filled before..."

She looked at her husband again, said: "I'm going to fuck him, baby, this is what you wanted. You are okay with it?"

I saw Henry swallow involuntarily, then nod his head once.

With that, I felt her jink her hips, and without having to manhandle me, she managed to get the tip of my cock inside her slick pussy, then slowly sink down to fill herself with me.

"Oh my God..."

I hadn't been lying when I'd mentioned how wonderfully tight she felt around me, and she hadn't been lying about me stretching her, though the veracity of her claim that she'd never had anyone so large was doubtful. We'd already done this before, but even so she looked at me with wonderment in her eyes.

But Michelle wasn't attempting to humiliate her husband by comparing his size.

Looking across at him, she mouthed the words "I love you", and I could see in her face how thankful she was to him, for giving her this experience. Once again, it made me wish I was her husband giving her such an experience.

Oh, Katie, could this have been us? If only I'd discovered the strange concept of wife-sharing, if only I'd realized how neglectful I'd been of your needs, if only I'd recognized that perhaps we needed a little third-party assistance to stoke your fires from time to time, to avoid dishonesty and cheating.

"Oh baby, I'm fucking him, I'm fucking another man..."

Henry looked so thrilled as his wife began rising and falling on my pole, like a man who had given his beloved a stunning necklace for their anniversary, seeing her wearing it proudly at a party.

"It feels so good... oh thank you, thank you, thank you..."

Her breasts bounced as she rode me, crying out to be held. Yet I wanted Henry to see just how hard her nipples were, just how turned on she was. Her flushed cheeks and wild eyes supported the picture of her as a real spitfire, an insatiable wife who was about the hottest thing either of us guys had ever seen.

I guess it was hot being watched, and to be used by this beautiful brunette in front of her husband. But as I pumped my hips to match her rhythm, pumping my hardness inside her, I kept finding myself imagining being in Henry's place.

She lay forward now, kissing me as we continued to

thrust together, pressing her chest down against mine as though to alleviate the throbbing of her stiff buds against the roughness of my chest hair.

Then she whispered in my ear: "Take me from behind. Fuck me, Sean."

I followed suit as she picked herself up, but was a little surprised to see her crawl over her husband's legs, her hands supporting herself on his thighs as she lined her behind up with the edge of the bed, so that I might stand there to take her.

She was looking directly in his eyes, now, and I can only imagine how powerful it must have been for Henry to see her like that, a couple feet away from his face, his friend stepping behind her to sink his cock inside her.

I dipped down for another brief taste of her wetness, adoring her flavor, which seemed to drive on my lust. Her pussy was red, puffy, used.

"Ooof..." she let out a grunt as I pierced her, shunting her forward, forcing her to grip her husband's legs tightly to support herself.

"Oh, he's so deep," she said, "I've never felt so full."

She cried and yelled as I pounded into her, but it didn't seem to be anything more than an honest expression of her feelings—she didn't need to enhance anything any more. This was real, this was an overwhelming adventure for us all.

She ordered me to keep fucking her, as though she needed to.

"Don't stop, don't stop, don't stop!"

I'm not sure how I lasted as long as I did, but I think the distraction of finding my thoughts switching back and forth between my own body and Henry's perception, of trying to imagine how he must be feeling to be watching this, probably helped me to maintain it.

Eventually, though, her climax was nearing. Her arms seemed to give way so that she slumped head down into the mattress, pushing her pert derriere up into the air as I continued to pump into her.

I placed a foot up on the mattress to aid my forceful pounding, which only accelerated as I sensed her orgasm approach.

Her cries became desperate, and then she was shaking, shuddering, convulsing, her tight pussy quivering around my hardness as I slowed, and allowed my own climax to ignite.

"Oh God, oh God..." she cried, then as though remembering her husband was there, added: "I can feel him throbbing inside me. He's going to come inside me, honey..."

I blew, both reacting to her instruction and the way she talked so dirty for him, something I don't think she really did with me.

Henry had a slightly vacant smile plastered to his face, but he looked a touch dazed as well.

"Oh I love you so much," she said to him, and I selfishly tried to ignore it. "Are you okay, baby? Was that how you hoped it would be?"

She was unfastening the fly of his pants even before I withdrew from her. I quietly excused myself, feeling that they might want a little privacy to reconnect, for Henry to reclaim her, and to discuss just how the whole thing had been for them.

I was tempted to stay and watch—and they seemed so into each other that I don't believe they would have cared if I did. But I didn't need to just then.

I was happy for them, though there was a bittersweet note in my feelings. I wanted what Henry had: not Michelle, specifically, though any man would want her physically. I wanted Katie to look at me as Michelle looked at Henry. To feel the joy of giving Katie wonderful experiences that were not limited by rigid monogamy.

How was it going to feel for me to see Michelle dating other guys? I might not have felt about her the same way I felt about Katie, but I did feel something for her, that was for sure.

I wanted to know what it was like, though. I wanted to know so that I would be prepared for my new resolve to win back Katie in the most unconventional of ways—by offering her marriage with benefits.

I might not be a brain surgeon or some mega high-achieving lawyer. I might not be wealthy or famous. Yet I now believed in myself, I believed I could provide Katie with something few other men could. I could offer her love, stability and as I had found with Michelle and Henry, the potential for some ferociously hot sex—with me, and with whoever else drew her fancy if she agreed to broaden our horizons.

What's Yours Is Mine

Keep reading for the first chapter of the next book, "What's Yours Is Mine"...

An unconventional relationship

I was out in a bar with Michelle in the middle of Soho when I ran into Laura Kitteridge.

Strange, but after so many months away from Katie, under the impression that our friends had sided with her after our separation, since they had for the most part always been her friends to begin with, it seemed a surprise to run into one of them and not have them blank me.

I'd left Michelle at the bar to duck out to the men's room, and then on my way back through the crowd in that darkened place, I felt a soft hand on my shoulder and my name called.

"Sean, it is you. I thought it was."

I turned to find Laura clutching a gin and tonic, her gray eyes saturated with pity and curiosity.

"Laura, how's things?"

She smiled, "Things are great, actually. Pete just got a big promotion, so we're finally in a place where maybe, you know, we can start on the next step."

"Big step. How many you think you'll want?"

"I don't know. Two, probably. I'm hoping for a little girl, Pete's hoping for a boy."

I nodded and looked interested, trying to encourage her to keep our brief conversation on the topic of herself, so that I might avoid an interrogation. I failed.

"Never mind me—how are things with you? You're looking fantastic."

"Thanks... I have a new fitness instructor. Very effective."

"I noticed you're with someone tonight..."

I shrugged, but then reconsidered downplaying the signs of my having moved on from Katie. I had to have some pride, and even if word did get back to Katie that I was seeing someone else, she had to expect that by now. I smiled, "I guess you could say I get on very well with my fitness instructor."

"Pretty cute," Laura beamed, and seemed relieved that I was dating again, despite the fact that she was Katie's friend more than mine.

"Michelle. She's pretty great, actually."

"She coming to the wedding?" Laura was referring to the upcoming nuptials of Alicia Milton, Katie's little sister, which I was only too aware was coming up in just a few days. I was supposed to be an usher on Alicia's request, but rather wished I'd been able to duck out and avoid seeing Katie's family after our break-up.

I guessed that Laura's question was more than just a polite inquiry – the question of whether my date would be my plus one at the wedding would confirm her exact status, at least in Laura's eyes. I said, "Well, we've only been seeing each other a couple months..."

Laura nodded, then swallowed nervously. She had something bugging her, and was clearly in two minds about sharing it with me.

"So..." I said, hinting that this was only really going to be a brief conversation, and that both of us ought to be getting back to our own evenings.

It was enough to prompt Laura into coming out with it.

"I'm really sorry..." she said in a low voice, her eyes blazing with the shock of what she was trying to impart to me. "It's just I did notice after you left to go to the restroom... well... she was kind of... well..."

"What was she doing?"

"I think she was chatting up another guy."

"Oh," I said.

"I'm sure it was nothing... I wouldn't mention it, but... well, you've already been hurt, Sean..."

"It's okay."

"She was giving him her number," Laura added.

I could have told Laura that the guy she'd been chatting up was simply a prospective customer, that she had been simply giving him a sales pitch for her yoga classes or her fitness classes. Only, the way Laura looked at me with such pity, marking me down silently as a failed husband and pitiful human being, I fancied startling her a little.

I gave a calm nod, attempting to look as though none of this was in the least bit surprising to me. It shouldn't have been, really, except that Michelle hadn't really made any moves to start seeing other guys beyond me and Henry yet. "Nothing wrong with that," I said. "She's polyamorous."

"Polyamorous?" Laura looked blankly at me.

"It's no big deal," I said, oozing nonchalance. "It's quite common over in the States, which is where she's originally from."

"Polyamorous, of course."

It sounded as though Laura was a little confused as to what the word meant, but was making as though she was okay with it because she was so polite. It wasn't exactly a common concept within the social circles through which she normally moved. She'd probably go home and Google the word, and even then she'd be wondering if I'd really been serious.

"Well, I'm glad that you're happy, anyway, Sean," she said, glancing over to the bar, where I could see Michelle clearly flirting away, looking up at a tall dark stranger with wide eyes and a broad smile—even touching his forearm gently as they chatted, offering him a clear signal though her wedding ring was actually visible on her finger.

"It was good seeing you, Laura."

"I guess I'll catch you at the wedding," she said.

"You certainly will," I nodded. "Looking forward to it."

As she scurried away, I just stood there with my drink, trying not to think about Alicia's wedding. I was dreading being submerged in Katie's family and friends so many months after she'd separated from me. And of course, Katie herself would be there, and I was dreading how that would feel.

I turned to watch Michelle having a lot of fun making eyes at the guy at the bar. Watching her, knowing how I'd felt about her in the early days when I'd come to live with her and her husband following the end of my marriage, made me feel that I'd definitely grown as a person over the past six months. I could appreciate her beauty, and the excitement she clearly felt in flirting with someone else. I had learned about this unconventional view on marriage and relationships that Michelle and Henry held, I had accepted it and even come to crave it myself.

But in this particular case, I knew my friend Henry might want to know what was going on during my night off, while he was stuck at work. I texted him.

>*Just came out of the bathroom to find your sweet wife standing at the bar and hitting on somebody.*

I didn't know how much he and Michelle had been planning for her to make the moves on somebody else, but I felt certain that whatever the case, Henry would get a kick out of knowing his wife was being naughty on her night out with me.

Henry's rapid reply to my text told me that he was probably sitting there at his desk at our newspaper, phone in front of him, monitoring the situation in case Michelle had felt like sending him any teasing texts. Ever since I'd taken Michelle for a dirty weekend in Paris, we knew how much Henry appreciated getting those little updates, keeping him in the loop, involving him in his wife's consensual infidelity, tweaking his jealousy muscle in the build-up to her ultimate debauchery.

>*Fantastic. She like the look of him?*

I replied:

>*Seems to. He's a big guy, just her type ;-)*

I took a few steps closer, but remained a healthy distance from the pretty brunette at the bar. I could see she had her own mobile phone sitting there on the bar next to her, and its screen briefly lit up to signal the arrival of a text message, no doubt from her husband.

Michelle glanced down at it, and then I saw her smile to herself before looking up at her new friend again, trying to look as though nothing had happened. As though her husband hadn't just sent her a text saying he knew she was flirting with a guy at the bar, and he approved unconditionally.

I had another text from him within a few moments.

>*Told her she should go for it if she wants to. You want to see her being a bad girl, Sean? ;-)*

My own reply:

>*Absolutely ;-)*

I saw her glance over her shoulder, trying to keep casual, as she looked for me in the gloom. Our eyes briefly connected, and I gave her a quiet nod and an amused smile that she should have found herself a new man so soon after I'd excused myself.

She grinned, and made it look as though she was responding to something the new guy had said, but I could see how buzzed she was at being cleared to misbehave if she wanted to. Then I watched as she excused herself to look at her phone and tap out a short text message even while their conversation at the bar continued.

Henry texted me:

>*Okay, she says she likes him, she's going to see what happens. He's called Rick, by the way. Keep me updated.*

>*Will do.*

Rick. She was so open towards him, touching him as they stood sipping their drinks, brushing his arm subtly but fairly clearly, leaning forward to offer him glimpses down her top, her eyes never leaving his.

It was amusing to notice just how much of her flirting I recognized from her doing it with me. Now, though, as I watched, I was detached from the process somehow—and therefore able to appreciate and even share in the excitement she felt, rather than being overwhelmed by the thrill of such a pretty girl coming on to me.

Rick seemed polite and clean-cut, and clearly couldn't quite believe his luck. To start with, he appeared to be expecting her to get up and leave at any point. Then he began to relax, the tension left his bearing.

The atmosphere for me was electric, so intense even though I was only a boyfriend, not the husband. Watching her sending signals to him, less and less subtle. Toying with her hair, licking her lips, arching her back to emphasize her cleavage.

The guy looked as though he'd won the lottery when she virtually dragged him out of the place, but Michelle did give a quick look around for me, to ensure I was on board regarding their move to the next place. I wasn't entirely sure where she was going, or what she was planning, but I knew for a fact she liked to go dancing.

Sure enough, she led him through the bustling Soho streets to a club nearby, close enough to make it easy for me to tail them.

I switched to soda while they were in the club. I didn't want to lose control, and I also felt a certain amount of responsibility for Michelle as her secret chaperone. But I could see Michelle knocking back shot after shot while they danced the night away, grinding up against each other, constantly gazing in each others' eyes, beaming smiles at each other.

It was a while before I even noticed that she'd removed her wedding ring.

I'd been keeping Henry updated all evening, and this little factoid was definitely worth sharing.

Henry's reply explained all:

>*I told her to, in case she freaked him out.*

It sent a shiver down my back for some reason. I think it was the sense that Henry really had offered his wife the freedom to decide what she wanted to do. If she wanted to go home with the guy, she could.

It wasn't long before her arms were around him, and a tentative little kiss on the lips descended into a forceful embrace between the two of them, Michelle going wild with her new man.

I could see the glow in her face as she made out with him, the slight sheen of perspiration over her forehead. She had to be tingling all over as his strong hands roamed all over her petite, trim body. And I was rock-hard just watching her.

Henry kept demanding to know what was going on, so I gave him as detailed a text commentary as I could.

But as the clock ticked over into the next day, I was startled by a firm hand clamping to my shoulder, and there was my friend standing right there next to me in the flesh.

"Henry!" I hissed. "What the hell are you doing here?"

He shrugged, "I think it's a touch of man-flu. Sue bought it, anyway. I'm off sick."

I rolled my eyes, then flicked my head to point him in the direction of his philandering wife, if he hadn't spotted her already.

"Magnificent, isn't she?" he said, then to me: "How are you feeling about it. I mean, you're with her, too."

I smiled, "It's pretty hot. But I can't help wishing I was watching Katie right now."

"Of course," he nodded, and said seriously: "And I think it's time you made a move in that direction, my friend."

"I guess it is."

They went deep into the night, until the club was winding down and the dance floor was beginning to empty.

It was probably a good time for Michelle to make a move, one way or another, since the rapidly depleting club was making it more and more difficult for us to watch what was going on without looking obvious what we were up to.

We looked casually away as she grabbed Rick's hand and pulled him toward the exit. But Michelle made sure that as they went, their route proceeded past us—and even between us, so that she brushed past Henry.

I saw her subtly stuff something into her husband's hand as she went, leaving the big red-headed goof staring at her, open-mouthed. As we watched her go, he showed me what she'd given him: her panties.

"Come on," I yelled, "you want to see where they're going, right?"

We caught up with, and managed to follow the couple as Michelle led Rick away from the club.

"You think they're going to a hotel?" Henry asked me as we did our amateur espionage act. "They've passed various taxis..."

"I don't know. I guess she's free to do that, right?"

"Right."

Michelle led her new man quite a way. She seemed to take delight in it, and no doubt as well because she knew we were there, following behind. We went down to Shaftesbury Avenue, and then past Piccadilly Circus. We proceeded along Regent Street and down the stone steps to the Mall, before venturing across and in to St James Park. Rick had incentive enough to keep up with Michelle, the way her short dress rode up her thighs—and we knew for a fact she wasn't wearing any underwear.

"Jesus, what is she doing?" Henry was out of breath as we got into the park, and my muscles were burning a little despite the fact that I'd become a regular attendee at Michelle's fitness sessions.

"It's either going to happen in the park," I said, "or she just wants to get on the District Line over there."

There was the St James Park Underground station directly across the park from us, but if she'd wanted to take Rick home on the Tube, she could have got on at Piccadilly Circus.

We watched them walk through the park, their pace dropping a little as they proceeded along the central lake. In the darkness, there were a lot of shady bushes around if she wanted to try something with him. And as it turned out, we only had to wait a few minutes for her to decide on the right spot.

Henry and I circled around, and eventually found a place in the bushes from where we might observe.

---

*W*e watched them kissing, taking up where they had left off at the nightclub, sucking on each others' lips with the wild abandon of alcohol, adrenaline and darkness. Henry was utterly transfixed.

"Don't we get hanged for treason if we get caught doing this in a Royal Park?" I whispered. Buckingham Palace was only a few hundred yards away, after all. This wasn't a huge park.

Henry said, "Are you kidding? Compared to what the Royals get up to, this is positively tame."

We watched as Rick's hand pulled gently on the hem of Michelle's dress, reminding us that she wasn't wearing anything underneath. How far was she going to take this? He pushed her back against a tree as he kissed her, those big hands spreading over her breasts, squeezing them through her thin dress.

"God, she's so dirty," Henry said, as we saw her hands fall down Rick's chest, to run over the bulge in his pants, checking out what he was carrying. "D'you really think you could handle Katie doing this kind of thing?"

I said, "I think so."

By the orange glow of the nearest streetlamp, which wasn't particularly close, we saw her unbuckle the man's belt, and then shove his pants down along with his underwear.

And there in her hands was Rick's formidable manhood, the swollen thing jutting straight out toward her pretty face, its tip glistening with pre-cum.

Henry quietly gasped as his wife took hold of that thing and started slowly pumping, looking up at Rick's face with an impish grin. She kissed around the man's abdomen, his upper thighs, circumventing his equipment as though to tease her watching husband.

Then she was focusing on the man's cock, touching the tip to her lips, rubbing the thing all over her soft face before taking it inside her mouth, bobbing down on his length as far as she was able. Henry was clearly loving the look of bliss on his wife's face as she took another man into her mouth.

In the relative quiet of the late night, with traffic around this part of the city almost nonexistent, we could hear the wet sounds of Michelle sucking on Rick's huge cock. We could hear his groans as she took him to Heaven and back, and hers, as she found sexual fulfillment in the act of misbehaving in public, right in front of her husband.

Rick was playing with her hair as she sucked on him, pulling it back out of her face, making ponytails in his hands, but Michelle controlled her pace on him. She was loving the act of being so wicked, of taking a stranger's cock in her mouth, rubbing it over her lips, her chin, her cheeks.

She sucked on him hands-free, stroking his thighs as she sank down on his shaft, then bobbed back up. She slipped the straps of her dress over her shoulders to reveal her bare breasts, and fondled herself while she swirled her tongue around his tip or compressed his full girth within her cheeks.

When her fingers curled back around his shaft, and she gently stroked the bulbous purple head of his cock over her velvet lips, a thick stream of creamy white suddenly spurted from his cock, taking her completely by surprise as it splashed over her face and in her hair.

It made her pull back and laugh, the man's remaining come dripping down over her mouth, her chin, her bare breasts.

Wiping it out of her eye, she said something to Rick that I didn't quite catch. The man seemed suddenly flustered, stuffing his softening cock back in his pants, but then barely managing to pull them fully up and clasp his belt together before he was off, fleeing the scene.

It left Michelle kneeling there chuckling, wiping some of the come from her face, licking her fingers then rubbing the rest into her breasts like it was skin cream.

"What did you have to go and laugh at him for?" Henry said as we approached her.

She was smiling, "No, I told him my husband would love hearing how I made him explode like that. That's what scared him off."

"Bad, bad girl."

I watched as Henry knelt down to stroke the hair back out of his wife's face, and she reached out to unbuckle his pants and retrieve his own hardness as some kind of replacement for her lost catch.

"He really got it everywhere," he said, touching the stickiness on her face, her neck, her breasts.

I watched for a little while as Michelle took the second

cock into her mouth within a matter of minutes, how she indulged in the wickedness of her actions—starting out by simply breathing in the smell of him, gently stroking his stiff shaft with her face, before lashing her tongue all over his length, kissing him softly, and slowly stretching her lips around that tip and sink down on it.

It wasn't a chore for her, it was a naughty treat. But with Henry, it was like going back to a familiar favorite after her little taster of something different.

Then keeping him in her mouth, Michelle reached back to slip her dress a little further up her body, to expose the sweet roundness of her behind, which she now wiggled to signify her needs.

I hesitated, suddenly very conscious of our location, and just how much danger there was that we might be discovered. There were so many CCTV cameras around central London—surely there couldn't be any that would cover this particular spot. The bushes gave us plenty of concealment except from one slight gap. Would there be a police patrol past this place? The area around Parliament, the government buildings and Buckingham Palace was among the most secure in the country.

It made me a trifle nervous, but the temptation of Michelle's offer was still too much.

I knelt by her, then leaned in to kiss the soft, warm flesh of her behind, inhaling the strong fragrance of her arousal. She was seriously wet from her evening's encounter. I couldn't help myself, and nudged in to snatch a taste of her sweet little pussy. Even with her mouth full, I heard her moan at my tongue pressing against her slippery folds, my hot mouth pressing against her as I sucked on her soaking lips.

I think I made her lose concentration in dealing with her husband, but he didn't seem to mind that she'd withdrawn from his cock, and that she was using it more as some kind of handle to hold on to while I lapped at her pussy. I could empathize strongly with him, because I envied his position. I knew he would be loving how much pleasure she was getting from another, exhilarated by the expression on her sweet face.

I wished I might be the husband in such a situation, but I was still more than happy to play the part of the lover on the side for a young woman as beautiful as Michelle. Fluttering the tip of my tongue over her moistened clit, pressing into her to drill my tongue as far inside her as it could reach, savoring her flavor as she stirred her hips slightly in response.

Feeling time was a little more scarce for us in this exposed place than we might be in private, I knelt up, and unbuttoned my fly to pull out my full length.

Michelle pushed her cute butt up in the air as I touched my hardness against her searing pussy, and wiggled it again to urge me inside her. I eased forward and slipped the tip of my cock into her wetness, looking up to find Henry watching intently.

She groaned, long and low as I thrust inside her, filling her completely. I was glad she was muffled by the big cock stuffed in her mouth, and it was as effective as any pillow in keeping her volume down while I began to move inside her.

At one point I paused, removing my cock to stroke her with it. Michelle looked round at me, urgency in her eyes as she demanded: "Do it. Take me now."

She was as aware as I had been of the risks we were facing doing this in one of the smaller of the Royal Parks, less than a quarter mile away from the Prime Minister's official residence, 10 Downing Street, and the Royal Family's main home, Buckingham Palace.

From that moment on, it seemed like a race. We had to do this and get out, quick. I pushed back inside her, gripping her tightly at the hips as I started up a forceful rhythm that seemed to take control of her movement on her husband's cock as she rocked back and forth between us.

It was Henry who came first, his face screwing up, his cheeks rosy red as his whole body tensed, and his cock throbbed as he hit his peak. Even from where I was, I could see her beaming up at him, knowing what was coming. Yet rather than swallow him, as she might ordinarily, Michelle consciously took him out of her mouth just at the last minute, so that his thick white come splashed over her face, just as the stranger's had before.

Her orgasm hit just as her husband's hot seed coated her, and her shivering, trembling body under me triggered my own end.

Feeling her apparent need to be simply filthy at the end of this public encounter, as I felt my climax taking hold, I pulled out of her, and allowed my own come to streak across the pale contours of her exposed behind.

---

*O*n the way home on an almost empty night bus, Michelle was silently enjoying the lingering of the faint aroma of the three men she'd taken in the park. The glow of complete satisfaction about her was wonderful to behold. Would that I could make Katie feel that way.

The pretty brunette was tired, shattered by her grueling night on the dance floor, her last reserves of energy taken by the adrenalized adventures in the park, so it wasn't long before she simply slumped against Henry, and drifted off to sleep.

"You've got to call her, my friend. At least call her."

I looked up at Henry, and saw that he'd read my mind. I guess it wasn't too difficult a guess for him to imagine I was thinking about her.

"I don't know..." I said. "I think I'd freeze up. I wouldn't be able to say what I wanted to say."

"You just have to relax. You don't have to come straight out and tell her you rather like the idea of sharing her, you know."

"I suppose not."

"That might come in time, but baby steps, old man."

"You're right, I know you're right."

"To begin with, you just have to reconnect with her. Become part of her life again. Friends, if nothing else."

I nodded. "Friends," I sighed. "You think it sounds strange that I don't feel like I have much in common with her any more? Our lives are so different."

Henry smiled, "You were married to each other. Are married to each other, still, unless you've signed something I wasn't aware of. You've got plenty in common. You love her—you just have to see how she feels about you. Maybe she's still got a soft spot for you."

I looked at Michelle, and the affectionate way in which she was curled up with Henry there on the back seat of the bus, and it did motivate me to change things up a little in my own love life.

"I'll try to see her tomorrow," I pledged, though the term 'tomorrow' wasn't a great one when you worked the night shift and days were nights, and nights were really days. "I'll be okay if it's face-to-face."

Henry said: "Are you tired?"

"Not especially."

The way our night shift schedule worked, normally we were out of the office at 6am, home for "dinner" around 8am, and after a leisurely winding-down period, we were asleep by about noon. So while that bus taking us home from our night out pulled up in Chiswick at an ungodly early hour for our sleepy Michelle, for Henry and I it was still too early for our regular sleeping period.

"So why don't I drive you round there? You can catch her just before she heads out to work."

"Well, I suppose..."

"She won't mind, I'm sure. And you can say you were just dropping by on your way home from work..." Henry had his determined expression and brutally confident tone, which always made it difficult to say 'no' to him. I couldn't, even if I did believe Katie would think it very odd for me to show up out of the blue, suddenly, at seven or eight o'clock in the morning. Even with me being a night shifter.

"I had thought maybe the evening might be a better..."

"Nonsense, no time like the present, eh?"

I sighed. With the force of Henry's optimism, I guess I was about to find out.

*ontinued in "What's Yours Is Mine", available now at all good ebook stores, via **MaxSebastian.net***

Available Now

What's Yours Is Mine

The sequel to "What's Mine Is Yours"

Sean Ruskin's all-consuming fantasy is to share his beautiful wife, Katie, with other men. The trouble is, he only realized this after she walked out on their marriage.

Converted to a less monogamous view of marriage by his best friend Henry and his wife, Michelle, Sean feels certain he can now offer Katie a new kind of relationship that will keep her satisfied in ways she could never have imagined.

But as Sean struggles with how to talk to Katie about how he now feels about her, he discovers a long-hidden secret about her that could thwart any attempt at reconciliation...

The red-hot conclusion to the wife-sharing romance "What's Mine Is Yours", from the author of *The Madeleine Trilogy*.

Web: MaxSebastian.net/whats-yours-is-mine

Another book you might enjoy:

A Lockdown Affair

A cheating wife turns hotwife…

Cam is shocked when he discovers evidence that suggests
his wife might be cheating on him — and during the lock-
down, of all times.

But as Cam investigates his suspicions, not only does he
begin to understand his wife's reasons for being unfaithful,
he also finds his desire for her growing exponentially.

Amazon bestselling erotica author Max Sebastian presents
a full-length novel full of sizzling suspense, as a stay-at-
home dad discovers the strange attraction of an unfaithful
wife.

Web: maxsebastian.net/a-lockdown-affair